P9-ELQ-057

A Darker Side

Also by Shirley Wells

Into the Shadows

A DARKER SIDE

Shirley Wells

Constable • London

Constable & Robinson Ltd
3 The Lanchesters
162 Fulham Palace Road
London W6 9ER
www.constablerobinson.com

First published in the UK by Constable,
an imprint of Constable & Robinson, 2008

First US edition published by SohoConstable,
an imprint of Soho Press, 2008

Soho Press, Inc.
853 Broadway
New York, NY 10003
www.sohopress.com

A copy of the British Library Cataloguing in Publication
Data is available from the British Library

UK ISBN: 978-1-84529-698-8

US ISBN: 978-1-56947-509-6
US Library of Congress number: 2007042573

Printed and bound in the EU

1 3 5 7 9 10 8 6 4 2

To my father

Chapter One

Martin Hayden felt as good as he looked. And he looked very good.

Tall and slim, with overlong, silky blond hair, he walked with graceful, flowing movements. If he'd been an animal, rather than a seventeen-year-old schoolboy, he would have been a beautifully groomed Afghan hound, grace and elegance personified.

His pale skin was clear and blemish-free, apart from a fading bruise beneath his right eye. Those eyes were the azure blue of a Mediterranean sea, and were highlighted by long, curling lashes. This morning, as he began the half-mile walk from Lower Crags Farm to the bus stop, a gentle smile played around generous lips, allowing a glimpse of perfect white teeth.

His school uniform, the dark green blazer, black trousers, white shirt and green and black striped tie of Harrington High School, accentuated his long, fluid limbs. As always, his tie was worn loosely, and the neck button on his shirt was unfastened.

He knew that when he boarded the bus, the girls would gaze at him with undisguised longing. A few of the boys would, too.

He looked as if he didn't have to try too hard. Yet try hard he did.

The lane was muddy, and he took care to avoid dirtying his shoes as he walked.

He reached into his brown leather briefcase, pulled out his MP3 player, put the tiny earphones in place and hit the Play button. The Kaiser Chiefs soon had him humming along.

Long fingers strayed to the bruise beneath his eye. It was barely visible, and no longer sore, but his anger was as raw as it had been a fortnight ago when David Fielding and his fellow thugs had managed to corner him.

Martin had been outnumbered six to one, and it had only taken minutes for them to kick him to the ground and pull off his clothes.

'Nancy boy!' they'd taunted. 'Queer fucking faggot!'

Tears, more from anger than anything else, had stung his eyes as they'd punched and kicked him.

When they'd finally grown bored, or scared of being caught, they'd run off, leaving Martin to pull on his clothes and stagger to the lavatories in C block to inspect the damage.

There was only a slight puffiness to one eye. It was a few hours before the bruises on his legs and ribs were visible. In the days that followed, he'd managed to laugh off his black eye as an accident on the football pitch.

'Bastards!' he muttered now, the memories still painfully fresh.

This morning, like every morning, his sister, Sarah, had read out his horoscope.

'Cancer. With the new moon – Marty, are you listening?'

'I'm listening,' he'd promised with amusement. 'Just cut the crap, sis.'

'Opportunity comes your way today.'

'And that's it?' he asked in amazement.

'With all the crap cut out, then yes,' she said lamely.

Unlike Sarah, Martin didn't believe in all that codswallop, but perhaps today there was something in it. But no, it was crap. Opportunity came his way every day. He made sure of it.

Today, for instance, crammed into his briefcase was a bottle of home-made wine. Nestling in the zipped compartment was a substantial amount of cocaine. It had taken a while, and a spot of blackmail, to acquire it, but it would be worth it. He'd read up on the subject. Cocaine, ingested in a sufficient quantity, could kill.

Martin Hayden was special. No one got the better of him. No one. It was a lesson David Fielding would learn the hard way.

Oh yes, revenge would taste very sweet indeed.

Chapter Two

Jill Kennedy walked into her cottage, dropped the bags containing milk, bread, the *Racing Post* and half a dozen tins of cat food on her kitchen table, and then spotted her mobile phone lying next to the kettle. What a relief. She'd thought she must have lost it in Burnley. Given the fact that she'd overslept and had to rush to a dental appointment, she supposed it wasn't surprising she'd forgotten it.

She glanced at the display and saw that she had messages.

As she called her voice mail, she switched on the coffee maker.

'Hi, it's me.' Me was Detective Chief Inspector Max Trentham, and the shock of hearing his voice had the hairs standing up on her arms. 'Give me a call, will you?'

The second message had been left twenty minutes later.

'Me again.' Me was still Detective Chief Inspector Max Trentham. 'Don't you ever answer this damn thing? Give me a call, will you?'

The third message was shorter and to the point. 'Where the devil are you?'

The fourth message had come through a matter of minutes ago. 'OK, you win, kiddo. I'll train a pigeon. Look out for it, will you? It'll have a note round its neck saying call Max.'

Patience wasn't one of Max's virtues. Off the top of her head, Jill couldn't name any of Max's virtues.

She made coffee and stood at her kitchen window, the mug cradled in her hands. It would do him good to wait.

More importantly, it would give her time to recover from the shock of hearing his voice.

Lilac Cottage was as pretty as it sounded, and she adored the stunning backdrop of the Pennines that, today, stood proud and aloof in the morning drizzle. She loved her garden, too. The old lilac tree, which was possibly responsible for the cottage's quaint name, showed no signs of life, but she knew it would come good with a little sunshine and warmth. It was the same with the clematis. At the moment, that was nothing more than a collection of untidy twigs entangled in the trellis, yet she had been amazed to see her shed covered in dark mauve blooms throughout the summer.

Her cottage sat on the very edge of the Lancashire village of Kelton Bridge, at the end of a narrow, unlit lane. Some people had thought she would find it too remote. They couldn't have been more wrong. She loved it.

After a holiday in Spain and then another few days on the Croatian island of Krk, it was good to be home.

It was no use; she wouldn't settle until she knew what Max wanted. She hit the button for his number and he answered almost immediately.

'A pigeon's just committed suicide at my feet. D'you know anything about it?'

'About time. Where have you been?'

Max couldn't even count good manners among his virtues.

'In case you've forgotten,' she pointed out patiently, 'I no longer work for the force.'

'You said you were coming back.'

'And I will. I just haven't decided when. At the moment, I'm enjoying writing my –'

'Enjoying writing? What bullshit! You're a well-qualified, highly respected forensic psychologist who bottled out because a bloke we arrested – a bloke who just happened to fit your profile – hanged himself!'

Jill had no response to that. His comments shouldn't have taken her by surprise; he wasn't noted for keeping his views to himself and she'd heard them many times before. Perhaps what he said had a grain of truth to it . . .

'Yes, well. What can I do for you?' she asked briskly.

'Where are you now?'

'At home.'

She had more than enough work to do, and she'd planned to do it sitting in front of her fire with her copy of the *Racing Post* to hand.

A thought struck her and she spread her *Racing Post* across the kitchen table.

'Spare me an hour, will you?' Max asked. 'I'm off to – You've heard about the missing schoolboy?'

'No.' She'd overslept. There had been no time for breakfast, so she hadn't listened to the local news and her car's radio was tuned to Radio Two.

'He's from your neck of the woods. Martin Hayden. Do you know him?'

'Hayden? No.'

'Lower Crags Farm.'

'No.' It meant nothing to her.

'The farm's about, oh, five miles from you. Anyway, Martin Hayden didn't turn up for school yesterday and I'm going to talk to his parents again. I thought you could come along.'

'Sorry, Max, but I can't. I'm too busy. As I've just told you, I'm a writer now.'

'So you are,' he said in a dismissive way.

It was true that she'd given up police work when Rodney Hill, wrongly arrested, had hanged himself. She'd helped them catch the right man, though. After Valentine, as the serial killer had been dubbed, had been put behind bars, Jill had considered going back to work for the force but, for the moment at least, she was happier out of it. Besides, she had a publishing contract and a screaming deadline.

She ran her fingers down the list of runners and, sure enough, Pigeon Post was running in the 2.45 at Haydock Park. At 33–1, it didn't have a hope in hell. All the same . . .

'What's so unusual about a missing schoolboy?' she asked. 'Why do you want me along?'

'I'd like to see what you make of the parents. They're very private, to put it mildly. Something's not right, but I'm damned if I can put my finger on it.'

'What do you mean, not right?'

'They're hiding something, I'm sure of it. Come along and see them, will you?'

She expelled her breath on a sigh. Max always knew how to arouse her curiosity. 'OK.'

'Great. Come over to the nick, will you? I've got a couple of things to do and then we can go.'

It took her less than twenty minutes to drive from her cottage to Harrington police station, and that included phoning the bookie and putting twenty quid on Pigeon Post.

She was about to walk into the building and find Max, but she changed her mind and waited in the car park. Too many people would be wanting to know why she was wasting her time writing self-help books when she could be helping to solve crimes. She'd heard it all before. Of course, there would be others who were glad that she and her mumbo-jumbo, as they called it, were safely out of the way at Lilac Cottage.

It wasn't long before Max was striding down the steps to the car park. A sudden gust of wind flicked his tie over his shoulder so that he had to pull it back.

He was tall, well over six feet, and slim, and his hair was thick and dark. That hair was greying at the temples, giving him a distinguished air. He wasn't the best-looking bloke on the planet, not by a long way, and Jill resented the way her stomach clenched at the sight of him.

'Hiya!'

He flicked the remote to unlock a black Mondeo and got in. Jill had forgotten he had a new car.

'So what happened?' she asked as she sat beside him and fumbled for the seatbelt.

'A seventeen-year-old, Martin Hayden, didn't show up for school yesterday.' Max fired the engine and pulled out of the car park. 'He set off at the usual time and his parents assumed he'd been there all day. When he didn't come home, they phoned one of his friends to see if he was there and it was then that they discovered he hadn't shown. The bus driver says he hung around for a few minutes, but didn't think anything of it when he didn't turn up. It's unlike him to miss school, though. Enjoys it. A bit of a swot, I gather. They called us at around seven thirty last night.'

In the confines of his car, Jill could feel herself growing more and more tense. She gave herself a strict talking to. Being with Max these days should be easy. It should have no effect on her whatsoever. She'd loved him, lived with him, been betrayed by him – but that was in the past. Now, he had no effect on her. None whatsoever . . .

'Seven thirty?' she queried, dragging her mind back to the missing schoolboy. 'Why not earlier?'

Max eased the car into a stream of traffic. 'I don't know. They seem reluctant to have us involved at all. As I said, they're very private.'

Max drove them towards the outskirts of the town.

'I haven't seen you for weeks,' he remarked. 'How's things?'

'Fine.' It was eight weeks to be precise. Eight weeks and two days. Not that she was counting. 'You? The boys?'

'Yeah, fine, thanks. And the boys are great.'

'And the dogs?'

'Yup, the dogs are good too. Your cats?'

'Yes, they're fine, thanks.'

Max drove in silence for a few moments.

'Well, that seems to have covered everything.' He gave her a sideways glance. 'Fancy a shag?'

She had to bite back a laugh. Damn him. 'Piss off, Max.'

'I'll take that as a no then.'

'So where is this Lower Crags Farm?' she asked, not giving him the satisfaction of a response.

'Right in the middle of bloody nowhere.'

The farm was only five miles from Jill's home village of Kelton Bridge, yet it might have been a different world. The view was similar to the one from Jill's cottage, yet the hills, those dark, brooding Pennines, were far more imposing.

Max swung the car off the road and stopped at a large wooden gate that barred a track. On one side of the gate was a sign declaring: *Lower Crags Farm*. On the other side, in bigger, black print was: *Private property. Keep out!*

'Very welcoming,' Jill murmured.

She got out to open the gate and closed it as soon as Max had driven through.

'It's a lovely spot,' she said as she got back in the car.

Max wasn't impressed. 'Give me tarmac and pavements any day.'

'You've no soul, that's your trouble.'

'Only one spare wheel, that's my trouble,' he replied, swerving to avoid a pothole.

The car bumped and jolted along the rutted track for about five hundred yards before Max brought it to a stop in front of the farmhouse.

'Who's with them?' Jill asked.

'No one. When we suggested a WPC stay with them, they wouldn't hear of it. They're not keen on doing a televised appeal, either. George Hayden, the father, said they didn't want their business broadcast for all the world to know, thank you very much.'

'That's an unusual view to take when your child's missing.'

'Exactly. That's why I want to know what you make of them.' Max glanced at his watch. 'We're doing all we can – the search party's set off, and the chopper's airborne – but it would be a damn sight easier with a bit of help from the parents.'

'You don't think he's done a runner then? Hitch-hiked south or skived off with his mates?'

'I'd like to,' he said grimly, 'but no. No, I don't.'

Chapter Three

The farmhouse, like a couple of nearby barns, had a sad, neglected air to it. The woodwork needed a coat of paint. A couple of half barrels guarded the front door, but the plants, whatever they were, were long dead. They sat forlornly in waterlogged compost.

Max lifted a black metal knocker and banged it against the wood. Seconds later, a tiny woman in her mid-forties opened the door.

'Detective Chief Inspector Trentham,' Max reminded her as she stared blankly at him. 'Harrington CID.'

She nodded, and Jill realized that her expression wasn't lack of recognition at all. It was panic.

'Jill Kennedy,' she introduced herself. 'May we come in? We'd like to ask a few questions about Martin.'

Mrs Hayden opened the door to allow them entry and they walked down a dingy and chilly hallway, and into a sitting room that was crammed with a lifetime's collection of bric-a-brac. There were porcelain birds and animals, cheap paperweights, ashtrays, jugs, bottles and vases. It was like walking in on a church jumble sale.

The furniture – leather suite, several wooden tables and a dresser – was functional rather than attractive, and had seen better days. About thirty years ago.

'Where is everyone?' Max asked curiously.

'George and Andy – that's my other son,' she added for Jill's benefit, 'are out in the fields. George didn't know what to do but, as he said, life goes on.'

'And your daughter?' Max was trying, and failing, to hide his surprise at the family carrying on as normal and leaving her alone.

'At work,' she said quietly.

'She's a hairdresser, yes?' Max asked, sitting down.

Jill sat on a leather sofa that had cracked and worn thin through years of use. She patted the space next to her and Mrs Hayden sat beside her.

'That's right,' she answered Max's question. 'Thursdays and Fridays are her busiest days. They used to close on Mondays but, because everyone else did the same, they stay open now and close on Wednesdays instead. Besides, there's nothing she can do here, is there?'

Except worry with her mother.

'Tell us about Martin,' Jill suggested. 'Anything you can think of. His friends, where he spends his spare time, what he's interested in – anything at all.'

Mrs Hayden was so quietly spoken that Jill struggled to hear her. Painfully thin, she was a woman who needed a good meal inside her. Her skin hung off her, and her wrists and ankles looked as if they might snap at any minute. Her hair, dark, shoulder-length and streaked with grey, was equally brittle. Her fingernails had been bitten down to the quick. She was wearing a heavy green skirt and a thick brown sweater that had worn thin at the elbows.

'We've phoned everyone he knows,' she was telling them, 'and the headmaster is asking the boys and girls if they've heard anything.' She bent forward, and began rocking back and forth, her bony hands running over equally bony knees. 'It's not like him to be late,' she added vaguely. 'He always phones. He's a good boy.'

'I'm sure he is,' Max said, adding, 'You said you'd try and find us a more recent photo.'

'Yes.' She sprang up, clearly glad of the activity, went to the drawer in the well-polished dresser, and took out three snaps.

'Sarah took these at Christmas,' she said. 'They're not as good as his school photo, but as I said, that'll be eighteen

17

months old now. I don't know why they didn't do one last year. It's not as if Martin missed it. He didn't miss a single day last year.'

Max looked at each photo in turn, nodded, and handed them to Jill.

'Oh!'

Max, picking up on the surprise in her voice, gave her a questioning look.

'He's – a striking young man,' she said, gazing at the pictures.

The boy in the photo, wearing a smile that would have done Mona Lisa proud, was far more than merely striking. He was beautiful. In one snap, he was leaning against the front door to the farmhouse wearing figure-hugging jeans and a black sweater, and he had a jacket hooked on his finger to drape decorously over his shoulder.

More than beautiful, he was perfect.

In the other two photos, he was equally posed. Yes, posed. The half-smile, a knowing, secretive smile, was the same.

'I bet he's popular with the girls,' Jill said lightly.

And the boys.

'He's very popular with everyone,' his mother said softly.

Well aware of it, too, Jill guessed.

'He's a special boy,' Mrs Hayden murmured. 'He knows it, too,' she added with the ghost of a smile.

Max was right; there was something unusual about this family. She was sure, too, that Mrs Hayden was keeping something to herself.

'May I look in his room, Mrs Hayden?' Jill asked, rising to her feet.

'Call me, Josie,' she said awkwardly, nodding. 'Up the stairs – first left. He shares with his brother. Andy's the untidy one,' she added.

Jill was pleased that Max kept Mrs Hayden – Josie – downstairs, telling her of everything that was being done to try and find her son.

She pushed open the bedroom door and was surprised at the size of the room. Even allowing for the sloping ceiling, there was plenty of room for two beds, wardrobes and chests of drawers. Each boy had taken one side of the room, and on Martin's side there was a desk. A few cables, still plugged in at the wall, showed that a computer had sat on it. No doubt the police had taken that away for examination.

Jill sat at the desk and opened the drawers. They were filled with notebooks, all used for schoolwork, some sheet music, pens and pencils, and a recorder. There was nothing of interest, and nothing personal.

She gazed around her, shuddering at wallpaper dotted with white roses that must have been clinging doggedly to the walls before the boys were even born.

CDs on the shelves told her nothing. His music of choice was the same as that of most seventeen-year-olds, the sort of stuff that had indecipherable lyrics and needed to be played at ear-splitting volume.

The small bookcase held a few surprises. Why, for instance, would a seventeen-year-old boy be reading Jane Austen's *Pride and Prejudice*? *Mansfield Park* was there, too, right next to *The Catcher in the Rye*. Perhaps they were part of his schoolwork. One by one, she took them from the shelf and flicked through the pages. Inside the copy of *Mansfield Park* was a handwritten inscription that said simply: *Enjoy.* It was signed: *DL.*

There was nothing personal in the room, but that didn't surprise Jill. Max had said they were a private family, and Martin looked – as far as you could tell from three photos – a secretive boy. Besides, he shared the room with his older brother. Posters of bands, girls, and especially boys, would prompt ridicule.

He's a special boy, his mother had said . . .

A vehicle drove up to the house and Jill went to the window to look out. Two men, father and son she guessed, jumped out of an ageing Land Rover. Martin's father and brother?

19

The older man was stocky with thick grey hair that needed a good cut. The young one was slimmer, but fit and strong-looking, with thick dark hair. Definitely father and son. The resemblance was strong. They had the same stubborn chin, and held themselves in the same manner as they walked.

In this house, among these people, Martin must be like an exotic bird of paradise.

Having gained little from looking at Martin's bedroom, Jill went downstairs.

'You'll not find him here, will you?' Mr Hayden was telling Max, but he stopped when he saw Jill, his eyes widening in astonishment. 'And what the devil do you think you're doing?'

'George!'

'I asked what you were doing?' he repeated, ignoring his wife's embarrassed plea.

Trying to find your son. Which is more than you seem to be doing.

'We need to find out as much as we can about Martin, Mr Hayden,' Jill said. 'It's a fact that seventeen-year-olds keep secrets from their parents. I did and I'm sure you did. He may have a girlfriend, for instance, or other friends you don't know about.'

'Are you suggesting he'd go off without telling his parents?'

'I'm not suggesting anything.'

'They're trying to help, Dad.' This was the first time Andy had spoken.

'Listen –' his father rounded on him – 'if you had the brains of your brother, you'd know to speak when you're spoken to and not before.'

So Andy wasn't special. He must be sick to death of living in his brother's shadow. Sick enough to do something about it?

'Andy's right, Mr Hayden,' Max cut in. 'We're doing all we can to find Martin. But we'll leave you now and go to the school to talk to his friends. If you need me, you have my number, and it goes without saying that we'll be in touch.'

He looked at Josie Hayden and his voice softened. 'Are you sure you wouldn't like a female officer to stay?'

'We're all right on our own,' her husband snapped on her behalf.

'If you're sure.'

'Just find him,' he added for good measure.

'Oh, we'll find him,' Max promised.

Josie, looking embarrassed, showed them out.

Despite the fine drizzle, it was a relief to step outside. They both stood for a moment, gazing at those steep hills, before getting in the car.

'I shall deck that bloke before long,' Max muttered, as he knocked the car into gear.

'Obnoxious, isn't he?' Jill was still taken aback by his rudeness.

They bumped back along the track and she got out of the car to open and close the gate behind them.

'What do you think then?' Max asked when she was sitting beside him fastening her seatbelt.

'I like Josie, but I think she's hiding something. I also think she's grateful to her husband for some reason. That's why he feels he can push her around. His behaviour embarrasses and irritates her, but she's too beholden to him to say anything. I agree with you; something's not right. They're keeping something quiet. A family row perhaps. I think Andy is searching for praise from his father. He's the one working alongside him, but it's clear he can't compare to Martin. I suspect there's animosity between the two brothers.'

'And Martin?'

'Martin is exceptionally attractive,' she said carefully. 'He knows it, too. Probably milks it for all he's worth. He's the golden boy, and he loves it. He's very confident. He's special and he knows it.'

21

Max nodded. 'Josie hinted that he was her husband's favourite. She excused his rudeness by saying he was a lot more distressed than we knew.'

'Who was on the phone while I was upstairs?' She'd heard the phone ring three times.

'Sarah, the daughter, was the first caller. The other two were the local rag.'

The hills and fields receded and they were soon caught up in Harrington's devious one-way system.

'I take it I'm coming to the school with you,' Jill said. She was happy enough to go with him, but it would have been nice to be asked.

Max took his gaze from the road briefly. 'You don't have anything better to do, do you?'

'Only a book to write, a deadline to meet, Christmas shopping to do –'

'Eh? It's the twenty-ninth of November!'

He was right; her Christmas shopping wasn't urgent. Her book was, though. However, they were almost at the school.

Chapter Four

It was just before two o'clock when Max pulled into the school's car park. As it was raining heavily now, he parked as close to the entrance as possible, in a bay with a large Reserved sign on it. Perhaps it was reserved for visiting coppers.

There were twelve hundred pupils at Harrington High School and it looked as if every one of them was suddenly storming the building. Originally the school had been a much smaller stone-built affair, but over the last thirty years brick extensions had been added. It wasn't the most attractive building in the town.

'Right,' he said, unfastening his seatbelt, 'we'd better have a chat with the headmaster first, then work down. OK with you?'

'Fine,' Jill replied, 'although I'll lay odds of a hundred to one that Martin Hayden is the model pupil.'

Max knew what she meant. In all the years he'd been a copper, nothing had ever happened to the young hooligans. It was the model pupils with their sparkling futures ahead of them that went missing or were abducted. Or worse.

'Better that,' he murmured, 'than hearing what a pair of no-hopers my two are.'

'True,' she agreed with a laugh.

Max's sons, Ben and Harry, attended Harrington High School, but as Max rarely, despite trying his damnedest, made it to parents' evenings, he didn't know the building or the staff well.

They dashed in and found themselves amid a crush of pupils. Fortunately, those pupils were giving the main office a wide berth.

'Detective Chief Inspector Trentham and Jill Kennedy, Harrington CID,' Max introduced them to the secretary, flashing his ID. 'Mr McKay, please. He is expecting us.'

'Of course.' She got to her feet, crossed to a door on her left, knocked and said, 'The police are here to see you, Philip.'

Turning back to Max, she said, 'Come this way, please.'

They followed her into Philip McKay's office and, after shaking hands and going through the preliminaries, which included a reference to Harry's excellence on the sports field but for some reason omitted mention of his academic achievements, were soon seated on chairs that were about six inches too low. Philip McKay, on the other hand, had a comfortable black leather reclining chair in which to relax.

He'd been headmaster at Harrington High for seven years now. A Scot who had lived in England for most of his life, he'd never bothered to lose his accent. In his mid-forties, he was a short, dapper chap. His grey suit and black shoes were of the best quality. Max knew he was married to a music teacher and that they had three children, all at Harrington High. He seemed to have the perfect life.

'This is a very worrying to-do,' he said, frowning earnestly, 'although,' he added, 'I'm sure you're doing everything you can.'

'We are,' Max assured him. 'What can you tell us about Martin Hayden, Mr McKay? Do you know of anything that might have been bothering him? Any trouble with bullying, that kind of thing?'

'There's no bullying at Harrington High, Inspector, I can assure you. We don't allow it.'

'I'm sure other schools will be eager to know how you stop it,' Jill put in. 'Kids will be kids. There's always going to be some trouble, surely?'

'Not here,' he said firmly.

'What happens when a child doesn't turn up for school?'
Max asked. 'When either of my boys have been off sick,
I've – well, my mother-in-law has phoned the school. What
if they simply didn't turn up?'

'We have twelve hundred pupils here,' Mr McKay
reminded him. 'If the child is a known truant –'

'Is there a lot of truancy?' Jill asked.

'We're well below the national average.'

'Which is?' Jill persisted.

'That average, I believe, is around the one point one
per cent mark. We're around the zero point nine per cent
mark.'

'Ten point eight children. That's not bad,' she allowed.

Philip McKay hadn't welcomed the interruption but that
faint praise helped.

It was her maths that impressed Max. A lifetime spent
working out profits from yankees, doubles and each-way
bets must have paid off.

'If a child is ill or unable to attend for some other reason,' McKay went on, 'it's the duty of the parent to contact
us. We will then authorize that absence. Now, if a child has
been absent for two days with no parental contact, we'll
send a letter or phone the parents.'

'So in Martin Hayden's case,' Max said, 'no action would
have been taken?'

'No.'

They talked of Martin's academic accomplishments. The
reports were glowing.

'He'll make head boy,' Philip McKay declared.

Max only wished he could share the headmaster's
optimism.

'We'll need to talk to members of staff and pupils,' he
said, getting to his feet.

'Of course. I briefed the staff this morning. You'll find
everyone more than willing to co-operate.'

'Thank you.'

The teachers were co-operative, but they all said the
same things. Martin was hard-working, pleasant and

25

happy. In short, he was the model pupil. They confirmed that there was no bullying at the school, and they passed on the names of Martin's friends, but nothing useful was forthcoming.

The last names on the list were Ms Donna Lord, Martin's English teacher, and Geoff Morrison, the PE teacher. As Ms Lord, who also taught drama, was in the middle of a rehearsal for the Christmas concert, they left her till last and were in the process of tracking down Geoff Morrison when Max's phone rang.

'We're drawing a blank on Martin Hayden, guv,' Grace's distinct tones informed him. 'No one's seen him since he left the farm. But I've found out something interesting about one of his teachers, a Geoffrey Morrison. All charges were dropped, so it could be nothing . . .'

'Go on,' Max urged. 'We're about to have a chat with him.'

'Seven years ago, at a different school, a lad accused him of indecent behaviour.'

'Really?'

'Yeah, and I've done some checking. Morrison lives with a bloke so he must be gay.'

'Must be,' Max agreed drily. 'OK, Grace, thanks for that.'

He snapped his phone shut and gave Jill the details.

'If he likes young boys,' she said grimly, 'he'll think Martin Hayden represents all his Christmases rolled into one.'

Geoff Morrison was striding, oblivious to the rain, from the football field to the swimming pool, wearing a red T-shirt and dark blue jogging trousers. Around the thirty mark, with very short dark hair and big muscles, he wouldn't have looked out of place on an army assault course.

Max and Jill waited under cover until he reached them, then Max introduced them and showed his ID again.

'Can you give me five minutes?' Morrison asked. 'I've got boys waiting for their swimming lesson. I'll get them in the pool and – well, we can talk there, can't we?'

'Can someone supervise them for a few minutes?' Max didn't want to get on to the subject of Morrison's sexuality with thirty boys listening in. He didn't want to get on to the subject of Morrison's sexuality full stop. 'I'd rather talk in private,' he explained.

'No probs. Jim will be along in a minute. He'll be OK with them.'

He strode off, flexing impressive shoulder muscles as he went.

'I hate that expression,' Max muttered.

'What expression?'

'No probs. There's no need for it.'

They waited for him and he was soon trotting back to them. He was one of those who would have to jog round Asda.

'Sorry about that,' he said, flashing strong white teeth at them. 'How can I help?'

'We're trying to build a picture of Martin Hayden – his friends, interests, that sort of thing,' Max explained.

'I'm afraid I don't know him well. He's not keen on sport, you see. He would far rather read a book than kick a football around.'

'Who does he mix with?' Jill asked, adding, 'You must know that. He's a striking boy. Handsome. You can't help but notice him.'

Max saw how he flushed slightly at that comment.

'He's often with Jason Keane so a word with him could be useful. Your best bet is to talk to his classmates.'

'Seven years ago,' Max began, 'I gather a young boy accused you of – what was it? Indecent behaviour?'

'Oh, that. Yes, a pupil. I'd dropped him from the first eleven football team and he didn't take it well. It warranted a paragraph in the local paper, but he knew he hadn't a leg to stand on.'

'A good-looking boy, was he?' Jill asked.

'Nothing special.'

'What would you call special? Someone like Martin Hayden? Tall and slim, graceful, blond hair?'

27

He laughed at that. 'I'm not interested in seventeen-year-olds, if that's what you're getting at.'

'Got a boyfriend, have you?' Jill asked.

His face turned the same shade of red as his T-shirt. 'As a matter of fact, I have. He's thirty-eight years old and works in the music industry. He's what I'd call special,' he added for good measure.

'Doing what in the music industry?' she asked.

'He sings in a band, produces records, writes songs –'

'The boy who made those accusations seven years ago,' Jill said, with a swift change of subject. 'What did he look like? Tall? Short?'

'Average, I seem to recall.'

'Dark? Blond?'

'I think he had fair hair, but I really can't see what this has –'

'Your boyfriend, what does he look like?'

'Now, listen,' he spat out. 'I have no idea where young Hayden has wandered off to. None at all. And I fail to see what my private life has to do with it.'

'You think he's wandered off?' Max asked. 'From what I've heard, he's not the type to miss school or not let his parents know where he is.'

'I can't tell you where he is,' Morrison said curtly. 'Now, is there anything else?'

'No, that'll be all for now. Thank you for your time, Mr Morrison.'

With a muttered 'You're welcome,' he strode off, rubbing tense neck muscles as he went.

'He's not your biggest fan, kiddo,' Max said as they watched him.

'I'm not his, either. I'd like to know about the boy who made those accusations. I'd like to see a photo, too.'

'I'm sure Grace is on to it.'

'I know Jason Keane,' she remarked. 'The family lives at Kelton Bridge in a huge stone house by the church. Stacks of money, I imagine, but a nice family. Jason's always seemed a pretty down-to-earth type. He's another good-looking boy. Gets on well with other kids in the village. He organized a charity car wash when Kelton was raising funds for Emma Bolton, a toddler with cancer.'

They headed back to the main entrance, looked at a plan of the school, and then set off for Room E4 where Max guessed Ms Lord taught kids how to punctuate such classics as CU2nite and CUl8er.

The door had a glass panel and Max peered through.

'Blimey, they didn't make teachers like that when I was a kid.'

Jill took a look. 'Just as well, Max. If they had, you'd still be struggling with the cat sat on the mat.' She rolled her eyes. 'Are we going to talk to her or would you prefer to stand here and drool all afternoon?'

Ms Donna Lord was in her late twenties or early thirties with long, blonde hair tumbling over her shoulders. It kept falling across her face and every time she tossed it back, pupils were treated to a glimpse of cleavage. She was sitting on the edge of a desk at the front of the class, wearing a tight blue skirt, blue blouse and high heels. Stockings, too, probably. Yes, Max would bet she was wearing stockings. If they stood there for a few more minutes, they'd probably find out because she kept crossing and uncrossing incredibly long legs. Max wouldn't be surprised if the lucky lad in the front row could already answer that question.

'We'll talk to her,' he said. 'You'll have to nudge me if I start drooling.'

Just as he lifted his hand to knock on the door, she spotted them, smiled an acknowledgement and slid off the desk. She said something to her pupils that made them laugh and walked over to the door, opened it and closed it behind her.

'You'll be the police,' she said, in a slightly husky voice. 'I'm sorry I missed you earlier but the Christmas concert is looming and, believe me, they need all the rehearsals they can get.'

Her voice was even better than he'd expected. Throaty, and very sexy. He wondered if she'd been born with it, or if she was a heavy smoker.

A discreet elbow in the ribs, presumably a drool alert nudge, prompted Max to respond.

'Just a couple of questions,' he told her.

When she'd told them about Martin, her star pupil, Jill had a question of her own.

'Is Jane Austen on the curriculum? *Pride and Prejudice*? *Mansfield Park*?'

'Sadly not,' Donna Lord said, 'but Martin's read those and enjoyed them.'

'Did you give him a copy of *Mansfield Park*?'

'I did, yes.'

'Why?'

'I thought he'd enjoy it.'

'Do you give all your pupils books?' Jill asked.

'Not all of them, no.'

'So if we ask your pupils if you've given them a book, what sort of percentage would say yes?'

Ms Lord shrugged.

'It's possible that Martin Hayden might be the only one?' Jill suggested.

'It's possible. I can't remember. Oh, I did give Alison Summers a couple of poetry books.'

'Why Alison? Why Martin Hayden? What makes them special?'

'Alison's keen on poetry. She entered a competition organized by the local library and her poem came second. As for Martin, I told you, he's my star pupil. He enjoys English – language and literature. It's rare in a boy. I had a spare copy of the book and gave it to him knowing it would have a good home. It is my job to encourage my pupils, you know.'

'Did you put an inscription in Martin's book?'

She laughed at that, and Max pulled himself together. He could do without another elbow in the ribs.

'I honestly can't remember,' she replied with amusement. 'Probably.'

'Does he have a crush on you?' Jill asked curiously.

'Probably. Young boys often have crushes, as you call them, on their teachers. They grow out of it.'

'Does he have a girlfriend, do you know?' Max put in.

'Not that I know of, but you need to speak to his friends. Jason Keane would know.'

'Thank you,' Max said, 'we plan to talk to him. OK, I think that's all. Thanks for your time, Ms Lord.'

'It's Donna.'

'Max,' he returned.

'I just wish I could be of more help,' she said, 'but I don't know much about his life outside school. I've met his mother twice, but that's all.'

'That's OK. Thanks.'

She gave Max a let's-go-to-bed smile – at least that's what it suggested to Max – and returned to the classroom.

As Max and Jill walked down the corridor, the sound of her pupils' laughter reached them.

'Right,' Max said, ridding his mind of Miss Sex-on-legs. 'We'll see these pupils and then get something to eat.' It was three o'clock and he was starving.

They'd been offered the deputy headmaster's office to use. Max gave the secretary a list of names and the pupils were duly fetched from class.

The first to arrive was Jason Keane. Tall and dark, he was, as Jill had said, a good-looking boy. He and Martin Hayden must make a handsome couple.

'Hello,' he said, surprised to see Jill.

'Hi, Jason. How's things?'

'OK, I think.'

'Good. I'm here helping the police,' she explained. 'We're trying to find out what's happened to Martin. He's a friend of yours, isn't he?'

He nodded, yet Max thought he looked nervous. That meant nothing, though. Even in these so-called enlightened days, when Max couldn't deliver so much as a well-deserved clip round the ear, a rare few were still in awe of coppers.

'We thought you'd be most likely to know how he thought,' Jill went on. 'Did he say anything, drop any hints, or suggest in any way that he might not be in school yesterday?'

'No. He definitely intended to come because we planned to go into town afterwards and look in HMV. The music store, you know?'

'I certainly know it,' Max told him. 'My sons would spend a fortune in that shop.'

He gave the lad an encouraging smile. 'Does Martin have a mobile phone?' His parents had said he didn't, but Max couldn't imagine a boy of that age without one permanently glued to his ear.

'No, he doesn't.'

'Do you, Jason?'

'Oh, yes. My mother insisted. Just for emergencies, really.'

'A wise woman.' Max smiled. 'Does Martin know the number?'

'Yes.'

'So if he had any sort of problem, he'd call you?'

'Yes, but he hasn't.'

'Apart from looking in HMV, what else do you both do after school?'

'Sometimes we go to McDonald's for a burger, but usually we go straight home. On Fridays, Martin –' He stopped short, looking as if he'd said too much.

'Go on,' Max urged him. 'What does Martin do on Fridays?'

'He has guitar lessons,' he admitted quietly.

'Really?' Jill was surprised. 'I didn't realize he played guitar.'

'Er, no. The thing is, his parents – well, it's his father really who doesn't approve. Martin keeps his guitar at my house, and I bring it in for him on Mondays, Wednesdays and Fridays.'

'Why Mondays and Wednesdays, Jason?'

'So he can practise.'

'I see. And it's a secret?'

'Yes.'

'That's OK,' Jill said, smiling to reassure him.

'Where does he have lessons?' Max asked.

'From a man in Church Street, a Mr Campbell. He's a strange chap, but Martin says he's a brilliant teacher.'

They talked for a few more minutes, but Jason could shed no light on Martin's disappearance.

'Let me know when you're organizing another charity car wash,' Jill said as he was leaving. 'Mine's never been so clean.'

'I will,' he promised, 'but we'll be charging a fiver next time,' he added with a grin.

The next boy they saw was Keith Palmer. He wasn't such a fan of Martin's.

'We usually sit together on the bus,' he told them, 'but that's all. We used to be good friends. Until last Christmas.'

'What happened at Christmas, Keith?' Jill asked.

'Martin was supposed to be taking my sister, Claire, to the school disco,' he explained. 'Something better turned up, though, and he dumped her at the last minute.'

'Something better?' Jill queried.

'Carole Moreton. Her parents are loaded.' He hesitated. 'Martin uses people. He thinks he's God's gift to the universe and only chooses friends that he thinks will do him some good.'

Was that true, Max wondered, or was Keith Palmer still bitter because his sister didn't go to the ball with Martin?

'Everyone will tell you he's wonderful,' Keith warned them, 'but he's not. If something exciting cropped up, he'd go off without a thought for letting anyone know.'

Max only hoped he was right.

The last pupil they spoke to was David Fielding.

'I suppose everyone's saying I beat him up,' he said shiftily, taking Max by surprise.

'Did you?'

33

'No.'

'Then why does everyone say you did?'

Fielding shifted uneasily in his seat. 'Me and me mates thought he needed a bit of a kicking, but we never hurt him. That's all lies.'

'When was this, David?'

'A couple of weeks ago. We only called him names. Faggot, queen, stuff like that. Honest. Anyway, he got over it. Must have, because on Friday, he said he wanted us to be mates and that we'd have a drink after school.'

Faggot? Queen?

'And when are you going to have this drink?' Jill asked.

'Should've been yesterday. He was supposed to be bringing some of his old man's home-made wine in.'

'And you didn't see him at all yesterday?' Max asked.

'No.'

'OK, David, that'll be all. You can get back to your English lesson now. Is Miss Lord your teacher?'

'Yeah.' He grinned.

'Then I'm sure you're eager to get back,' Max said, allowing himself an inner smile. 'Off you go!'

Chapter Five

It was almost six o'clock when Jill turned off the main road towards Kelton Bridge. She'd intended to go straight to her cottage but, on an impulse, she stopped at The Weaver's Retreat. The Haydens might be a very private family, but there was little that escaped the residents of Kelton Bridge, and the pub was the best place to hear the gossip. The second best place was the village post office, but Olive Prendergast's tittle-tattle tended to come highly embellished.

'The usual, is it, Jill?' Ian, the landlord, asked, his hand already on the lager pump.

Jill didn't really know what she fancied. It might as well be lager as anything else.

'Please.' She looked in dismay around the empty bar. 'Where is everyone?'

'It were busy earlier,' he replied, pouring her a half-pint of Stella, 'but there's often a lull around now.'

'Thanks.' She handed him a fiver as he put her glass on the bar.

'Still raining, is it?'

'Worse than ever. We'll have to build an ark soon.'

He smiled at that. 'It's supposed to improve tomorrow. Should be colder and windier, but dry.'

'Fingers crossed then.' She perched on a stool at the bar and took a sip of lager. 'Have you heard about Martin Hayden, the boy from Lower Crags Farm?'

'Aye, me and Dennis were talking about it earlier. It's a funny do. Mind, he's a bit of a wild one, by all accounts, so he could have gone off anywhere.'

'A wild one?'

'He seems to have gone that way lately,' Ian said, nodding. 'He's been thrown out of a couple of pubs in Harrington in the last couple of months. Mind, that'll be the landlords' fault, if you ask me. They're too happy to turn a blind eye to under-age drinking. I know he could pass for eighteen, but landlords are supposed to ask for ID from anyone who looks younger than twenty-one. Anyway, he got thrown out twice that I know of. You know what kids are like when they've had too much to drink.'

'Yes, I can imagine. Do you know the family well?'

'No.' He polished his side of the bar as he thought. 'Occasionally, very occasionally, Andy, his brother, has a drink in here. George Hayden's been known to call in but he's not a particularly chatty or popular bloke.'

Jill was all too aware of that.

'What about the boy's mother?'

'Josie? She seems nice enough, but she doesn't have a lot to say for herself.' He grunted. 'George makes sure of that.'

The door banged open and Tony Hutchinson breezed in. 'Hi, Jill. Ian. Where is everyone?'

While Ian explained again that they'd missed the rush, Jill looked at the tie Tony was wearing. As headmaster of Kelton Bridge's primary school, he dressed in suit and tie every day, and Jill was fascinated by his ties. They came in all colours of the rainbow and, if they didn't happen to match his shirt, they were guaranteed to clash violently with socks that had been fluorescent yellow. In his midfifties, he was a good-looking man, but those socks . . .

'We were talking about Martin Hayden,' Jill said as he sat on the stool next to her and took a swallow of his pint. 'Do you know the family, Tony?'

'I taught the three children,' he said, licking froth from his top lip. 'They were OK, but I don't know the parents well. They keep themselves to themselves. They've never involved themselves in school or village activities.'

'What do you make of young Martin?' she asked.

36

'An honest opinion? He's a spoilt brat.' He took another swallow of beer. 'Not in a material way perhaps,' he added thoughtfully, 'but – oh, perhaps he's not spoilt exactly, but he's got one hell of a high opinion of himself. A bright boy, though.'

Nothing he said surprised Jill.

'The daughter's a hairdresser,' he went on. 'She's done Liz's hair a couple of times.'

'Oh?'

Now that did surprise Jill. Liz, Tony's wife, was always immaculately coiffeured and Jill had assumed that only a top stylist was allowed near it.

'Yes. Apparently, she's into astrology. A nice enough kid, though. It's just the males in the family that no one would want to associate with.'

'What about Andy?' she asked curiously.

'He'll be as big a bully as his father one day.' He grimaced. 'Sorry, but you did ask my opinion.'

And she was grateful for any opinion.

'What do you think, Tony? Might Martin have escaped the farm and done a runner?'

'It wouldn't surprise me in the least,' he replied easily. 'Martin Hayden looks out for Martin Hayden and Martin Hayden alone. He wouldn't think twice about anyone else.'

Perhaps he'd done exactly that. Jill hoped so.

Now it was Tony's turn to ask the questions. 'Is this idle curiosity or have you returned to police work?'

'I discussed Martin's disappearance with the force,' she said, 'but no, I'm not working for them.' She grinned, knowing exactly what Tony thought of the self-help books she wrote. 'I'm too busy writing.'

'From top criminal profiler to crutch for housewives who are feeling a tad stressed by life.' He tutted. 'You must be mad!'

'Quite probably.'

She finished her drink and declined Tony's offer of another. With a deadline looming and a day's work missed, she needed to get back to her cottage and her computer . . .

A bit of housework wouldn't come amiss, either, she decided when she walked into her cottage.

The cat flap clicked open and closed, and she scooped Sam into her arms. He was getting even fatter if that were possible.

'Are you feeling neglected?' she murmured. 'Never mind, a spot of dieting wouldn't hurt.'

At the sound of the tin opener, her other cats, Tojo and Rabble, appeared.

With the animals happy, she made a coffee and drank that, then quickly tidied the sitting room.

As she did so, she thought back to her meeting with Martin Hayden's family, or part of that family. She hadn't met the sister.

Yesterday morning, Martin's mother had said goodbye to her son, as she did every morning and, as yet, they'd found no one who had seen him since. On the half-mile walk from the end of the farm's drive to the bus stop, Martin had vanished. But boys didn't vanish. The road in question was a winding, narrow B-road, but someone must have seen him.

How long would it take him to walk that half-mile? Ten minutes? His mother had said he'd left in good time to catch the bus, and it hadn't been raining then. They had several centimetres of rain yesterday, but it hadn't started until after ten o'clock. According to his mother, he often listened to music on his MP3 player as he walked. He wouldn't have been rushing.

George Hayden wasn't behaving like a distraught father. Why? Because he knew, or thought he knew, where Martin was? Had there been a family row? Was that what Josie Hayden was hiding?

Jill's phone rang and she saw from the display that it was either her mother or father.

'Hello, love, I wondered if I'd catch you. Not out tonight then?'

'Apparently not, Mum,' Jill replied, amused. 'How are things in Liverpool?'

'Oh, all right. What about you?'

'Busy,' Jill told her, as she always told her. It was usually true, but she knew she should make more time to visit her parents. 'Dad OK?'

'Ha! And how should I know? He's been fishing every night this week. I tell him, I don't know why he bothered to marry me. But then, he wouldn't have a resident skivvy if he hadn't. And you'll never guess what the devil did – oh, that reminds me, you know Tom Peters who lives at number four? He married that flighty piece with the red hair?'

'Nope, means nothing to me.' Mum forgot that she hadn't lived on the estate for seventeen years.

'Well, it seems as if he's giving her a dose of her own medicine. He's carrying on with – oh, I don't suppose you'd know her. She only moved in a few months ago. All tits and arse, your dad described her. And he's probably right at that. She's got a couple of kids and not a sighting of the father. Name's Tracy.'

'It's all happening on River View then,' Jill said with amusement.

'We certainly see life,' Mum agreed. 'And then there's – well, well, well! Look what the cat's dragged in.'

Jill assumed that her father had returned from his fishing trip. Rain or shine, day or night, he and his mates hauled fish from the water, congratulated each other, and then threw them back. Pointless!

She waited for the inevitable bickering between her parents. Devoted to each other they were, but outsiders would never know it.

'You daft bugger,' she heard her mother say softly.

No wrangling?

'Here, Jill, talk to your dad a minute.'

'Hi, Dad. Catch a big one?'

'I caught nothing,' he said with disgust. 'Not a bite all night. That pike was hanging around, though. I'll have him one of these nights. Anyway, how's my girl?'

'Your girl's wondering how you've managed to escape a lecture from your wife.'

'Easy,' he said with a chuckle. 'I stopped at the filling station on the way home and bought her a half-price bunch of flowers and a box of chocolates.'

'Ah!' Jill laughed. 'What woman could resist such sophistication?'

'I had a couple of quid on Starlight in the 1.30,' he explained the reason for such extravagance, 'and it romped home at sixteen to one.'

'I thought of backing that, but I didn't get a chance to look at the runners properly. However,' she added, enjoying the chance to gloat, 'I did manage to put a few quid on Pigeon Post.'

'Eh? Never! God, that was a good price, wasn't it?'

'Thirty-three to one. It won by a short head.'

'Well I never! A pity you didn't get a good look at the runners. The way your luck is at the moment, you'd be quids in. So what kept you busy?'

She explained about Martin Hayden's disappearance. 'So I've been to see his family. I'm unofficially helping the police.'

'Oh?' he said knowingly. 'Any particular copper?'

Jill smiled to herself. Her dad, like everyone else on River View estate, had an inbuilt distrust and dislike of the police but there was one exception.

'Yes.'

'Ah.'

'It was strictly business,' she assured him, 'and there's no need to mention it to Mum or she'll be ordering her wedding outfit.'

'You could do a lot worse, sweetheart.'

'I could do a hell of a lot better, too.'

Her parents, her sister – everyone was convinced that Max was the catch of the century. No matter what Jill said, no one would believe it was over, that she no longer loved him. She *had* loved him. She'd believed there could never be anyone else for her. But he'd had an affair, or if not an

40

affair then a sordid one-night stand, and it was over. It had been over for a long time.

She felt a familiar sick feeling in the pit of her stomach. Even thinking about his betrayal was something she'd rather not do.

'So how's Mum? Really?' she asked, changing the subject.

'Doing great,' he answered, and Jill could sense that, for once, he was telling the truth. She'd had an operation on her lung. Thankfully, it had been successful.

'And the ciggies?' Jill asked.

'Not had a puff since!'

Jill smiled at the pride in his voice. 'Good for her.'

'Mind you,' he added, 'she's gone from sixty fags a day to forty Mars bars a day.'

They talked for a few more minutes, then Jill chatted to her mother again before ending the call . . .

Max had met her parents a few times, and he'd liked them probably as much as they'd liked him. 'A good honest bloke,' her dad had called him.

'And how would he know?' Max had joked when Jill had passed on the compliment. 'He lives on River View. That lot make the Krays look like charity workers.'

He had a point.

River View was a rough estate, and it was getting worse. A look in the local paper was enough to convince people that the majority of petty criminals hailed from the estate. Her parents had moved there when they married and wouldn't entertain the idea of moving. Mum carried on as if she lived in her personal soap opera and Dad liked to think he was tougher than any of them . . .

She deliberately turned her thoughts back to Martin Hayden. Assuming there had been a family row, and it seemed likely, where would a boy like Martin go? He would want to teach his parents a lesson, yet he would want his comforts, too. So where would he go?

Or perhaps he hadn't gone anywhere. Perhaps George Hayden was trying to teach his son a lesson. Perhaps he knew exactly where he was.

Chapter Six

At Lower Crags Farm, Josie Hayden was busy in her kitchen. She'd fed her family – except her lovely Martin – and was washing up. Her hands refused to stop shaking and a long and painful scream was desperate to escape. Yet she kept busy.

From her window at the sink, she could see the moon sliding out from behind the clouds.

The door opened behind her and she instinctively stiffened.

'Let me help, Mum.'

The concerned voice of her daughter almost had her screaming. 'Thanks, love.'

Josie was relieved it was Sarah and not George, but she didn't want help. She wanted the pile of plates to be never-ending so that she could stand here, staring out into the darkness, until her son came home.

'You OK, Mum?'

'Yes, love. You?'

'Yeah.'

No sooner had Sarah uttered the word than she was in tears, her arms flung around Josie's waist, her head pressed tight against her chest.

'There, love,' Josie soothed. 'Try not to think the worst, and try to be strong for your dad, eh?'

'I am trying,' Sarah sobbed, 'but I'm frightened, Mum. So very frightened.'

'I know, love.'

Sarah rubbed at her tears with her knuckles. 'What's wrong with you and Dad? You're not even speaking to each other.'

'It's hard,' Josie said, leaping to George's defence. 'Things like this will bring some people together. But others, like me and your dad, tend to worry in silence.'

Sarah thought about this.

'But Dad seems so angry with you.'

He was angry all right. Furiously angry.

'No, love. Now, let's get this lot out of the way, and then take them a cuppa, eh?' she said, changing the subject.

Sarah rubbed at her tear-marked face again, but she picked up a tea towel.

They washed and dried plates and cutlery, put everything away and made a pot of tea without saying a word. What was there to say? They both shared the same terrors . . .

That night, Josie lay in bed and pretended to be asleep while George tossed and turned alongside her.

She'd heard Sarah go downstairs, probably to make herself a drink. What about Andy? she wondered. Was he sleeping or was he lying there, like she was, dwelling on all the frightening possibilities?

She sometimes thought her whole life had been one long nightmare . . .

'You've got the curse!' Uncle Terry had cried.

Of course, the curse to which Uncle Terry had referred was her periods. He'd been horrified to realize she had started menstruating. Not that it had stopped him. But perhaps there had been more to his words than even he had known. Maybe she had been born under an ancient curse.

She'd been twelve years old when Uncle Terry had first come to babysit. He wasn't really her uncle, or even a blood relative. He was a friend of her mother's.

An only child, with a father God knew where and a mother who liked to be out either working or enjoying herself most evenings, Josie was a lonely girl. Yet she preferred the loneliness. She dreaded the nights that Uncle Terry stayed with her.

'Come and sit on my knee,' he used to say, and Josie's refusals had merely angered him. So she'd sat on his knee . . .

Josie still felt sick when she remembered the way his hand slid along her thigh and to her secret place. She still wanted to vomit when she thought of his fingers touching her. His breath had smelt of stale cigarettes, and it had been animal-hot against her face. She still had to bite back a scream whenever she recalled the searing pain as he forced himself inside her.

'Don't tell Mummy,' he would gasp, thrusting away, his hand clamped over her mouth to silence her screams of pain.

She didn't tell Mummy. Until she was fourteen years old and pregnant.

'You're a dirty, filthy-minded little liar!' Her mother's hand had stung Josie's face.

Josie was taken away to have the baby. Other than a quick glimpse before the nurse carried it from the delivery room, she never saw her child.

When she returned home, it wasn't mentioned. Her mother refused to discuss the matter. Twice Josie tried to talk about it and her mother's reaction was the same each time. Josie received a sharp slap across the face and was threatened with much worse if she ever dared to utter such filth again.

Not a day, not even an hour went by during which Josie didn't wonder about her baby, but she never spoke of it to anyone. Few nights passed when she didn't have nightmares . . .

Life improved when she left school and took a job with a firm of solicitors. She worked hard and the senior partner encouraged her to go to the college and study shorthand and typing.

How the world has changed, she thought. Everyone used computers these days. They would have no need for

44

the diligent, hardworking secretary with her excellent shorthand and typing speeds and her neat handwriting.

Josie was soon promoted, and Sue Johnson arrived in the office to take her place.

Pretty, bubbly and fun-loving, Sue was Josie's first real friend. Sue would return to the office after her lunch break with a cream cake for each of them. She spent a fortune on women's magazines, for the fashion, diet and make-up tips, and always passed them to Josie when she'd finished with them.

It was Sue, hell-bent on showing Josie the meaning of fun, who persuaded Josie to go to the Hallowe'en party.

The music had been too loud, Josie remembered, and she and Sue had both had too much to drink. Sue had wandered off to dance with a young man, and Josie, her confidence vanishing with Sue, had been about to hide in the Ladies when George approached her.

'All on your own?' he'd asked. 'Must be my lucky night.'

He was a stocky, red-faced man with thick dark hair. Older than her, too. He'd flirted with her and made her laugh. For the first time, she had felt like an attractive young girl who people would find interesting. He was nothing like Uncle Terry.

They made love in the back of his car, a big old-fashioned Rover with cold leather upholstery, and then, in a flurry of apologies, George had driven her home.

He'd been the perfect gentleman, and Josie had tumbled into her bed that night with a smile on her face. Their love-making hadn't been memorable, or even particularly enjoyable for her, but she'd felt enlightened. At long last she knew that it wasn't a matter of gritting her teeth against the terrible pain. She had fallen asleep giggling about those cold leather seats . . .

It was the following morning, with the effects of the alcohol replaced by the icy light of day, that the horror of what she'd done hit her.

She had been thoroughly disgusted with herself. People would think her a cheap tart who would go with anyone

45

for a couple of drinks. She had behaved like her mother, and Josie knew how people sniggered behind her mother's back. She knew the names they called her.

Amazingly, three days later, George phoned her at home. He hadn't known her surname, yet he'd searched the phone directory for her address.

'Lucky for me your surname's Dee and not Wood,' he'd joked awkwardly.

He had asked to see her again, but Josie hadn't felt able to face him. It was difficult enough talking over the phone. She'd mumbled a few embarrassed apologies, promised to call him if she changed her mind, wished him well, and ended the call.

Two months later, she discovered she was pregnant.

It had been a day much like this one, with an unrelenting downpour, yet she'd sat outside the health centre with the rain masking her tears. She'd been dazed and confused.

The nightmares started again. In each one, a baby was torn from her body and thrown into a furnace . . .

Josie, at her wits' end, resorted to phoning George. They met in a dingy café long since closed and Josie, her face burning with embarrassment, spilled it out.

'What do you want? Money, I suppose,' George had grunted.

'I don't know what I want,' Josie admitted. 'I didn't know where else to turn. I thought you should know, that's all. But no, I don't want your money. What good would that do?' She'd risen to her feet, tears stinging at her eyes. 'I'm sorry, I shouldn't have called you. I'll have to think about things.'

Josie hadn't expected anything more, and she would have left it at that, but he caught her by the wrist and made her sit down again.

'You'll have an abortion?'

'I will not!'

She'd already lost one baby; she wouldn't lose this one. People could say what they liked. They could go to hell for all Josie cared.

'Then we'll have to get wed,' he announced. 'Aye, we can be wed in a few weeks.'

The idea horrified her. They were complete strangers. They'd made love, committed the most intimate of acts, yet they were strangers. In normal circumstances, with both of them sober, they wouldn't have looked twice at each other.

At almost ten years her senior, George was too old for her. He was a farmer and Josie knew nothing of the land. She didn't want to know, either. She had dreams of her own and farming didn't feature in them. What she longed for was a place of her own, a flat in town, one that was close to her office. She was saving every penny she could for her dream home.

With a baby though, she could wave goodbye to her dream.

Could she marry George? If she did, her problems would be solved. She wouldn't have to face her mother's wrath, suffer ridicule from friends and neighbours or worry about supporting them both. She could keep this baby and give it a father. They would be respectable . . .

They were married four weeks later and Josie was moved into Lower Crags Farm. She left her job and devoted herself to caring for George and his parents. All George wanted was a woman who cooked, washed and cleaned, but she was grateful. Sickeningly grateful.

When Andy was born, she was even more grateful. Her son was adorable, and she loved him with every breath in her body. He was a thing of beauty in the dismal landscape that was the farm.

He was the image of George yet, strangely, George seemed to draw no comfort from that fact. He wasn't a loving father, she realized. He could easily ignore Andy for days at a stretch. The baby's face lit up as soon as he saw his father, yet George was oblivious.

When Sarah was born, two years later, George's reaction couldn't have been more different. He fell in love with her on sight. It seemed that he'd been saving all his love for his little princess.

47

Josie was saddened by his reaction to Andy, but she continued to be grateful. If George had said 'Lick my boots,' she would have fallen at his feet in gratitude.

Life had ticked along, dull but safe, until that bright, sunny day seventeen years ago . . .

Chapter Seven

Max bit into a bacon sandwich and held a serviette beneath his chin to catch any drips that might be heading for his shirt or tie.

His boss was in a bad mood. Max could sympathize. He wasn't in a very good mood himself. He didn't like kids vanishing from the school his sons attended.

'Why did no one see Martin Hayden?' Phil said, glowering at him. He hated people eating in his office. 'That's impossible, surely.'

'It's pretty remote out there,' Max reminded him. 'But one chap did, a Thomas Smith. He works at the garden centre and drives that way every morning. He saw Martin closing the gate to Lower Crags Farm. The only interesting thing he said was that a car – light blue, grey or silver – was parked a couple of hundred yards from there. The car was well off the road, under trees and difficult to see. He thought it was a couple having a quick snog before they reached the office or something.'

'What make of car?' Phil demanded irritably.

'Your guess is as good as mine. Quite small, he said, but he couldn't tell us the make, model or registration number. He's not even sure of the colour. He said he was past it before he really noticed it.'

'Get it checked,' Phil snapped.

'We're doing our best. Meanwhile, I'm off to speak to Martin's guitar teacher. In fact –' Max glanced at his watch and saw blessed escape beckoning – 'I'd better get a move on. He's expecting me in half an hour.'

'Keep me informed,' Phil said when Max was already on his way out. 'Max!'

'I will, I will!' Max closed the door behind him and stuffed the last of his sandwich in his mouth.

Despite what he'd told Phil Meredith, he had plenty of time before he needed to be at Church Street so he caught up with everyone else or tried to.

He managed to find Grace, and wondered again about parents who had given this firecracker such a name. Perhaps, after giving birth to six boys, Mrs Warne had thought her daughter graceful in comparison. Tall and reed-thin, with a broad Geordie accent and what, at best, could be termed a no-nonsense approach to life, she had never yet allowed a criminal to get the better of her. Used to bossing six older brothers around, DS Warne took crap from no one.

'Anything on Campbell?' he asked her.

'Nothing interesting, guv. He used to teach music at a private school in Cheshire until he took early retirement. No mortgage. Financially sound. No form.'

'OK, thanks. Where's Fletch?'

'Canteen.' She grinned. 'Asleep probably.'

Max smiled at that. Fletch's wife had just presented him with another daughter and Fletch hadn't had a wink of sleep since. Max had warned him, but Fletch had merely called him a cynical bastard and laughed it off.

'That reminds me,' Grace said, looking around her before going to the bottom drawer of her desk. 'Trudi will be off on maternity leave in a couple of weeks. We're having a whip round.'

'We're always having whip rounds,' Max observed, reaching for his wallet. 'And, um, who is Trudi?'

'WPC Dover. Joined us from Hull six months ago. Tall. Redhead.'

Max could place her, just. He handed over a fiver and made his escape before anyone else rattled a tin at him or sold him raffle tickets.

Jill had promised to meet him at Church Street and he called her number.

'I'm running late,' she told him, 'but traffic permitting, I'll be there by half past.'

'OK, no rush. See you in a bit then.'

'Right. Oh, and Max, have you got a photo of the lad who made those accusations against Geoff Morrison?'

'I have, yes. I'll bring it along.'

Max did an about turn and went back to Grace's desk. 'Grace, that photo of Paul Sharp – did you do some copies?'

'I did, guv.' She sorted through a pile of stuff in her in-tray and finally handed him a copy of the photo.

'What do you think?' he asked her, gazing at the photograph again.

'Nice-looking kid,' she said thoughtfully, 'if a bit dreamy. Looks older than sixteen.'

'Are you going to have a word with him?'

'I'm on to it,' she promised. 'He's working for a travel agent's in Manchester now.'

Clutching the photo, Max set off once again.

He parked outside Toby Campbell's house with five minutes to spare. There was no sign of Jill, so he sat in the car and waited, using the time to gather up a pile of junk from the passenger foot well. Having grabbed a handful of empty polystyrene cups, chewing-gum wrappers and sandwich containers, he realized he had nowhere to put them. There wasn't a litter bin in sight along Church Street. In the end, he dropped them on the back seat.

The houses in the street had been built in Victorian times. They were large terraced houses with steep steps leading to the front door. Number four was the same as the rest, and the exterior at least looked to be in good order. The white paintwork was fresh, the windows clean and a large tub planted with purple heathers added a splash of colour.

Jill pulled up just as the radio presenter announced that the news was coming on. Max switched it off. He'd already heard the headlines: more funding for police forces. He'd heard it before. If they were lucky, each force would end up with enough to train a puppy.

'Sorry I'm late,' Jill said as she joined him. 'Any news?'

'Nothing. We've organized a reconstruction for this afternoon, but that's a long shot.'

A curtain twitched at the front room window of number four.

'Looks like he's waiting for us,' Max said. 'Come on.'

They walked up the steps and rang the doorbell. And waited.

'Sorry,' the gentleman said when he finally opened the door, 'but I was down in the cellar.'

'Detective Chief Inspector Trentham and Jill Kennedy, Harrington CID,' Max said, offering his ID for inspection. He often wondered why he bothered. For all the notice anyone took, he could show them a bus pass with a photo of Marilyn Monroe on it.

'Yes, yes. Come in, please.'

When they were in the hall, Mr Campbell switched off a light and closed a door that must lead to the cellar.

'Do you live alone, Mr Campbell?'

'Yes.'

Ghosts at the window then. Great.

'Nice place,' Max added, looking around him. The decoration was too fussy for his taste, but it was neat and clean.

'Thank you. Come into the sitting room.'

They walked into the sitting room, and Max looked out of the window to confirm that this was indeed the room from which the curtain had moved. Definitely ghosts. In the unlikely event that it wasn't ghosts, either Toby Campbell was lying about being in the cellar, or there was someone else in the house. Martin Hayden?

Toby Campbell was in his late fifties or early sixties, and was obviously stuck in a time warp. He was wearing cream trousers, white shirt, a cravat and a pale lemon jacket which seemed to date from the 1950s, and his grey hair was overlong.

'Sit down,' he offered. 'Can I get you a coffee? Or tea?'

'Coffee would be great, thanks,' Max said, smiling. 'As it comes – no milk or sugar.'

'The same for me, please,' Jill answered his questioning look.

'Do you mind if I use your bathroom?' Max asked him.

'Not at all. Top of the stairs, second left.'

'Thanks.'

He didn't look worried that Max might stumble across a seventeen-year-old. All the same, it wouldn't hurt to look.

Max opened the door on the first left and guessed it was Campbell's bedroom. Checking the wardrobe confirmed this. The jackets and suits represented every colour of the rainbow. Unfortunately, there was no one lurking between the hangers.

He opened other doors. One led to a second bedroom which, judging by the dust lying on the oak drawers and bedside table, hadn't been used for a while, and another bedroom was filled with unopened boxes and bulging plastic bags.

When he went into the bathroom, a quick look round revealed no second toothbrush or anything out of the ordinary.

He flushed the toilet and opened the bathroom cabinet. Nothing of interest.

When he crossed the landing, heading for the stairs, a huge ginger cat scuttled in front of him, pausing only to spit. Had the cat moved the curtains?

By the time he returned to the sitting room, his coffee was already waiting for him.

'Thanks.' Max picked up the cup and made himself comfortable on a well-worn leather sofa. 'As you know, we're investigating the disappearance of Martin Hayden. We believe he came to you for guitar lessons.'

'That's correct. Every Friday at four thirty.'

'Did he say anything to you to indicate that he might not arrive this Friday?'

'Nothing. I've heard the news on the radio, of course, but I'm still half expecting him to turn up.'

'What are your impressions of Martin, Mr Campbell?' Jill asked.

'Toby, please. Impressions, hmm.' He put two fingers to his chin and gave the question his serious consideration. 'He's a very confident boy, and also ambitious. With Martin, everything has to be done now. I keep telling him, he needs to take time to smell the roses.' He smiled. 'But he won't take any notice of me. Old man, he calls me. He's only teasing, bless him, but there are precious few seventeen-year-olds who don't think they know it all.'

'Would you say you were close?' Jill asked. 'Would Martin confide in you?'

'There has always been a special bond between master and pupil. Yes, I like to think he'd confide in me.'

'Has he told you anything out of the ordinary lately?' Max asked. 'Anything that might be bothering him or something that's happened to him?'

'Nothing I can recall,' he replied thoughtfully, sipping from his bone china cup. 'There was a spot of trouble at the school, I know that. Martin's one of those boys that his peers will pick on. He's bright and beautiful. A few boys taunted him, I gather. A punch was thrown and Martin had a bruised eye. It angered him, but he's probably forgotten all about it by now. At the time, he vowed vengeance, but – yes, I'm sure that's forgotten.'

'What about his family?' Jill asked. 'Does he talk of them often?'

'He speaks of his sister, Sarah. I gather they're quite close. It was only recently that I knew he had an older brother. As for his parents, I think he rubs along with them OK.'

'They didn't know he was having guitar lessons,' Max put in.

'Ah, yes, I am aware of that. I once asked Martin why he

was keeping it from them, and he said he wanted it to be a surprise.'

'Is he talented?' Jill wanted to know.

'No.' Toby Campbell smiled wistfully. 'He's keen. He's decided he wants to play the guitar, and play it he will. There's no passion there, though. He'll be competent, but that's all.'

'And where would his passions lie, do you think?' Jill persisted.

'His passions? Hmm. I'm not sure he's passionate about anything. He's ambitious yes, but he has no passion. At times, he seems quite a cold-hearted individual.'

'If he were in trouble, might he come to you?' Max asked.

'I'd like to think so.' Again, Toby Campbell wore that wistful smile. 'But I doubt it. Naturally, if he does, I'll contact you immediately. His poor parents must be out of their minds with worry.'

'Yes,' Max agreed.

As they were leaving, Max again remarked on the house. 'Friends of mine were thinking of buying a house just down the road from you,' he explained, 'but they were a bit concerned it might be too small. This is a lot bigger than it looks though, isn't it?'

'Oh, yes. And you can extend out the back.' He headed for a doorway. 'Come and look at the kitchen.'

Max duly oohed and aahed over the size of the kitchen and the scope for expansion.

'And with the cellar, there's plenty of storage space,' Toby Campbell pointed out. 'One couple has converted the cellar to a games room, I believe.'

'Really? Would you mind if I had a look?'

'Be my guest.'

The cellar was like a small antiques shop. Old chairs and tables vied for space with bookcases.

'It's mostly my parents' old furniture,' Campbell explained. 'I really must get round to sorting it out one day . . .'

When Max and Jill stepped outside and walked down the steps to their cars, Max wished he had a quid for every time he'd interviewed someone only to feel he'd wasted his time. He'd be a millionaire by now.

'Do you really know someone who's thinking of buying a house round here?' Jill asked.

'No. I just wanted a gander at his cellar.'

'Ah.'

'I've got a photo of Paul Sharp, the boy who made those accusations against Geoff Morrison.' He unlocked his car and reached for the photograph. 'A good-looking boy,' he murmured, handing it over.

'Isn't he just?' she agreed. 'Almost as good-looking as Martin Hayden. If there was anything in those allegations, and Morrison *is* interested in boys, he'd be a huge temptation.'

'Grace is talking to him. He's twenty-three now and works in Manchester.'

Jill nodded. 'I'd like another word with Martin's mother. Is that OK with you? I'm sure she's holding something back.'

'Of course.' Max realized he was holding his breath. 'So, um, perhaps we could meet up later to discuss it. This evening? I'll buy you dinner,' he added hopefully.

'Sorry, Max, I can't.' She was smiling, but it was an awkward, strained little smile. 'I've made arrangements for this evening.'

Made arrangements? What the hell did that mean?

'Who's the lucky man?' he asked lightly. 'Anyone I might know?'

Her hesitation was only brief. 'Yes.'

He seemed to stand on the pavement for an age waiting for more.

'Scott Williams,' she said at last.

It seemed another age before his vocal cords recovered sufficiently from the shock.

'You're joking!' But he knew she wasn't. 'Well, isn't that just great. I try my damnedest to rid the streets of scum and he puts the scum straight back on the streets. God, of all the people. Ask him how he sleeps at night. Still, I assume there's no need to ask. You'll know how he sleeps at night. A damn sight better with you by his side, no doubt.'

'Why, you arrogant –'

'I need to go and catch some criminals to keep the defence lawyers in luxury,' he snapped. 'Let me know if you get anything from Josie Hayden.'

He jumped in his car, had a brief view of Jill scowling as she marched back to her car, and sped off.

Scott Williams? What the hell did she see in a smooth, conceited prat like him? Perhaps he was a stud in the bedroom.

Max wished that thought had lain dormant.

Chapter Eight

When Jill stopped her car outside Lower Crags Farm, she was still fuming. What right had Max to offer an opinion? She was free to spend her time with anyone she chose. If she and Max had still been living together, then maybe, just maybe, he would be entitled to give his views. But they weren't living together. And why weren't they living together? Because he'd leapt into bed with Miss Young-and-Very-Attractive at the first opportunity.

And *he* had the audacity to pass sarky comments on *her* sex life.

She could sleep with half the population of Harrington or Kelton Bridge – or indeed the whole of Lancashire – and it was still none of his damn business. How dare he be so arrogant as to assume that it was?

'Bastard!' she muttered, giving her car door a hefty slam.

She strode across the yard to the front door, took a couple of deep breaths to calm herself, lifted the knocker and dropped it against the wood.

Josie Hayden opened it before the sound had even died away. The poor woman looked on the point of collapse.

'I'm afraid there's no news,' Jill said quickly, 'but I was wondering if I might have another word.'

'Come in,' Josie said. 'Can I get you a cup of tea?'

'That would be lovely. Thank you.'

Jill followed her into the kitchen. The table in the centre of the room was well worn, and the cupboards were old and free-standing, but everything was spotlessly clean. There wasn't so much as an unwashed cup to be seen.

The window at the sink overlooked the driveway and Jill guessed that the poor woman had spent hours at that window, waiting and hoping.

'Is everyone at work today?' she asked and Josie nodded.

Josie was wearing her hair tied back and a dress that had once been a dark blue but had been washed so many times that it had faded to grey. Jill supposed that if her own child was missing, she wouldn't care how she looked, either. If it were Ben or Harry, she'd be out of her mind. She had no idea how Max would cope.

Not that she had any intention of thinking about him.

She made small-talk as they waited for the kettle to boil and the tea to brew.

'Sit down and join me,' she suggested, taking a place at the table.

With reluctance, Josie sat down. It was clear, however, that she didn't like sitting still. Those long, bony fingers kept tugging at a thread on the sleeve of her dress. The skin around her bitten fingernails looked raw.

Jill reached for her hand, as much to stop her pulling at that thread as anything else.

'Josie,' she said slowly, 'if you know anything at all, you must tell us. Was something worrying Martin? Has something happened? Has he had a fight with his father? You must tell us, you know that.'

Josie jumped to her feet and wrapped her arms around herself. She paced the kitchen, lips clamped tightly shut.

'You must tell us,' Jill insisted. 'We're on your side, Josie, you know that. Everyone wants Martin where he belongs. Back with his family, with his mother.'

Josie gazed out of that window for a few moments before turning round to face Jill.

'Yes, something happened,' she whispered. 'Martin – he isn't –' She broke off and tugged at her sleeve again. 'George, my husband, he isn't Martin's father.'

Whatever Jill had been expecting to hear, it wasn't that. She'd known that something was wrong in this family, but she hadn't considered that. Yet it made sense, and she could have kicked herself for being so dim. Martin was the odd one out, the exotic bird of paradise among the drab sparrows.

'And Martin hadn't been told until now?' she guessed.

'He hasn't been told at all,' Josie confessed.

'You're grateful to George,' Jill said, 'but you don't love him, do you?'

Josie shook her head. 'I've tried,' she said helplessly, 'but no, I don't love him. He married me out of a sense of duty. I was pregnant with Andy, you see, and I married him because . . .'

'It was the done thing?' Jill guessed.

'If you like,' Josie murmured, and Jill knew there was more.

Josie had put a plate of home-made flapjacks on the table and Jill helped herself to a piece. She remained silent, hoping Josie would tell all. Eventually, her patience was rewarded.

'Seventeen years ago,' Josie explained, returning to her seat at the table, 'I met someone. His car broke down and he walked up the lane to borrow our phone. There weren't mobile phones in those days. Or if there were, not many people had them.'

Jill didn't comment. She wanted Josie to do all the talking.

'He used the phone, we chatted while he waited for the AA, and then he went on his way.' There was pain etched on her face at the memories. 'A week later, he came back to thank me. He brought me flowers – red roses and lacy white gypsophila. No one had given me flowers before.'

Jill could believe that. George certainly didn't look like the hearts and flowers type.

'And you fell in love with him?' Jill asked.

Of course she did. He'd brought sunshine – well, red roses and gypsophila – into her sad life.

'Yes,' she confessed. 'He was a salesman, so I suppose he had to have the gift of the gab. He wouldn't have kept his job otherwise, would he?' Her eyes clouded. 'When he was in the area, we'd meet up at the Harrington Hotel. He'd book a room.'

It was difficult to imagine Josie having an illicit affair in the luxurious Harrington Hotel. She looked too weary. Jill wondered what she had been like seventeen years earlier.

'We'd been seeing each other for almost six months when I found myself pregnant.'

Again, she fell silent, her gaze on some distant spot as she relived the memories.

'With Martin?' Jill asked, and Josie nodded.

'I thought Brian loved me.' She gave an embarrassed, self-conscious shrug and Jill could only guess at the pain of her humiliation.

'He refused to believe the child was his,' she explained, 'and he stormed out of the hotel. Fortunately, George assumed it was his, and I was grateful for that.'

'And you didn't see Brian again?'

'Not until Martin was a year old,' she confided. 'Martin was in his pushchair. We bumped into him in the street, outside Mothercare of all places. Brian looked at Martin and he knew immediately. Martin's the image of him, you see. He said, "He's mine," and he sounded surprised. I said, "No, Brian, he's mine," and I left him standing in the street.'

Was that Josie's one act of defiance?

'But then, a month ago, a letter arrived from Brian completely out of the blue. After seventeen years, can you believe that?'

Jill was finding it difficult. She was finding all of this difficult to believe.

'What did he want?' she asked.

'He was wanting – demanding to see his son.'

'And? Did he?'

'No. It's rare that a letter comes for me and so I didn't think. I just opened it when me and George were sitting at the table. George saw it.'

'What was his reaction?' But Jill could guess.

Josie was on her feet again, those thin arms wrapped around herself.

'He was furious,' she whispered. 'He burned the letter and has barely spoken to me since.'

'And Martin?'

'He doesn't know. Unless George said something – but no, I'm sure he doesn't know.'

'Oh, Josie, why haven't you told the police this?'

'George wouldn't let me,' she said simply. 'He'll kill me if he finds out I've told you.' Her eyes were bright with unshed tears. 'But I'm past caring,' she burst out. 'I'd rather be dead than live like this.'

'Tell me about Brian,' Jill suggested gently. 'Where does he live and work? What's his surname?'

'Taylor,' she answered shakily. 'Brian Taylor. He's living in Harrington now. Chase Gardens. I only know that because I saw it on his letter. I don't know the number.'

There was a grandfather clock in the hall that Jill remembered from her first visit to the farm and its loud tick echoed through the house. It was driving Jill mad so God only knew what effect it was having on Josie's nerves. Perhaps the years had made her immune.

'Do you still love him?' Jill asked quietly.

Josie was a long time answering.

'It doesn't matter now, does it?'

Jill supposed it didn't.

'Where do you think Martin is, Josie?'

Her answer, when it finally came, was chilling.

'I think he's dead. I think I'm being punished. God's punishing me!'

Chapter Nine

The last thing Jill needed was a dinner party. She hated the things. She hated having to dress up, she hated having to make polite conversation with strangers, and she hated having to remember to compliment the hostess on the food when she'd rather be in her cottage eating beans on toast.

She tried Max's number again, but he wasn't answering. After this morning's comments on her love-life, she was still furious, but she did need to talk to him about Josie. Brian Taylor had become chief suspect.

There was no point leaving another message for Max so she went upstairs, showered and put on her black dress. She needed more clothes. Perhaps at the weekend, she'd go on a shopping spree and sort out her wardrobe. And instead of pulling her usual trick of coming home laden with new jeans and shirts, she must buy some clothes suitable for a social life.

Scott's silver BMW pulled up outside the cottage on the dot of seven o'clock.

'You look gorgeous!' he declared, giving her a quick kiss on the cheek.

So did he. Absolutely gorgeous. His blond hair was due for a cut, but she liked it long. He was tall, although not as tall as –

Why, she thought irritably, did she have to compare everyone to Max?

Unlike Max, Scott wouldn't lie to her. He wouldn't spend the night with someone else when he was supposed to be with her. At least, she didn't think he would. He certainly wouldn't presume to tell her who *she* should spend *her* time with.

The three cats wound themselves around her legs as she gathered up her bag, phone and keys. They totally ignored Scott, and he ignored them right back.

He was looking at his watch, a chunky Rolex that she suspected he wore because it was the best watch money could buy, not because it was an attractive piece of jewellery. Fortunately, she didn't have to keep him waiting. Scott, she guessed, was one of those people who had never been late for anything in his life.

The evening had turned chilly and she was pleased his car was warm.

'So what's going on?' he asked, as he drove them down her lane. 'Are you playing at being author or helping the police?'

She wasn't *playing* at anything and his choice of phrase irritated her.

Jill didn't know Scott well. In the course of her police work, they'd come into contact a few times, and they'd had lunch twice in the last six months. Why he'd asked her to accompany him this evening, she had no idea. More to the point, she didn't know why she'd accepted. Perhaps it was because she needed a social life. Perhaps it was because he wasn't Max. Perhaps she was finally over Max and could begin to think about the future with another man in her life. Or perhaps it was merely an eye-candy thing.

'I'm busy writing,' she answered carefully, 'but I've also been to Harrington High and Martin Hayden's home. It's all unofficial, but the case intrigues me.'

'Why?'

'The people involved are interesting.'

He shrugged, and she gained the impression that strangers held no interest for him.

The Millingtons' house was on the outskirts of Harrington and they arrived at seven thirty, along with two other couples.

Henry, their host, was taking coats and getting them drinks when Jill's phone rang.

'I'm sorry,' she said, 'but I need to take this call. It's work.'

She spotted a brief flash of irritation cross Scott's face, but Henry was obliging.

'Take it in my study, Jill,' he offered, pointing to a door on her left. 'It's quieter in there and you'll have more privacy.'

'Thank you.'

'Hi,' she said coolly, closing the study door behind her.

'I hope I'm not interrupting anything,' Max said.

'No.'

It was strange, listening to them now, to remember they'd once been so close, so deeply in love.

'Sorry I didn't get back to you earlier,' he said, 'but we've had a development. Martin Hayden's briefcase has been found.'

'Oh, God.' But it didn't necessarily mean anything. If he'd been planning to take the first train to the bright lights, he wouldn't have taken school books with him. 'Where?'

'In a skip in Burnley Terrace.'

Jill knew the street. She often left her car there instead of queuing up for the car parks.

'This isn't looking good, is it? I've spoken to Josie and it seems that George Hayden has just found out that Martin isn't his son.'

'You're kidding me. When you say "just", how recent are we talking?'

She told him about Josie's affair with Brian Taylor and about the letter he'd written, breaking seventeen years of silence.

'George is barely speaking to her,' Jill said, 'which explains a lot. She said he'd kill her if he knew she'd told us.'

'I wouldn't put that past him,' Max said grimly. 'And you say Brian Taylor lives at Chase Gardens?'

65

'Yes.'

'OK, thanks. Oh, and this briefcase,' he added. 'The contents were much as you'd expect – books, a couple of CDs, an apple, that sort of thing. But there was also a bottle of home-made wine and cocaine.'

'Coke?'

'Enough to put him away with the fairies for a good long time.'

The door opened behind Jill and she turned to see Scott.

'We're waiting for you,' he told her.

She had a sudden longing for that pub meal with Max. She would much rather be bouncing ideas around with him than wasting time making small-talk with strangers.

'Right, we can't have our favourite defence lawyer kept waiting,' Max said abruptly. 'I'll be in touch.'

He cut the connection, annoying Jill far more than Scott's impatience had.

'All ready,' she told Scott, giving him the best smile she could manage, which wasn't up to much.

Jill could eat a four-course meal in fifteen minutes if she took her time. This one lasted three hours. Forty-five minutes per course. Forty-five minutes to eat a few melon balls. She could feel life passing her by.

To be fair, her hosts and fellow guests were friendly, interesting people, but Jill's mind was elsewhere. Apart from wondering if Reluctant Guest had reached the winning post first in the 2.45 at Wolverhampton – netting her a hundred and thirty quid if he had – she was trying to put herself inside Martin Hayden's head.

Had he seen his natural father and been persuaded to take off for the promise of a better life? If Brian Taylor had promised him the moon, Martin would have left without a backward glance, she felt sure of that.

Cocaine and home-made wine? So much for the lad destined to be head boy of Harrington High School.

She dragged her attention to the man at her side whose name she had already forgotten.

'I was born in Kelton Bridge,' he was telling her. 'I used to spend hours on the hills with my dog. My best friend, Wilf Hayden, and I used to take old bottles up there for shooting practice. Wilf used to borrow his father's shotgun.' He chuckled. 'It's a wonder we didn't shoot the dog. Or ourselves.'

'Wilf Hayden?' Jill was instantly alert. 'Is he any relation to the Haydens at Lower Crags Farm?'

'He was. Sadly, he's dead now. When Wilf died, his younger brother, George, took over the farm.'

The way he spoke, Wilf Hayden had died some time ago. 'How old was he when he died?'

'Twenty-one,' he told her grimly. 'A tragic accident. He and George had a couple of old motorbikes and they used to ride them around the quarry at Stacksteads. There was a sheer drop and, one day, Wilf lost control of the bike and went over the edge. He didn't stand a chance.' He took a sip of wine. 'Tragic, it was.'

'How awful. George must have been devastated.'

'Yes. He was two years younger than Wilf so he'd have been nineteen at the time.' He brightened. 'But every cloud and all that. The farm always meant everything to George and at least he inherited that. Oh, I'm not saying it could take the place of his brother,' he added hastily, 'but, well, I'm sure it helped.'

'I know what you mean,' Jill assured him.

Exactly how much had the farm meant to George Hayden though? Enough to cause an 'accident' out at the quarry?

They chatted about the area in general and then Jill enthused over Kelton Bridge, her cottage and her neighbours until it was time to leave . . .

It was a few minutes after midnight when Scott stopped the car outside Lilac Cottage.

'Thanks, Scott,' she said, stifling a yawn. 'I enjoyed it. They're lovely people.'

'You were miles away,' he scolded gently.

'Sorry. Was it so obvious?'

'Not to the others, no. Is something bothering you, Jill?'

'Oh, it's only work. A good night's sleep will soon have me back to normal.'

'Ah. I take it I'm not being invited in for coffee then.'

The thought of inviting him inside hadn't even entered her head. It was so long since she'd had a boyfriend that she'd forgotten the basics.

'Next time,' she promised, not bothering to hide this yawn. 'I've an early start in the morning.'

'I'll call you tomorrow,' he promised.

'Thanks. And thanks for this evening. I enjoyed it. Really.'

He leaned over and kissed her cheek. 'You're a hopeless liar,' he whispered.

She couldn't argue with that.

Chapter Ten

'Dad, can we go to Blackpool today?'

'Yeah, you said we could.'

'Blackpool?' Max groaned. 'I couldn't possibly have said such a thing. What do you want to go there for? It's a horrid place.'

'It's brill!' Ben argued.

'You said we could, Dad,' Harry reminded him again.

In a moment of madness, when he was bribing his sons, Max supposed he probably had.

He made himself another coffee and leaned against the sink to watch Ben and Harry eating toast as if they hadn't been fed for months. The dogs, Fly and Holly, were watching every mouthful, too.

'Tell you what,' Max said, 'we'll get some ice-creams out of the freezer and, instead of throwing money in those machines, you can throw it in my pockets. You'll never know you haven't been to Blackpool.'

'Oh, Dad!' Harry scoffed.

It looked like a trip to Blackpool then. Max could think of a hundred things he'd rather do, but at least he'd be spending time with his kids and that's what weekends were for. He'd planned to do a few jobs around the house. Rehanging cupboard doors and tidying out the shed couldn't be termed quality time, though.

'I need to make a couple of phone calls first,' he told them, resigned, 'and then we'll go.'

His mobile rang and, while he would have welcomed an

excuse to avoid Blackpool, he didn't want work to tear him from the boys again.

It was Jill.

'Hi. Good night last night?' There was no need to sound downright unfriendly, but he couldn't help himself. If she'd been seeing anyone other than Scott Williams ... It wouldn't have made a jot of difference, an inner voice scoffed.

'Interesting,' she replied. 'George Hayden had an older brother, apparently. Years ago, when George was nineteen, his brother was killed in an accident. They were both riding motorbikes near an old quarry – there was a sheer drop and his older brother was killed. George inherited the farm, of course. He could easily have been responsible.'

'Hmm, that is interesting.'

'I thought so. And Martin Hayden –'

He'd known it wouldn't be a social call, but he was pleased she had the case on her mind. Scott Williams couldn't be too exciting a date.

'The cocaine in his briefcase won't have been for his personal use,' she was saying. 'He'll have been selling it or something.'

'What makes you so sure? He wouldn't be the first seventeen-year-old on coke. Not by a long chalk.'

'Martin Hayden is ambitious and in control. He plans everything, even the way he poses for a family snap. Coke would take away that control. It will have been in his briefcase for his advantage, not his *dis*advantage.'

Max considered that. 'He might have been planning to add a kick to the proposed drinking session with David Fielding.'

'That wasn't going to be a friendly, fun drink with his new pal. In fact,' she added thoughtfully, 'I bet he didn't intend to drink anything. If Fielding did beat him up and, from what Toby Campbell said, we assume he did, Martin will have been out for revenge.'

'You don't like our Martin, do you?'

70

'I shall be as relieved as everyone else when he turns up safe and sound.'

She'd said when, not if, Max noticed.

'I don't know him and haven't spoken to him,' she reminded him, 'so I can't really comment, but I'd suspect him of having a narcissistic personality disorder.'

He sighed. 'Which translates as?'

'Such people believe themselves to be special and limit any associations to people they consider worthy. They exploit others, they believe others envy them, and they're too caught up in their own self-importance to have empathy.'

'That sounds a bit drastic.'

'I could be wrong, but that's my view for what it's worth,' she said briskly. 'And he won't have been planning to snort that coke. I'd stake my life on it.'

'OK, thanks.'

'Let me know if you hear anything,' she said.

Before he could say he would, she ended the call. The line went cold. Dead.

'Right, give me ten minutes,' Max said, smiling at his kids. It wasn't their fault Jill was seeing Scott Williams.

While he phoned the station to see if anything new had turned up, Ben and Harry took the dogs outside. As soon as he'd finished on the phone, he joined them. It was bitterly cold.

'Let's get this mess cleaned up,' he suggested.

They cleared the lawn of balls and sticks that Fly had chewed to pieces. The dog chased around them, barking at every falling leaf that caught his eye, but Holly, devoted to Max and used to being a one-man dog, followed him around as if they were doing heel-work at Crufts.

With that job out of the way, they left the dogs with Kate, Max's uncomplaining mother-in-law, and set off for Blackpool.

The motorway was moving freely for a change and Max felt his spirits lift. It was refreshing to drive somewhere for pleasure. Even Blackpool. He was pleased with his new car, too. As yet, he didn't know what half the bells, buttons

71

and whistles actually did, but it was fun finding out. He set the cruise control then messed about with the radio. Grace would be impressed to learn that he was now alternating between Radio Two and Planet Rock.

'What's happening at school?' he asked the boys, lowering the radio's volume.

'Not a lot.'

Did Harry seem cagey or was that his imagination?

'What about drugs?' Max asked. 'Have you heard of anyone dabbling with drugs?'

'Some of the older kids get grass sometimes,' Harry told him, 'but I don't know their names,' he added quickly.

Poor Harry. Being a copper's son must be hell.

'I don't want names,' Max said casually. 'I was just curious.'

'Do you want us to get you some, Dad?' Ben asked and, even without looking in the rear-view mirror, Max knew his son was grinning.

'Now there's a thought. I could get you both locked up in a cell and have the house to myself. No noise, no moaning about homework, no pocket money to hand out, and no trips to Blackpool.'

'Ha, ha.' Harry groaned.

Max didn't have any real worries about his kids. They had too much sense to mess around with drugs, and they had too many other things to interest them. Harry lived for his football and could play the game all day and watch it all night. Ben lived for his dog. He was taking Fly, the manic rescue dog, to obedience classes. A couple of weeks ago, Fly had won a rosette at the club's show and it currently had pride of place in the lounge. Put Fly in a ring and he grasped commands such as Sit, Stay and Down. Bring him home and he was stone deaf.

Harry had always been the more confident and outgoing of the two. Ben, possibly because he was younger and had been more deeply affected by his mother's death, was quieter and more sensitive. Thanks in part to Fly, however, he was now growing more confident.

Max doubted if either boy would attain academic heights, but he didn't care about that. Like all parents, he wanted them to be happy. And safe. While he had no real worries about them experimenting with drugs, and he was fairly sure his constant nagging about talking to strangers had sunk in, he'd still breathe a whole lot easier when he knew what had become of Martin Hayden. The longer the boy was missing, and this was day four, the less Max liked it.

'Right, Blackpool here we come,' he announced as they arrived on the outskirts. 'Let's hope we can park.'

He parked easily, and scoffed his concerns. Who in their right mind visited Blackpool at this time of year?

Usually, when they walked along the sea front, Max found himself dodging girls in short skirts and cowboy hats. The hats didn't appeal but Max appreciated the short skirts. Today, however, Blackpool was deserted.

Despite his misgivings, they had fun. After walking along the street eating hot dogs, the boys filled up on disgusting blue ice-creams and then they hit the amusement arcades. When their money ran out and Max refused to hand over more, they all braved the cold wind and walked along the sand.

The boys enjoyed themselves, although they would have been happier if they could have ridden the Pepsi Max, allegedly the tallest and fastest roller coaster in Europe, but Max thought seaside towns were depressing in winter.

'Time we went home,' he told them eventually. 'It's not fair to leave Nan with the dogs for too long.'

His mother-in-law never seemed to mind being lumbered. So long as he and the boys were happy, Kate was happy. All the same, he didn't like to take advantage.

It was almost eight o'clock when they got home. The phone call came at 8.10 p.m.

A body had been found.

Chapter Eleven

Jill was looking forward to a lazy Sunday. Scott had invited her out for the day, but she'd told him she was busy. The lie, that she was visiting her sister, had tripped off her tongue effortlessly, surprising her. She wouldn't waste time worrying about that, though. The sun was shining so she decided to brave the icy wind and walk to the newsagent's for her paper.

She'd got as far as the Manor when she saw Olive Prendergast, Kelton Bridge's postmistress and leader of the local grapevine, purposefully striding out.

'Morning, Olive. Nice to see some sunshine, isn't it?'

'Nice for some. Martin Hayden won't be seeing any, will he?'

Jill's heart skipped a dull beat.

'Haven't you heard?' Olive asked, and Jill shook her head. 'They've found his body in the canal. It was on the seven o'clock news. Not that they've said it's him,' she added, 'but it can't be anyone else, can it?'

The sun had vanished behind a dark cloud that had appeared from nowhere. Poor Josie. She would see it as God's idea of vengeance.

'I hadn't heard,' Jill said.

'You do surprise me.' Olive wrapped her scarf more tightly around her neck. 'That detective you hang around with made a statement. I assumed he would have told you.'

'Not yet.' Jill smiled sweetly and resisted the strong urge to pull that scarf even tighter around Olive's neck.

'They're a funny family,' Olive went on. 'That George Hayden, you wouldn't want to tangle with him.'

Jill might have asked what she meant but Olive was another you wouldn't want to tangle with. She rarely had a good word for anyone.

'It takes all sorts, Olive. I'll get along to the shop before the rain comes . . .'

She hurried on her way, feeling thoroughly depressed. For Josie's sake, she had longed to hear that Martin had been found safe and well.

She met Ella Gardner in the shop and, typically, Ella's thoughts were with the family.

'Loss is a terrible thing,' she said, 'but the loss of a child is unthinkable.'

Having recently lost her husband to cancer, Ella knew all about bereavement.

'And for a family like that . . .' She shook her head.

'What do you mean, Ella?'

'They keep themselves to themselves,' she explained. 'That's not a bad thing, I suppose, but they'll have no one to help them cope. It'll be lonely out at the farm. I'll stop by and offer condolences, but I doubt I'll be welcome. Still, you have to offer any support you can.'

'Josie will appreciate it,' Jill said.

'We'll see.'

Jill walked home more slowly, her thoughts with Josie.

She was halfway along the lane when she saw Max's car outside her cottage, and she quickened her step.

'Sorry, I've been out for my paper.'

'You on your own?' he asked, as she opened the door and let them in.

'Yes.' No doubt he assumed she'd spent yet another passion-filled night with Scott. She might have told him she had, but what did it matter?

'Have you heard the news?' he asked.

'Yes. I just met the resident gossip. It's definitely Martin?'

'Yes, he was in the canal. And no, he didn't jump. His skull had been fractured long before he hit the water.'

Max hadn't said so, not in so many words, but she knew he'd been expecting something like this. She supposed she had, too.

She threw her newspaper on the table.

'I'll get you a coffee. Do you want something to eat?'

The question took him completely by surprise.

'Eat? Er, no, thanks, but a coffee would be good. Yeah, thanks.'

She knew exactly why he was surprised; they were barely being civil at the moment yet she was suddenly going through the social niceties. This was no time for pettiness, though. She understood how he was feeling. As yet, they didn't know what they were dealing with, and that was the scary part. A boy from the same school that Harry and Ben attended had been murdered. A boy only three years older than Harry.

Max sat at the table, jean-clad legs stretched out in front of him. She put a coffee beside him.

'How's Josie taking it?' she asked.

'How can you tell? It's almost as if she was expecting it.'

'She was,' Jill said softly. 'She thinks God's punishing her for her affair with Brian Taylor. So what have you got?'

'Anyone who heard it on the news will believe that yours truly is following several leads, but I've got naff all.' He thought for a moment. 'We won't get details until tomorrow, but we're assuming he got in a car – before he reached the bus stop – and was taken to some place. He was beaten pretty badly, and then his skull was fractured. We don't know about the murder weapon as yet. We're assuming he knew his killer and went with them willingly.' He pulled a face. 'And what's my catchphrase?'

'Never assume.'

'Quite. The SOCOs found nothing along the lane, but that's not surprising. It rained most of the day.'

'Great.'

'So we reckon he was taken, possibly in the car that Thomas Smith spotted, killed somewhere else, and thrown in the canal at the back of the old mill. He was long dead by the time he hit the water. As you know, his briefcase was dumped in a skip in Burnley Terrace.'

'Why wasn't it thrown in the canal with him?'

'I don't know.'

'So who stands to benefit from his death?' she said, thinking aloud. 'George Hayden for a start. With the evidence out of the way, he might be able to forget his wife's infidelity. And as he's killed before –'

'Jill!' Max shook his head, bemused. 'You don't know he caused his brother's death. The coroner decided it was an accident.'

'That was very convenient. Very fortunate for George, too.' She wasn't convinced by the coroner's verdict. 'Andy Hayden then. He might stand half a chance of getting some attention with Martin out of the way.'

'No. George and Andy Hayden are both in the clear.'

'His natural father then. Maybe he's worried that his wife will find out. Is he married?'

'Yes. He's on his second marriage. They married about four years ago.'

'Then perhaps he's told his wife he can't have children or something. Maybe he doesn't want her finding out. It's very coincidental, him suddenly wanting to meet his son – seventeen years too late. Oh, and I'd like a word with Martin's sister,' Jill told him. 'I haven't met her.'

'Dim but nice,' Max summed her up. 'Not much of a looker, but very fashion-conscious.'

'But don't forget,' Jill pointed out quietly, 'that I'm a writer now and I have a deadline. I'm only doing this out of curiosity.'

'I'm planning a word with Meredith tomorrow,' Max told her, 'and I think he'll want you in on this one, Jill. He'll want it solved in double-quick time.'

'It will have to be on a freelance basis. I really don't have the time, Max.'

'Whatever.'

Jill thought back to the time they spent at Harrington High School.

'Martin isn't – wasn't,' she corrected herself, 'as pure as the driven proverbial. That cocaine didn't come cheap. He has no job and only a small amount of pocket money each week. Yet he can afford guitar lessons and cocaine. He was up to something.'

'I couldn't agree more. Blackmail?'

'Possibly.'

'But who?'

Jill gave him a sideways look. 'You're the detective.'

'So I am.' A wry smiled touched his lips.

'There's the PE teacher, Geoff Morrison,' Jill said. 'If he *is* into young boys, and if Martin Hayden found out, he might be a target for blackmail.'

'I've already marked him out as a suspect.'

Sam wandered into the kitchen, leapt on to the table and sat looking very regal. Realizing he wasn't impressing anyone, and that there was no hope of being the centre of attention, he soon ambled into the sitting room.

'You don't think it's a random killing, do you?' Max said. It was more statement than question.

'No, I don't. You don't either, Max. If Ben and Harry didn't go to Harrington High, it wouldn't have crossed your mind.'

'I suppose so.' He checked his watch. 'I've promised to take the kids out to lunch,' he said. 'I don't suppose you fancy keeping us company?'

A refusal sprang to her lips and hovered there, unspoken.

'Yes, that sounds good. Thanks.'

He frowned at her, looking as if he would never fathom the workings of her mind.

If he asked why she'd agreed, she would tell him she was starving, that she'd got no decent food in and that she wanted to see Ben and Harry. All were true.

The real reason was that she didn't want to be left alone to think about Josie. And every time Max walked away, she was left with a void. Even now.

So much for her handsome, witty, charming defence lawyer, she thought grimly.

'McDonald's or Burger King?' he asked, and she laughed.

'On your bike, Trentham. I want roast beef and all the trimmings followed by something sweet, sickly and disgustingly expensive.'

Chapter Twelve

On Monday morning, after briefing the team, Max paid his second visit of the day to his boss's office.

'We need Jill in on this one, Phil.' There was no point beating around the bush.

'God damn it, Max, I knew you'd say that.' He shook his head. 'The answer's no.'

'No? Why?' A thought struck him. He wouldn't. Surely he wouldn't. Yeah, he would. 'You mention the word shoe-string and we'll all be bloody lynched.'

'I haven't mentioned it!' Phil looked insulted, as if the thought hadn't crossed his mind. 'The answer's no and that's that. If word gets out that Jill's on the case, everyone will think we're after a serial killer. People will panic.'

Max knew he had a point.

'It's your job, Max, to convince parents that everything's under control.'

'But everything's far from under control,' Max said drily, 'and if another kid –'

'That's unlikely.'

'But not impossible.'

'Not impossible,' Phil agreed, 'which is why we need this wrapped up asap.' His eyes glinted like cold steel. 'If you don't think you're up to the job, I'll bring in someone else. Got it?'

'But –'

'Got it, Max?'

Sod it!

'Yes. Got it. Loud and clear.'

Max slammed out of his office. Sod it.

He coaxed a coffee from the machine, took it back to his desk and tried to calm down.

Phil had a point, he knew that. If word got out that Jill was on the case, rumours of serial killers would be rife. All the same, he'd be a lot happier with her on the team. She could read people. A few words, a couple of minutes watching body language, and Jill knew that person. But it wasn't the end of the world. Max could read people, too.

'You ready, guv?' Grace asked.

'Yeah.'

Grace gave him one of her inquisitive looks. 'What's wrong?'

'Phil Meredith.'

'Ah.' She grinned. 'You shouldn't be so hard on him, guv. After all, it's not easy running this outfit on a shoestring.'

'Ha! Come on. Let's go.'

He and Grace would go to Harrington High and talk to Geoff Morrison. Meanwhile, the rest of the team knew what they had to do. Max was forever getting bollocked for not having faith, for believing he had to do everything himself. He didn't. While he was with Morrison, someone else would find out about that blue car, someone else would find the murder weapon . . .

Grace drove them towards Harrington High School.

'I've tracked down Peter Davy,' she told him. 'He's holi-daying in Scotland, but he's due back tonight. I got his mobile number and he's agreed to see me first thing in the morning.'

'Good.'

Peter Davy had been a pupil of Morrison's, in the same year as Paul Sharp, the lad who had made those accu-sations. According to Sharp, Peter Davy had also been popular with Morrison.

'Your boys are at Harrington High, aren't they?' Grace asked him.

'They are, yes.'

'Did they know Martin Hayden?'

'Ben didn't. Harry knew him by sight, but had never spoken to him.' Max was glad about that.

Realizing that he could hardly hear himself think, he hit the radio button to silence it.

Grace grinned across at him. 'Sorry, guv, but I don't think this picks up Radio Two.'

'Well, I won't say it's crap and it all sounds the same or I'll think I've turned into my dad. It is though.'

'Don't your boys listen to it?'

'Not if I'm within earshot,' Max assured her.

She pulled into the car park and they got out.

'I hated school,' Grace said with a shudder.

'Best years of your life.'

Max knew exactly what she meant, though. He hadn't enjoyed it, either. Like Harry, he'd been happy on the sports field and bored rigid in the classroom. Ben, still in his first year at the school, seemed simply bored rigid. He resented anything that took him from his beloved dog.

Their first stop was the headmaster's office, and Philip McKay was looking exceedingly ruffled this morning. He was also looking exceptionally smart, ready, no doubt, to face the television cameras and tell the world how devastated the school was at the loss of its star pupil.

'None of this has sunk in,' he said. 'If I can't accept it, it's no wonder the children are so dazed. We're trying to carry on as normal, but it's difficult if not impossible. Staff and pupils alike are very distressed. Understandably so.' His eyes narrowed. 'I know you're only doing your job, but I'm not sure that a police presence is helping matters.'

A police presence? Max had spotted one uniformed PC standing at the main entrance.

'This is a murder inquiry,' Max reminded him, 'which means you'll have to get used to us.'

'Just because the lad attended this school –'

'Could mean nothing,' Max finished for him. 'We're aware of that. Now then, can I ask you about Geoff Morrison?'

'Geoff?' That threw him. 'Well, yes, of course.'

82

'How long has he been at the school, Mr McKay?' Grace asked, notebook poised.

'Four years. Why?'

'He came from Manchester? Yes?'

'Yes.'

'Are you aware,' Max asked, 'that, at his previous school, a sixteen-year-old pupil accused him of indecent assault?'

Philip McKay opened his mouth, but no words came out.

'Mr McKay?' Grace prompted.

'Are you sure?' he asked at last.

'Yes. It came to nothing,' Max informed him, 'and Morrison claims it was sour grapes. Apparently, the boy was miffed because he'd been excluded from the school team.'

'I see.'

'We've spoken to the person in question,' Grace explained, 'and he still stands by his story. Nothing came of it, he says, because his family knew it was Morrison's word against theirs.'

'I see.' Philip McKay tapped a pencil against his desk. 'I knew nothing of this, but I wouldn't, would I? If nothing came of it, if it was an innocent mistake, well, I wouldn't.'

He looked at Max, and Max knew there was something else. He just knew it.

'Have you ever had any concerns?' Max asked.

'No. None.'

Liar.

'We need to speak to him.'

Philip McKay nodded. 'Yes, of course.'

Max and Grace were at the door.

'Wait!' Philip McKay waved them back to their seats. 'There *was* something.'

Bingo.

Max and Grace sat.

'Geoff, as you'll know, likes to keep in shape. He runs a lot.'

'And?' Grace prompted.

'One evening, more than a year ago, he was running through the park and . . .' He paused, and looked at Grace. 'He was caught short. Call of nature, you know.'

Max could guess what was coming.

'A third-year pupil and his father were walking their dog there,' the headmaster continued. 'Unfortunately, Geoff hadn't picked a terribly secluded spot. The father got a bit irate. He thought Geoff was . . .' Again, he paused.

'Having a wank?' Grace suggested casually, adding at his disapproving glare, 'Masturbating?'

'Yes.' His distaste for the uncouth Geordie officer was obvious. 'We had a chat and it was sorted out when Geoff explained he'd been answering a call of nature.'

'The pupil's name?' Max asked.

'What does it matter? As I said, it was all sorted out. Geoff is a well-respected teacher and the idea that he might have been – well, it's preposterous.'

'I'd like to talk to the boy's father,' Max insisted. 'His name?'

'The boy was Mark Jones,' he said with a heavy sigh, rising to his feet. 'I'll get his father's name and address for you.'

'Thank you.'

They sat and twiddled their thumbs for a couple of minutes, until Philip McKay returned with the necessary information.

'Thank you,' Max said again. 'We'll talk to Mr Morrison now if that's OK.'

'I'll have him brought here,' he was informed curtly. 'I don't think there's any need for staff or pupils to know that you've singled him out.'

'Fine.'

The door was closed none too quietly behind him.

'Having a wank,' Max tutted with a grin. 'Really, Grace.'

'I thought the conversation needed moving forward, guv. We'd have been sitting here till Christmas if we'd waited for him to describe what happened. I'll tell you

84

something else, for a highly respected teacher, this Geoff Morrison has a lot of bad luck.'

'He does,' Max agreed. 'Too much for my liking.'

A few minutes later, Geoff Morrison walked into the office. He was wearing a white T-shirt and dark blue jogging bottoms. From the sweat on his face, he'd either been running or he was nervous. Given his job, Max supposed it was reasonable to give him the benefit of the doubt and assume the former.

'Sorry to interrupt again,' Max began pleasantly, 'but we'd like another word. Please, sit down.' He indicated the seat behind the desk, the comfortable leather recliner.

Morrison sat, but he didn't look comfortable.

'How can I help?' he asked.

'We need a few points clearing up,' Max told him. 'Firstly, we've spoken to Paul Sharp. You remember him? You claimed he was upset because you'd omitted him from the school team. He claims indecent assault.'

'He's lying,' Morrison retorted. 'And what's more, he knows it. If there had been anything in it, they would have had me up in court.'

'He says it would have been a waste of time,' Grace explained, 'and that it would have been the word of a sixteen-year-old, as he was at the time, against a teacher, someone in authority.'

'Pah!'

'Have you had any other – slurs on your character?' Max asked.

'No.'

'The thing is,' Max went on, 'we've heard that a young boy and his father saw you answering a call of nature in the park and misunderstood the situation.'

'Oh, that.' Morrison laughed, but he looked as if the temperature in the office had suddenly increased to skin-burning levels. 'My own stupid fault, I suppose,' he said. 'I was dying for a pee and thought I could wait till I got home. I couldn't, and in the end I headed for the nearest bush. I didn't think there was anyone about.'

'And why would people think you were doing anything other than having a pee, do you think?' Max asked.

'People always think the worst,' Morrison answered simply. 'In this day and age, when you can't turn on the radio or television or open a newspaper without seeing, hearing or reading about paedophiles, people automatically jump to the wrong conclusions. Everyone's a thief, a killer or a paedophile.'

'A slight exaggeration perhaps, but I see your point,' Max said.

'It's no exaggeration. People always believe the worst. And teachers are a prime target. Parents are neurotic when it comes to leaving their cherubs in someone else's care. No teacher is good enough for their precious little ones.' He took a white handkerchief from his pocket and wiped the sweat from his face. 'You can check these things out. I've nothing to fear.'

Why was that? Because Paul Sharp had simply been out for revenge? Because Mark Jones and his father had completely misinterpreted the situation? Or because there was no proof to substantiate the stories?

'Martin Hayden,' Max said. 'Did he know about Paul Sharp's accusations or about Mark Jones's – mistake?'

'No.'

'You're sure?'

'No, I'm not sure,' Morrison said irritably, 'but I can't see how he'd know. Paul Sharp's claims were made when Martin was still in short trousers. As for Mark Jones and his father – well, that was something and nothing. I explained what had happened and that was never mentioned again.'

'If Martin Hayden *had* found out,' Max went on, 'do you think he would have mentioned it to you?'

'I've no idea. What are you getting at exactly?'

'Might he have been tempted to blackmail you? After all, you wouldn't want the world and its wife knowing – no matter how innocent it all was. It would look bad, wouldn't it?'

'You're right; I wouldn't want people to know. It's all ridiculous, but as I said, people jump to conclusions.'

'So might he resort to blackmail?'

'I've no idea. It's all a bit hypothetical, isn't it?'

He was rattled and uncomfortable, but that was to be expected, Max supposed.

'So he wasn't blackmailing you?'

'What? Are you mad? Of course he wasn't. What sort of fool do you take me for? Blackmailed by a pupil? A schoolboy? For God's sake!'

'For a schoolboy, Martin Hayden seemed quite affluent,' Grace said. 'Do you have any idea where he might have got extra cash? Perhaps a job he didn't tell his parents about? Something like that?'

'I couldn't say.' He let out his breath on a long sigh. 'Look, I'm sorry about what's happened to him, we all are, and I'll do all I can to help, obviously. I dread to think how his parents are suffering. But I really can't think of anything that might help you. As I've told you before, I didn't really know the boy well. He wasn't an outstanding pupil when it came to sport. He had little interest in sport or me, and I'm afraid I had little interest in him. I wish I could help, really I do, but I can't.'

'You can,' Max assured him. 'I need to eliminate as many people as possible from this inquiry so you can tell me where you were last Wednesday.'

'I've already told you. Or if not you, the coppers who were here taking statements.'

'Humour me,' Max said pleasantly.

'I was here. I left home at the usual time, about eight fifteen, and got here at about eight fifty. I stayed here until gone five and then I drove home.'

'And home is?' Grace asked.

'Mount Pleasant,' he told her. 'It's about twenty minutes away, unless you try it in the rush hour. And you've already spoken to Alan, my partner. He's confirmed that.'

'OK.' Max got to his feet, a pleasant smile pinned in

place. 'That'll be all for now. Thanks for your time, Mr Morrison. We appreciate it.'

'You're welcome. I only wish I could be of help. Right, I'll bid you good day.'

He had his hand on the door handle.

'Oh, one other thing, Mr Morrison,' Max said. 'What colour car do you drive?'

'What?' That laugh again. That nervous, forced laugh. 'Red. Why?'

'Just trying to eliminate people,' Max told him.

Chapter Thirteen

Jill was about to sit down to an unappetizing lunch of eggs on toast when her doorbell rang. She hoped her visitor wasn't hungry.

She was amazed to see Phil Meredith standing on her doorstep, his face wreathed in smiles.

'Whatever brings you to Kelton Bridge, Phil?'

'I was passing so I thought I'd drop in and say hello.' He followed her inside. 'You've got it looking very nice,' he said, and although she knew he preferred the modern executive boxes with their en-suites, he sounded sincere.

'Thanks.' She nodded at the table. 'You'll have to watch me eat. Are you hungry? Can I get you something?'

'No, thanks. You go ahead.'

That was a relief. 'A coffee?'

'No. Really.'

No one 'just passed' Lilac Cottage. The lane was a dead end. Nor did people visit Kelton Bridge without good reason.

Jill was on her fourth mouthful when he got to the point of his visit.

'You're pretty busy with your next book, aren't you?'

'I certainly am, Phil.'

'Ah, that's what I thought.' He seemed pleased to hear it. 'That's what I told Max. He assumed you'd be able to help on the Hayden case, but I told him you were far too busy.'

Jill wasn't convinced. She knew damn well that if Phil wanted her on the case, he'd waste no time in telling her so. To him, her book was of no importance whatsoever.

'Besides, as I told Max,' he went on, 'I don't think your involvement would be a good idea. You've too high a profile and you're associated with Valentine. People would immediately think we were hunting a serial killer. This Hayden case is going to receive a lot more media coverage than will be comfortable as it is.'

He smiled in that jovial, all pals together way he had.

'Mind you, Max wants you in on every case he has.' He tutted. 'That man has no idea of the budgets we work to.'

'Max has never thought highly of budgets,' Jill agreed, 'especially when there's a killer on the loose.' She could see that her sarcasm was lost on him. 'And this case will be especially delicate,' she reminded him, 'because a young person is involved.'

'Seventeen. That's almost an adult.'

'Almost, but not quite. No one in Lancashire will be happy until whoever killed Martin Hayden is locked up. The population will be nervous. Edgy. And meanwhile,' she murmured, 'Max has to send his boys to Harrington High School.'

'I appreciate that.' The all pals together smile was gone and he rose to his feet. 'Right, good to see you, Jill, and really, you've got this cottage looking very nice.'

'Thanks.'

Jill saw him out and waved when he'd turned his car around and was driving off.

He hadn't actually forbidden her to have anything to do with the Hayden case. Had he? No. He'd merely said he didn't think her involvement was a good idea.

Given that, she'd have to make sure her involvement was kept very low-key. In other words, she'd have to make sure he didn't find out.

Feeling better for having sorted that out, she finished her lunch, made a couple of calls while she drank her coffee, and set off for Lower Crags Farm.

As she drove, she tried Max's number, but he wasn't answering. She'd catch him later.

She knew he'd be busy, just as she knew he'd only taken time off yesterday because he'd promised the boys lunch. Jill was glad he had; it was the first decent meal she'd had in ages. Well, except for the dinner party with Scott. It had been fun, too. They'd been laughing and joking, like a real family.

The only thing that had marred the day had been the appearance of Martin Hayden's English teacher, the undeniably sexy Donna Lord. She'd arrived at the restaurant with a female friend just as they were getting ready to leave, and she had been all over Max like a bad case of hives.

'I didn't realize you two were an item,' she'd said, looking Jill up and down and clearly finding her rival lacking.

'We're not,' Max replied immediately.

Excuse me, Jill had wanted to shout, but we *were* an item, and we just might be an item again. The only reason we're not *currently* an item is because Max fancied a night of unbridled sex with a tart like you.

Of course, she said nothing.

It came as a bit of a shock though to realize she was thinking they might get together again one day. Had she always believed that? Did Max believe that? Or did he believe it was all over? Perhaps the choice was no longer hers to make. Perhaps he'd rather have Donna Lord.

For the next few minutes, Donna had teased the boys, and then, finally, they'd been able to leave.

No one mentioned the encounter, but why should they?

It had depressed Jill though, and she almost wished she'd stayed at home. But no, she missed those boys so much. Every time she saw them, which wasn't often, maybe only a dozen times a year, it was as if she'd never been away, as if she still lived with them.

At times, she wished she did.

The best times had been when they'd all had breakfast together before she and Max left for work and the kids left for school. Or perhaps the best times had been those lazy Sundays. Or perhaps –

It didn't matter. The worst time was when Max came home and told her, oh, so casually, that he'd spent the night in a hotel with another woman. The good times didn't make up for the pain.

Jill wondered if Josie Hayden was thinking about the good times with Brian Taylor . . .

When she arrived at Lower Crags Farm, it was Sarah Hayden who answered the door. Her eyes were red and swollen as if she hadn't stopped crying since her brother's body had been found. Jill supposed she probably hadn't. Her unwashed hair hung lankly down her back. The fashion-conscious girl was wearing black jeans and a shapeless black T-shirt. She was twenty, but looked younger.

'Jill Kennedy, Harrington CID.' Harrington CID? Tsk. Phil Meredith would throw a fit. 'I wanted to call and offer my condolences.'

'You'd better come in.' Sarah took a wad of crumpled tissues from her jeans pocket and blew her nose before showing Jill into the kitchen where the entire Hayden family was sitting around that well-scrubbed pine table.

'I don't want to intrude,' Jill told them, 'but I did want to offer my condolences. I'm so very sorry about Martin.'

'Sorry won't help, will it?'

Jill hadn't expected much more from George Hayden.

'George, will you just stop it?' Josie pleaded, a hint of steel in her voice that hadn't been evident before.

'Aye, I will at that. Come on.' He gestured to his son. 'There's still work to be done, you know.'

With that, he and Andy stomped out of the kitchen in their huge, heavy boots.

'He's upset,' Josie apologized for him. 'He didn't mean to be so rude.'

Jill would have liked to talk to George and Andy Hayden, but it wasn't her job. Officially, she wasn't even on the case. She could hardly demand that the two men answer her questions.

They were both suspects in her eyes, despite having watertight alibis. She'd seen such alibis dissolve before. They might be upset, although it was difficult to spot, but they both gained from Martin's death in some sick, perverted way. George might be able to forget that he'd brought up another man's son, and Andy no longer had to live in his brother's shadow.

'It's good of you to call,' Josie added.

It wasn't good at all, and Jill knew a pang of guilt. On the other hand, Josie would want Martin's killer found as much as she did.

'How are you coping?' Jill asked gently.

'We're coping.'

Josie was a changed woman. Jill had expected her to crack under the strain, but no, she was showing a surprising strength. Perhaps, with the family falling apart around her, she was determined to hold them together.

'What about you, Sarah?' Jill asked. 'You and Martin were very close, weren't you?'

'Yeah.' She sniffed into those tissues. 'Who did that to him? Eh? Who did it?'

'We don't know,' Jill admitted, 'but we'll find out.' She took a deep breath. 'Did Martin do drugs, Sarah, or anything like that? You were close to him. He'll have told you things he wouldn't tell his parents, wouldn't he? Yes, I'm sure he would. When my sister and I were growing up, we always confided in each other.'

'He'd have told me, yeah,' she said, 'but no, he weren't doing drugs. He were too clever for that.'

'Did he ever have a drink or a cigarette?'

'Nah. Oh, I know there were a bottle of Dad's wine found in his briefcase,' she rushed on, 'but it weren't for him. He were planning to make this kid at school drunk on it.'

'Do you know the kid's name? A friend, was it?'

'It weren't no friend. Martin called him a little shit.' She grimaced. 'Sorry, Mum, but that's what he called him. Fielding or something, his name were.'

93

David Fielding. He was the boy who'd thought he and Martin were the best of friends.

'Would you do me a favour, Sarah? I'd like to walk to where Martin used to catch the school bus. Would you show me the way?'

Sarah looked at her mother and then shrugged. 'If you like.'

Any idiot could find their way along the road to the bus stop, and Jill had already been to the spot, but she wanted to talk to Sarah alone. She wasn't the brightest of girls and, if she knew anything, it would come tumbling out.

The farmhouse was a dark, sad building and it was always a relief to step outside. It was bitterly cold today and the sun wasn't bothering to do much about that. A stiff breeze was blowing, too. All the same, it was good to step outside into the fresh air.

'How's your mum doing really?' she asked as they set off up the drive.

'OK,' Sarah replied. 'Better than any of us really. Dad's took it hardest because Martin were his favourite.'

'Didn't they ever row?'

'Oh, yeah. Dad used to go mad when Martin brought books home from school that Dad thought made him look like a sissy. Martin liked English – that's what he were planning to do at uni – and his English teacher gave him a couple of books.' She smiled sadly. 'Dad threatened Martin with his belt if ever he brought home poetry books.'

They reached the gate at the end of the drive. Sarah, who'd obviously been doing this since she was big enough, clambered over the gate. Jill, glad she'd worn trousers, did likewise.

'What about sport, Sarah? Did Martin like that?'

'Not really. He quite enjoyed tennis, but they didn't do that very often. Me and him used to play tennis in the summer. We haven't got a court or anything like that, but we used to play down in the orchard.'

She began snivelling into her tissues again.

94

'I can go on my own if this is too hard for you,' Jill told her gently.

'It don't matter.'

Jill couldn't tell how the girl was feeling, but she suspected that coupled with the distress would be the high that comes with the death of a loved one. That high, with people rallying round, people making you the centre of attention, will usually last until after the funeral. It's then that the grief really hits home.

'Didn't he like swimming?' Jill asked. 'I thought everyone loved to swim, and they've got a nice pool at the school.'

'He didn't mind swimming, but he hated the teacher. Reckoned he was a perv.'

Along with everyone else by the sound of it. 'Who was that? Mr Morrison?'

'Yeah. Martin reckoned he stood and ogled the boys in their swimming trunks.'

'He sounds a right creep.'

'He is. Martin said –' She broke off, looking embarrassed.

'Go on.'

'Nah, it's rude. Martin were a right devil at times.'

'What did he say?'

'Well, he said that when he went into the pool, he always made sure he had – um, an erection. A stiffy, he called it. He reckoned it drove the perv mad.'

Jill smiled at that, but she couldn't help thinking that Martin Hayden had been a dangerous boy to know. Dangerous enough to blackmail his PE teacher? Had Martin thought he was a pervert? Had he heard about those accusations?

'Did he ever say anything to Mr Morrison about it?'

'Nah, it were just a laugh.'

Jill wondered if that was true.

'The bus stops at the end of the road,' Sarah said, pointing.

'At the T-junction? That makes sense.' There was no point making Sarah walk any further. 'Let's turn back then.'

It was cold, but at least it wasn't raining. For all that, the grass verges still squelched underfoot. It was a beautiful spot though, and hard to remember that the bustle of Harrington was only five miles away.

'He bought me this,' Sarah said, reaching up to reveal a gold necklace that had been hidden by her sweater. 'Martin did. Nice, isn't it?'

'It's lovely.' It was too showy for Jill's taste, but it was gold, and heavy. 'I bet it cost him a lot, too. He was one wealthy schoolboy.'

'He'd got some money off someone,' she explained, 'and treated me. Out of the blue, it were.'

'How lovely. I wish I knew that person,' Jill said lightly.

'Yeah, me an' all.'

'I don't suppose he said who that person was?'

'Nah. He told me I was best not knowing.'

Probably very wise words.

If it were any other boy, she would be convinced that someone would know the identity of the person who'd given him the money. Close friends would know. With Martin, she wasn't so sure. He *might* have confided in Jason Keane, but she doubted it. Martin was one of those rare creatures who could keep a secret.

When they reached the farmhouse, Josie was sitting exactly where they'd left her.

Perhaps Sarah found the sight of her mother too upsetting to bear as she quickly made an excuse to go to her room.

'She's a good girl,' Josie said softly, when they were alone.

'Yes.' Jill sat opposite her. 'How's Andy taking it, Josie?'

'He's shocked, of course, but he'll be OK. They were never close.'

'Did they fight?'

'No, it never came to that. They weren't really close enough to quarrel. They went their separate ways and were happy like that.'

'What about you and George? How are you getting along?'

Josie grimaced at that. 'He'll speak to me in front of the kids. Other than that, he ignores me. He's taken to sleeping in the spare room. We've told the kids that his snoring is keeping me awake.' She shrugged. 'He's never been a demonstrative man so I don't suppose the kids have noticed much different. Well, we're all different at the moment, but you know what I mean.'

'Yes.'

'We'll get over it,' Josie told her. 'People do, don't they?'

Some did, some didn't. When the loss of a loved one hadn't even been faced for forty-eight hours, however, no one believed they would.

As ever, Jill had the feeling that Josie knew a lot more than she was telling.

'Have you heard from Brian Taylor?' she asked.

'No.'

Surely, the boy's natural father would have been in touch. Only a month ago, he'd been desperate to meet his son.

'You haven't contacted him to let him know what's happened?'

Josie shook her head.

'He will have heard about it,' Jill pointed out, 'unless he's managed to miss the TV and radio reports. I'm surprised he hasn't been in touch.'

'He didn't bother for seventeen years,' Josie said, her tone curt, 'so I don't suppose he'd bother now. What is it to him? Martin's just a stranger to him.'

She spoke in the present tense, Jill noticed, as if Martin was still alive. Perhaps she hadn't accepted it yet.

On the other hand, she'd been expecting to hear that he was dead. Wasn't it supposed to be God's idea of retribution?

'Josie, who do you think did this?'

'I don't know,' she said, and there was a crack in her voice. 'But I wish to God they'd taken me instead!'

Chapter Fourteen

'You're upset, aren't you?'

'Oh, for God's sake!' Geoff Morrison pushed past Alan and hit the button to switch on the kettle. 'No, I'm not upset. I've had a hard day and I want a coffee. Is that OK with you?'

Alan went into the lounge and, just to prove he was sulking, he switched on the vacuum cleaner.

Geoff would go and make peace in a minute, but for now, he needed quiet. It was all right for Alan; he hadn't had the police breathing down his neck half the day.

A shiver crawled over his skin. All those questions. All those crude insinuations.

He looked around the kitchen. There wasn't a thing out of place. That was another sign all wasn't well. Alan was tidy by nature, but if his world was turning smoothly, he worked on his music. If there was any emotional blip, he cleaned.

There wasn't a speck of dust to be seen. All utensils were in their correct places. The kettle gleamed, as did the toaster. He could see his own reflection in the cooker's glass door. Even the plants had had their leaves polished.

Soon, Geoff guessed, he'd get the 'I like to keep things nice for you' routine. He wasn't in the mood for it. Not tonight.

He was supposed to get all he needed from this relationship. Sometimes, it seemed as if all he got was suffocated. At first, he'd been quite touched by Alan's jealousy. Now, it had worn thin. He only had to look at another bloke, and sometimes he didn't even have to do that, for Alan to start sulking. The sulking was usually followed by a blazing row unless Geoff managed to calm things down.

As soon as he'd finished his coffee, he went upstairs and ran a hot bath. Alan, he knew, would be fuming at his lack of interest, but why the hell should he be the one to make things right all the time? Why couldn't Alan make some effort for a change? Why couldn't he trust him? He hadn't even asked how his day had been. For God's sake, he could have been arrested for all Alan knew or cared.

He poured a generous dollop of oil in the water. It was supposed to aid relaxation. Geoff doubted it would work.

He pulled off his clothes, letting them drop on the floor around him, climbed into the bath, and lay back with his eyes closed. All he could see was Martin Hayden laughing at him . . .

He'd been shaking all day, long before those coppers had turned up to talk to him. Had they seen the way he'd been trembling?

He was still shaking now. The bath water was as hot as he could stand it, yet he was still shivering. The longer he lay there, the more angry he became. On top of everything else, why should he have to put up with this crap from Alan?

Lying in the hot water, he didn't know whether to hurl something at the walls or burst into tears. He was an emotional wreck.

The bathroom was spotless too, so there was nothing to hurl at the walls. Apart from his clothes lying in a heap on the floor. He could throw a bar of soap at the mirror, but that wouldn't help matters.

Every muscle in his body ached from the tension. He'd like to go for a long run, but that would annoy Alan even more. Besides, at the moment, he'd rather stay close to home. There was no pleasure in running through the town centre. He liked to run through the park or out in the countryside, but if anyone spotted him, they'd assume –

Well, God knows what they'd assume.

One thing was certain, he was safer at home.

He lay in the bath for a full forty-five minutes and then, very reluctantly, climbed out. A towel wrapped around his waist, he gathered up his clothes, threw them in the laundry basket – the empty laundry basket, he noticed – and padded across the landing to the bedroom.

When he was dressed, he stood at the window for a few moments, gazing out at the street. Their house was in a quiet cul-de-sac. Nothing was happening out there.

From the orange glow given off by the street lights, he could see that the garden was a mess. It always was at this time of year. Other gardens in the road looked equally drab and lifeless. Except number three's. It was the third of December and already they had a string of lights in a tree and a flashing reindeer standing on the lawn.

He walked down the stairs, and put his head round the door of the lounge. Alan was reading the newspaper.

'Do you want a coffee?' Geoff asked.

'No, thanks.'

With a sigh, Geoff went to the kitchen and made one for himself. That was another thing; when Alan was in one of his moods, he never accepted a coffee. In five minutes, he'd go and very pointedly make one for himself.

Geoff carried his coffee into the lounge and sat down.

'How was your day?' he asked.

'Fine, thanks. Yours?'

'Pretty crap, if you must know,' Geoff told him, growing angry all over again at his short, snappy answers. 'I had the police questioning me again.'

Alan looked up, his interest piqued. 'And?'

'And it's pissing me off,' Geoff snapped. 'I had the detective who's been on the telly, and some bloody Geordie woman. Detective Sergeant Warne or some such name.'

'Why are they picking on you?' Alan asked. 'Christ, how many people knew you had the hots for Hayden?'

Geoff's temper was about to snap.

100

'I did not have the hots for Hayden,' he said, speaking slowly and with exaggerated patience.

'I saw you looking at him,' Alan cried.

'So I looked at him once. Bloody hell, that's not a crime, is it?'

'No, it's not a crime,' Alan said coolly. 'It's just not very nice when you're supposed to be with me. How would you like it if I eyed up every bloke in the vicinity? I suppose it wouldn't bother you, would it? Let's face it, you've never been as committed to this relationship as I have.'

That did it.

'For fuck's sake, Alan, shut up! If I looked at the kid, it was only because I was surprised to see him there. Martin Hayden in a gay club? Come on. I've told you before, he was a pretentious, arrogant tosser. I had no interest in him whatsoever. None.'

'He had plenty of interest in you,' Alan retorted. 'I saw the way he looked at you.'

'He did not!'

'He did. He would have been all over you the next time he saw you. When I wasn't around.'

'But he never saw me again, did he?'

'No. And now you're upset because he's dead.'

'I'm upset, if that's what you insist on calling it, because the coppers are hounding me.'

'Big deal. You know they can't touch you. And why? Because yours truly lied through his teeth and said you were here with me.'

Geoff stood at the window staring out into the darkness. His heart was pounding with anger. Or perhaps it wasn't all anger. Perhaps he was being too hard on Alan. After all, he *had* lied to the coppers. He'd said he had been with him that morning until eight forty, long after Martin Hayden's bus had left without him. If Alan had told the truth, that Geoff had left the house at seven so that he could go for a run before the school day started, he'd really be in the shit.

'Don't take it out on me,' Alan said. 'You asked me to lie to the police for you, and I did. For all I know, you could have been meeting –'

'I wasn't meeting anyone,' Geoff said on a weary sigh. 'I don't want anyone else. I'm not interested.'

'Really?'

Geoff was growing to hate that pathetic whine. 'Yes, really. I've told you a million times.'

He heard the sofa creak. A second later, Alan's hand was resting on his shoulder.

'Let's give it a rest, shall we? Let's lighten up?'

Geoff sighed. 'Yeah.'

'We could go out for a drive,' Alan suggested, his voice soft and suggestive. 'You keep your hands on the wheel. I'll let mine wander.'

It was tempting but, knowing Geoff's luck, the police would stop the car and find his dick in Alan's mouth. All the same, it might take his mind off Martin Hayden . . .

Where was Alan the morning Martin Hayden vanished? He'd said he was at home all morning, but Geoff had set off, got a few minutes down the road, and realized he'd forgotten a letter that needed posting. When he'd let himself in, Alan hadn't been there. So where *had* he been? Had he followed him? Had he been checking up on him? More importantly perhaps, why was he too scared to ask?

'OK,' he agreed. 'Let's go . . .'

Chapter Fifteen

It was almost seven that evening when Max called at Jill's cottage.

'You should be at home having quality time with the boys,' she told him. She was ridiculously pleased to see him, though.

'I've phoned them. They're OK.'

The TV was on and the local news came on. Martin Hayden's murder, not surprisingly, was the lead story. A head and shoulders of Max, standing outside Harrington nick and speaking of the progress made, had him looking very calm and in control.

'Is that idiot never off the telly?' he muttered.

Jill smiled at his poor attempt at humour. 'You did a good job there. Sounds like you're a breath away from catching the killer.'

'Ha.'

'Ah.'

He spotted her laptop open on her desk. On it were notes she'd made about the Hayden family and anyone else involved in this case. He wandered over and took a closer look, scrolling down the page.

'I had a word with Phil Meredith this morning,' he murmured, his attention still on the screen, 'and, surprise, surprise, he doesn't want you working on this case.'

'I know. He called here at lunchtime. Seems to think people will panic if they know I'm involved.'

'I suppose we should be grateful he didn't mention his bloody shoestrings.'

'Oh, he did say you have no grasp of basic economics. We had a nice little chat – just before I went to Lower Crags Farm.'

Smiling at that, Max turned his back on the laptop. 'It sounds to me as if his authority is being undermined.'

'Probably. Mention it to him in the morning and see what he says.' She headed for the kitchen. 'Are you driving?'

'Of course.'

'Pity. I was about to open a bottle of wine. Still, I suppose I can manage on my own.'

'One glass of wine won't hurt me,' Max said, a pace behind her.

The sitting room was warm and cosy, but they sat at the table in the kitchen.

'So what do you know?' Jill asked.

'Not a lot,' Max admitted. 'I spoke to Morrison this morning. Apparently, about a year ago, he was having a slash in the park and a pupil and his father happened across him. They thought he was having a wank, he insists he was having a pee. A chat in the headmaster's office sorted it all out. Funny how he keeps cropping up, though.'

'No, it's not funny. I spoke to Sarah Hayden and she said Martin thought he was a perv. According to her, Martin used to make sure he had an erection when he had swimming lessons. He used to like winding Morrison up.'

'He was full of his own importance, wasn't he?'

'He was. Not a likeable boy at all.' She took a sip of her wine. 'Oh, and he called David Fielding a little shit. I knew he wasn't planning a friendly drink with him. According to Sarah, he planned to get him drunk.'

They both mulled this over. It was always the same; the more questions asked, the more questions needing asking.

'He had money, too,' Jill went on. 'He bought his sister an expensive gold necklace and said he'd got the money from someone. He wouldn't tell her who, said she was best not knowing.'

'Blackmail, I think. And I still have Morrison as chief suspect.'

'Brian Taylor's mine. Have you spoken to him yet?'

'No. He's been at a sales conference in Italy. It's all right for some. He's due back late tonight so I'm seeing him in the morning.'

'Was he in Italy last Wednesday?'

'No, he flew out on Thursday morning.'

'How very convenient. What colour car does he drive?'

'Silver. Oh, and that's another thing. When asked what colour car he drove, our favourite PE teacher, Geoff Morrison, said red. When we checked, we discovered that he'd changed his car at the weekend. Before then, he drove a blue one. The damn thing's been valeted to within an inch of its life but we're having it checked out.' He looked at her. 'Other than that, I've got diddley squat.'

She sympathized.

'I'm sure the answer lies at Lower Crags Farm,' she mused. 'Nothing fits at the place. Nothing at all.'

A stranger walking into that house would have no idea that a member of the family had been brutally murdered. George and Andy were continuing to work. Josie was carrying on much as normal. Only Sarah looked as if she'd shed a tear for young Martin.

'I had a chat with Andy,' Max told her. 'He's as bloody private as the rest of them, but he hated that brother of his.'

'Hate's a strong word. His or yours?'

'Mine,' Max admitted, 'but I'm right. He hated him.'

'Because Martin got all the attention?' And why exactly was that? she wondered. 'Martin was supposedly the favourite, yet Andy's the one who looks like his dad, and the one who works alongside him. Odd. Except, of course, that George married Josie because she was pregnant with Andy. Perhaps he blames Andy for tying him to Josie.' She sighed. 'I don't believe in divorce as an easy option, but I think it should be obligatory in their case.'

'They're an odd family,' Max muttered. 'But the more people that disliked Martin, the more I like it. The more convinced I am that someone wanted him out of the way, and the more convinced I am that the kids at Harrington

High School are safe.' He looked at his watch and emptied his glass. 'I'd better be going. I'll be in touch if anything happens.'

She watched him go and wondered if Donna Lord had made her move yet. That she would make a move, Jill had no doubt. She'd made it sickeningly obvious that she was interested in Max.

Not, Jill reminded herself, that it was any of her business.

Chapter Sixteen

Max sat in his car outside Lilac Cottage for a moment. Whenever he drove away, he always thought how wrong it was. They should be together. That Jill lived here in Kelton Bridge was madness. They were made for each other. Even Jill must admit that they'd been great together.

Yes, he'd been unfaithful to her, but there were valid reasons for that. She called them 'lame excuses' and he called them 'valid reasons'. He'd been working too hard and drinking too hard, and Jill had been having nightmares because Rodney Hill had committed suicide. Between them, they'd been unable to cope with the pressure. Very few couples would have coped.

As a means of a brief respite, Max had spent a few hours with someone else . . .

With a sigh, he fired the engine and drove off. It was pointless going over and over the same ground. They should be together. End of story.

His phone rang and he hit the button.

'Max, I don't know if this is someone taking the piss or not,' Dave, currently manning the desk at headquarters, told him, 'but I've spoken to a bloke who calls himself – are you ready for this? – Accrington Stanley.'

'That's all I need. What a bloody day! Yes, it's genuine,' Max told him. 'To you, Accrington Stanley is a football team, the pride of Lancashire. To me, he's a pain in the arse who occasionally, very occasionally, gives us some good info. His name's Stanley and he originates from Accrington. Hence Accrington Stanley.'

'Oh. Right.' Clearly, Dave was none the wiser. 'Anyway, he said he had some gen on Martin Hayden. Told you to meet him at the usual place.'

'Thanks, Dave. I'll find him.'

There was no 'usual place', but Max guessed that Accrington would be at The Red Lion or The Nag's Head, and Max would have to go through the usual cloak and dagger routine to hear what he had to say. Among Accrington's many faults was a penchant for old cops and robbers shows like *Starsky and Hutch* or *The Sweeney*.

Max tried The Red Lion first, but there was no sign of him. He struck lucky at The Nag's Head.

Accrington was propping up the bar, an almost empty glass of Guinness in his hand. They made eye contact and then Accrington shuffled away from the bar.

While Max waited for the barmaid to finish talking on her mobile phone, he looked around him and tried to tot up the number of years the customers had spent in various prisons. A lot.

'A pint of Black Sheep, please,' he said, when the young girl finally deigned to serve him.

He handed over his money and stood at the bar to drink what was an exceptionally good pint. The service was poor, the glasses never looked particularly clean, and the customers were small-time crooks, but at least the landlord kept a decent pint of beer.

Max was halfway down his pint before Accrington looked around him, put his glass on the bar and made a show of saying goodnight to a few people.

Max had to wait five minutes – not a second less – before following him. Yes, it had to be a case of too much *Starsky and Hutch*. Still, Accrington did provide them with useful information now and again, so Max had to take part in the charade. Accrington refused to speak to him any other way. 'Walls have ears,' he'd say.

Max gave him ten minutes – it wouldn't hurt him to wait – and then left the bar and walked to the alley at the back where Accrington was smoking one of his hand-rolled cigarettes.

'How are you doing, Accrington?'

'You weren't followed, were you?'

'Followed? Me? Don't talk daft.' Who he thought might be interested enough to follow him, Max had no idea. 'So what have you got? Something to do with the Hayden boy, I gather.'

'Yeah. I've seen those pictures of him on the telly and I'll tell you this.' He broke off to look around and make sure they weren't being overheard. 'That George Hayden – I know him – and that young lad isn't his son.'

Max was disappointed. They already knew that.

'That boy looks nothing like his dad,' Accrington went on, his voice low. 'Not that that accounts for much,' he admitted. 'I look nothing like my dad. He's a right ugly bugger.'

Accrington had a large bulbous nose sitting on a red, flabby, unshaven face. His ears made cauliflowers look like exotic orchids, and his many chins wobbled with each word. And his father was the ugly one?

'I saw the lad's mother's photo,' he said, his voice a whisper now, 'and I've seen her –' Again, he stopped to look around him. 'I've seen her with the lad's real father. And I know he's the real father because the lad's the spitting image of him.'

'Wait a minute. You've seen Mrs Hayden with Martin's real father? Recently?'

'Twice I've seen 'em together.'

'Where, Accrington? And when?'

'Churchyard,' he whispered. 'I mows the lawns at St Saviour's and keeps the place tidy.'

Max knew that. Accrington would rob his own grand-mother, except of course his own grandmother was prob-ably laid to rest at St Saviour's, but he'd been mowing lawns there – gratis – for years.

'And?'

'There's a bench where all the old graves are. It's a very deserted spot. No one'd see you. I only see 'em because I heard something and went to have a gander. They was sat there as large as life. Heads bent. Talking. I couldn't hear what they was saying, mind.'

'When was this?'

'I go every Tuesday afternoon to tidy up a bit. They was there last Tuesday and the one before that.'

'Last Tuesday?' The day before Martin Hayden was killed? 'Are you sure?'

'Of course I'm sure. I would've told you before, Max, but it only came to me today. As I said, I knows George Hayden, but I'd never seen his wife, or his son. Her picture was in the paper today and I recognized her from St Saviour's. I knew then why the lad that was murdered looked so familiar. I tell you, Max, he's the image of his real father.'

Well, well, well.

'The thing is, Max,' he whispered, 'when there are them sort of skeletons in the cupboard, well, it strikes me, your killer'll be close to home.'

Good point, Accrington.

'Mm, thanks for that.' Max took a twenty pound note from his wallet and handed it over. 'You'd better have a drink on me. Oh, and if you see them again, let me know, will you?'

'You can count on me!' Accrington tapped the side of his bulbous nose and strode off.

Max walked back to his car, deep in thought.

Last Tuesday, Brian Taylor met up with Josie Hayden for at least the second time. On Wednesday, Martin was murdered. On Thursday, Taylor very conveniently left for Italy.

But he was due back in England this evening. In fact, his plane should have touched down by now. Max would be very interested to hear what he had to say . . .

So deep in thought was he, Max had driven past Asda when he remembered he'd meant to stop and buy some Scotch and wine. His mother-in-law bought all the groceries they needed, but she was hopeless when it came to keeping the alcohol cupboard stocked.

He drove on to the roundabout, doubled back, and then parked in Asda's car park.

It didn't take long to pick up a couple of bottles of Scotch and half a dozen bottles of wine, and he was standing at the check-out, the one for baskets only, wondering how people could cram so much into one small basket, when an incredibly sexy voice said, 'Having a party, Max?'

He turned around to see Ms Lord with a well-filled trolley. Even sex goddesses, it seemed, needed groceries. Looking at the contents of her trolley, Max guessed she was something of a fitness freak. There was no sugar or sodium to be seen. Lots of fruit and vegetables, several bottles of water that would taste no better than tap water, but no chocolate, cakes or biscuits.

"Fraid not,' he said, smiling. A party for two didn't sound like a bad idea, though.

She was wearing a short black skirt, a white, breast-hugging blouse and ridiculously high heels. No wonder her legs looked so long.

'I saw you at the school today.'

'Really? I didn't see you.'

'I was stuck in a classroom overlooking the car park.' She glanced at her watch. 'Do you have time for a coffee?'

'Here?'

'Why not?'

At this rate, he'd never get home. But a coffee wouldn't take long. Besides, this was business.

'Sounds good to me.'

'Great. Give me a couple of minutes – there are just a few things I need – and I'll meet you as soon as I've paid for it all. Mine's a latte.'

He watched her walk back to the deli counter. Her legs looked longer than ever. Phew, it was a tough job being a copper.

When she breezed into the cafeteria, however, his job was the last thing on his mind.

111

She parked her trolley by the side of the table and sat opposite him.

'Thanks,' she said, picking up her cup. 'After fighting my way round here, I always need a coffee to revive me.'

Max nodded at his carrier bags. 'I always need something a little stronger.'

Her lips were full and covered with a glossy pink lipstick. Other than that, she didn't wear a lot of make-up. She didn't need to.

'Are you on your way home?' she asked.

'Yes. To two boys and two dogs.'

'It was good to see you on Sunday. I didn't know you and the psychiatrist socialized.'

The psychiatrist? Jill would love her for that gem.

'Only now and again, but we used to be – close.' Until I was daft enough to spend a night with someone far less appealing than you, he added silently. The memory of that night, of how low he had fallen, still sickened him.

'You must get lonely,' she murmured, taking a sip of her coffee.

He laughed at that. 'If I didn't know better, I'd think you were chatting me up, Ms Lord.'

'You know perfectly well that it's Donna. And I am chatting you up.'

'Then I'm flattered. Donna.'

'So you should be,' she said, laughter dancing in her eyes. 'I'm very fussy about my conquests.'

With a body like that, she could afford to be.

'What were you doing at the school today?' she asked, changing the subject.

'Talking to a couple of people. Typing up loose ends.' He shrugged. 'Nothing exciting or important.'

'You were talking to Geoff Morrison for one,' she said. 'What's poor Geoff done wrong? He has nothing to do with Martin Hayden's murder, does he?'

'Not that I'm aware of.' He considered asking her about Morrison, but thought better of it. 'Do you enjoy your work?' he asked instead.

'Love it,' she assured him happily. 'I get on better with children than adults. We have fun.'

'It's the boys I feel sorry for. If I'd had a teacher like you, I would have struggled to concentrate.'

She laughed. 'Some of them do struggle,' she admitted. 'Didn't you fantasize about your teachers when you were at school?'

'Hardly! Of the only female teachers I remember, one was built like a tank, another was the envy of the boys because she had a moustache and the third was ninety if she was a day.'

Donna spluttered with laughter. 'Ah, poor Max.'

She gazed at him for long moments, and he wondered what she was thinking. He gazed right back, and he knew exactly what he was thinking. There was nothing remotely professional about it, either.

'Here.' She reached inside her handbag and scribbled her phone number on the back of a business card. 'If you get too lonely, give me a call,' she said, handing it over. 'We could meet up for a drink or something.'

The front of the card advertised Harrington's fitness centre.

'Thanks. I will,' he promised. 'But I'd better be going now.'

'Don't forget to call me,' she said.

'I won't. See you.'

As Max walked back to his car, he wondered what the appeal was. It wasn't purely sexual. Yes, she had a terrific body but so did countless other women.

He tucked the card she'd given him safely in his pocket. It was unlikely he'd use it, but he'd hang on to it just in case.

Chapter Seventeen

Brian Taylor lived in a four-bedroomed, executive detached house on Chase Gardens. The houses, twenty-four in a cul-de-sac, were identical. Boxes. Very nice boxes, admittedly, but not to Max's taste. He preferred something older, something with more character. Still, each to his own.

'It's number four, Fletch,' he said, as Fletch drove past and, for some reason, pulled up outside number ten.

'Is it? Are you sure?'

'Yes.' Or he had been sure until Fletch put the doubts in his mind. 'You need more sleep, Fletch. How are Sandra and the new addition by the way?'

'They're great.' Fletch's face had a distinctly dreamy expression as he reversed the car along the road. 'I know I wanted a boy this time, but girls are great, aren't they?' He grinned at Max. 'And the new addition's name is Chloe.'

'I knew that,' Max lied.

'Right, number four,' Fletch announced. 'It does look more promising – I mean, with a silver BMW on the drive and everything.'

'It does,' Max agreed drily.

'I still can't understand why you don't bring him in, guv. He has to be number one suspect.'

'Oh, he is. But we've got nothing to pin on him. And he'd be sure to want a brief there. We'll see how it goes here first.'

Max preferred to see people on their own territory. He always had and he always would.

They had nothing with which to charge Taylor. To all intents and purposes, Brian Taylor's son had been murdered. There was nothing to suggest that he was in any way involved. Only a lot of coincidences.

They rang the doorbell and Taylor answered almost immediately. He was talking into his mobile phone, but he gestured for them to step inside. Whoever was on the other end of that phone was struggling to get a word in.

He was a good-looking man, fair-haired and dressed casually in jeans and a crisp blue shirt. His suntan said he hadn't spent all his time in the office while in Italy. He wore glasses and a thin gold chain, very similar to the one Max wore, around his neck.

While he spoke on the phone, and Max gathered it was a business call, he ushered them into a huge lounge. Apart from two sofas in spotless white leather, a massive TV, a tiny hi-fi system, and a glass coffee table, the room was empty. It looked like a showroom rather than a living room. Max thought of his own house and wondered where these people kept their clutter. Perhaps people like Brian Taylor didn't accumulate clutter.

Try as he might, Max couldn't imagine this man in the throes of passion with someone like Josie Hayden. It was obvious that there had been passion at some point, however. As Accrington Stanley had said, Taylor was the adult version of Martin Hayden.

'Sorry about that,' he said, snapping his mobile shut. 'I'm working from home today and, having been away for a few days, there's a lot to catch up on. The voice mail's on now so we won't be disturbed.' He gestured to one of those spotless sofas. 'Please, sit down. What can I do for you?'

Fletch sat and, after only a brief hesitation, Max did, too. White leather. Who in hell's name had white leather? Someone who didn't have two boys and two dogs, he supposed.

'As you know, we're investigating the murder of Martin Hayden,' Max began.

'Yes. It's dreadful, isn't it?' He sat down on the other sofa. 'I imagine you know he's my son?'

Max nodded. 'Did you ever meet him?'

'No.' He wore a slightly wistful expression but didn't seem too concerned about that. 'No, I never saw him. Ah, that's a lie. I saw him once when he was about a year old. At the time, the last thing I wanted was children. I certainly didn't want Josie's child. She was happily married, and so was I. Well, I wasn't *happily* married, but the last thing I needed was that complication. But I saw him with Josie in town when he was about a year old, and I knew then that he was mine. He looked very much like me, you know.'

'Yes, the resemblance is striking,' Max agreed. 'Did you make any attempts to see him?'

'Recently, yes. I suppose that, as you get older, family means more. I often think that, if I killed myself on the motorway tomorrow, I'd leave nothing behind. So yes, I wrote to Josie about a month ago asking to see him.'

'What was her reaction to that?' Max asked.

'Nothing. She didn't answer my letter or call me or anything.'

'I see. So what did you do then?'

'I'm sure she's told you all this.' He sighed, somewhat dramatically. 'I phoned her and told her that if she didn't meet me, I'd turn up at the farm and see Martin for myself.'

'And she met you?'

'Yes. I'm afraid I didn't give her much choice. The last thing she wanted was me turning up on the doorstep. So yes, we met – this sounds silly, but we met in the grave-yard at St Saviour's. No chance of anyone seeing us there, you see.' He frowned at Max. 'But I'm sure Josie has told you all this.'

Max ignored that. 'How many times did you meet?'

'Twice.' He twisted a watch, a Rolex by the look of it, around his wrist a couple of times. 'The second time was last Tuesday, a week ago today, the day before young Martin was murdered.'

'Why twice?' Fletch put in.

116

'The first time, she was being awkward about me seeing Martin. I said I'd meet her there the next week – give her time to think about things, you know. She'd calmed down a bit by then and seemed to accept that I had a right to see him. She was resigned to it, I suppose you'd say.' He sighed. 'I went off to Italy and, the next thing I knew, Martin had been murdered.'

'How do you feel about that?'

Taylor thought for a moment. 'I'd be lying if I said I was devastated,' he admitted. 'I never knew the boy. He's a stranger – was a stranger to me. I suppose I feel cheated, to tell you the truth. It seems a cruel blow. Selfish, I know, but just when I wanted to see him . . .' He shrugged. 'Very selfish of me.'

'How would you describe your relationship with Mrs Hayden?' Max asked.

'Past or present?'

'Both.'

'Seventeen years ago, I found her amusing,' he explained. 'She was very naive, especially sexually. She'd never been unfaithful to that husband of hers.'

'I see.'

'To be honest,' he went on, 'it was just a bit of fun. You know, some afternoon entertainment. I had no idea that Josie thought it was anything more.'

'Have you had many affairs?' Fletch asked.

'A few. I'm a salesman which means I travel about a bit, and hotel rooms can get pretty boring, believe me. It's nice to have something to alleviate the boredom.'

'And Mrs Hayden was something to alleviate the boredom?' Fletch guessed.

'It sounds callous, but yes. Yes, she was.' He thought for a moment. 'My first marriage was heading for the divorce courts at a fast pace.'

'What about now?' Max asked. 'How do you get along with Mrs Hayden now?'

'She was very cool with me,' he replied. 'Cool, angry. Hurt probably. I'm not her favourite person, not by a long way. She talked a lot about Martin. She said he was like me – in looks and temperament.'

'Really?' How odd. Josie Hayden wasn't a fan of Brian Taylor, yet she thought her son was like him in temperament. Which part of that temperament had young Martin inherited?

'How did you hear about his death?' Max asked.

'The oddest thing. When I was in Italy, I called my brother. Nothing unusual about that as we often speak on the phone, but just as we were ending the call, he jokingly said something about a murder in Harrington. Said the victim, a young boy, looked just like me and that I should watch out. I asked the name and he told me. Of course, he doesn't know that Martin was my son.'

They spoke for another half-hour, but nothing new came to light. Brian Taylor seemed a damn sight more open and honest than Josie Hayden.

Max was on the point of leaving when his phone rang.

'Excuse me.' He walked over to the window to answer it.

'Max,' Grace greeted him breathlessly, 'you won't want to hear this.'

He'd already guessed as much. When Grace called him Max instead of the usual guv, he knew something serious had happened.

'Go on.'

'We've got another dead body.'

Max felt the world shift slightly. 'Not another –'

'No,' she cut him off, guessing he was expecting it to be another pupil from Harrington High. 'It's Josie Hayden.'

'Suicide?' But he suspected the answer to that was something else he'd picked up from Grace's tone.

'No, guv.'

Chapter Eighteen

Jill sat on a stool at the bar in The Weaver's Retreat. It was just after nine o'clock and the place was packed with regulars who called there after their evening meal.

Liz and Tony Hutchinson came in and, after the usual greetings and moans about the weather, the three of them sat at the table nearest the fire.

'I wouldn't be surprised if we didn't have snow soon,' Tony remarked.

'It feels cold enough.' Jill held her hands out to the burning logs.

Inevitably, talk turned to Martin Hayden.

'Tony told me that Sarah does your hair, Liz,' Jill remarked.

'Occasionally.' Liz nodded. 'She's good with colour,' she explained, 'although I prefer Jon to do it when I'm having anything more drastic than a quick trim.'

'What's she like?' Jill asked. 'Does she talk of her family much?'

'No. She's one of those rare beings – a hairdresser who doesn't insist on (a) knowing your business and (b) telling you hers.'

'I heard something yesterday,' Tony put in. 'I'm not sure if it's true or if it's idle gossip, but someone said Andy Hayden was spending a lot of time in Benedict's.' He took a swig of beer. 'That takes a bit of believing, doesn't it?' He grimaced. 'God knows what would happen if George found out about it.'

Benedict's was Harrington's lively gay club, and Tony was right. It took some believing.

George had made his thoughts known to Martin about what he called sissy poetry books. Why was George thinking along those lines? George and Andy were father and son, both working the farm, but they weren't close. Was Andy gay? Was that why George was so hostile towards him?

'It could be nonsense,' Tony added. 'It was Glen, the mechanic at the garage, who told me.'

'Andy Hayden isn't gay,' Liz told them with certainty. 'For a while, at least a year, he was seeing Lucy Rodgers.'

At Jill's frown, she explained, 'She's a nurse at the vet's in Harrington. I know her because we had to take Tony's mother's cat there quite often.'

'And they've split up?' Jill asked. 'Recently?'

'Yes. She had a whirlwind romance with a new vet at the practice and they're due to be married at Easter.'

'I wonder how Andy took that.'

'I don't know, but badly, I imagine. He used to worship her.'

'Really?'

Before Jill could comment further, her phone rang. It was Max.

'Where are you?' he asked.

'At the pub. You?'

'Shivering outside your cottage. I need to talk to you.'

'OK, I'll walk up. Let yourself in. There's a spare key under the pot on the right-hand side of the door – the one with the winter pansies in it.'

'Bloody hell, Jill. Why in hell's name don't you erect a sign – all burglars, rapists and murderers welcome?'

She chose to ignore that. 'Put the kettle on,' she told him 'and I'll be there in five minutes.'

'What I need doesn't come out of a kettle,' he said grimly, and she could hear him unlocking her door.

Jill cut the connection, said a hasty goodbye to Tony and

Liz, left her unfinished drink on the table and stepped out into the cold.

It didn't take long to walk the half-mile home, and she found Max in the sitting room nursing a glass which held a generous measure of whisky. She knew, just by looking at him, that something was very wrong.

'What's up?'

'Josie Hayden's dead,' he said flatly.

Jill dropped on to the sofa, still wearing her coat and scarf.

'Dead?' The heating had been on all day and her cottage was warm, but she shivered and thought her teeth were about to start chattering 'Suicide?'

Max shook his head.

'Murdered?' She couldn't believe it.

'Do you want a drink?' he asked, and she nodded.

Max went to the kitchen for a glass and poured her an equally generous measure from a bottle he must have brought with him. She was sure she had no whisky in the house.

'Thanks.' She took it from him, had a swallow and felt the warmth in her throat.

After a few moments, she took off her coat and scarf, and sat on the floor in front of the gas fire with her drink cradled in her hands.

'Your friend found her,' Max said quietly. 'Ella Gardner.'

'Oh, no!' Ella had said she planned to call and offer her condolences. 'What happened?'

'Josie was at the farm alone. George and Andy were at a sale of farm machinery in Cumbria, and Sarah had gone back to work for the first time. It seems Josie let someone in –'

'Someone she knew?'

'We don't know. Possibly. Anyway, they slit her throat.'

'No!' Jill was starting to shiver all over again.

'We'll know more tomorrow after the autopsy, but it seems she was cut badly after she was dead.'

'Cut where?'

121

'Everywhere. Face, arms, legs, breasts, genitalia.'

'Dear God.' No wonder Max looked wiped out. 'Poor Sarah. Poor Ella, too. What a shock. Is she OK?'

'Ella's fine – very calm considering. Sarah's not so good. Understandably.'

'Poor kid.'

They talked some more, and had another drink.

'What about Brian Taylor?' Jill asked. 'You saw him today, yes?'

'Yes, and he seemed a damn sight more forthcoming than Josie.' But they both knew that meant nothing. 'I suppose it's just possible he drove straight to the farm before we saw him and killed her. I can't see it, but it's possible. We're taking him in for questioning. We'll keep him overnight and I'll see him in the morning. Actually, I'd like *us* to see him in the morning.'

She nodded. 'OK.'

'George and Andy Hayden have a shed load of witnesses so we can discount them.'

'You can't discount George Hayden, Max!' Jill didn't care how many witnesses the man had. 'His brother dies and, bingo, George inherits a farm that meant everything to him. He discovers his wife's been unfaithful and that he's brought up someone else's son and, bingo, they're both wiped out.'

Max was shaking his head.

'He may not have done it himself,' she allowed, 'but he could easily have paid someone else to do it.'

'I don't think so.'

Jill didn't know what to think. 'At least we know the answer's at the farm and not the school.'

'Not necessarily, Jill. You see, that's not all.'

'Oh?'

'No.' He rubbed his hands across his face in a gesture of weariness. 'Another pupil from Harrington High has been reported missing.'

'No!'

'Yes. A James Murphy.'

122

'James? But I know him. And his parents.'

'I thought you might.'

It was only the fourth of December but Jill's first Christmas card had been delivered that very morning. It was from Emma, Gerald and James Murphy.

'He stayed late at school for football practice,' Max explained, 'but he should have been home by five thirty. His parents were planning to take him and a friend to the cinema. James hasn't turned up.'

Dear God. What were they dealing with?

Chapter Nineteen

Jill could have slaughtered Max. Technically, it wasn't his fault she felt like this, but she had to blame someone. If he hadn't called at her cottage last night, she wouldn't have had a drink. And if he hadn't coaxed her into letting him sleep in her spare room, she wouldn't have had another drink. And another.

This morning, she had the hangover from hell. He, on the other hand, looked as fresh as the morning dew.

It was hot and stuffy in Phil Meredith's office and a lot of the conversation was going over Jill's head. She needed water – lots of it – and fresh air.

She'd been at the morning's briefing, and that had been depressing. They had a huge tangled mess to unravel. Millions of questions and no answers.

But it was always that way.

'I've had the headmaster of Harrington High on the phone,' Phil snapped, 'saying he wants some answers. He's not the only one. The school will be deserted today. We'll have a major panic on our hands if we don't move quickly.'

'All suggestions gratefully received,' Max said pleasantly.

'Don't get bloody funny with me!'

'I'm not,' Max said, taking a breath. 'My kids are at Harrington High so I know how the parents are feeling.'

A reminder that Harry and Ben attended the school seemed to calm Phil slightly. It didn't do much for Jill. It didn't look as if it had done much for Max either.

'The answer is at Lower Crags Farm,' Jill said quietly. She couldn't talk any louder; her head hurt too much. 'It has to be.'

'There's no link between the Haydens and James Murphy,' Phil scoffed, dismissing that.

'There has to be. We just haven't found it yet.'

'Jill.' Phil spoke as if he were addressing a five-year-old. 'A schoolboy is murdered. His mother is murdered. Another schoolboy is –'

'He's missing,' she said. 'That's all. Missing. He's not necessarily dead.' Although she guessed that the three of them feared the worst. She hoped not, for Gerald and Emma Murphy's sakes. 'The answer has to be at Lower Crags Farm.'

'We can't afford to waste time on the farm, Jill!'

'Grace is going to the school after she's been to the post-mortem,' Max told Phil, speaking calmly, 'to see if we can establish a link between Martin Hayden and James Murphy.'

'And Brian Taylor was brought in last night so we'll go to town on him,' Jill said.

'We've got divers in the canal, just in case,' Max went on, 'and we've got people talking to parents. They might supply that link.'

'He vanished straight after football practice at the school,' Jill put in, 'and he's another good-looking boy so it may be sexual. That puts Geoff Morrison high up the list.'

Phil shook his head in despair. 'A forty-four-year-old woman has been butchered. That wasn't some bloke with a liking for boys, was it?'

'She might have found out who the killer was,' Max pointed out.

'Then it's a pity she wasn't working in this bloody place!' Phil glared at them both. 'I want some answers and bloody soon,' he snapped, waving in the direction of the door.

Max looked at Jill, and she shrugged. Presumably, Phil had finished with them for the moment.

'Oh, I've told everyone that overtime payments have been authorized,' Max remarked casually. 'That's OK, isn't it?'

'Just get on with it!' Meredith snapped.

He was a pain. First, he didn't want Jill on the case; then he decides he not only wants her on the case, he wants her to have all the answers yesterday.

'I need a coffee,' she said as she closed Meredith's door behind them.

Max grinned at her. 'You wanna go easy on the booze in future, kiddo.'

'Yes, well. I don't get as much practice as you.'

He glanced at his watch. 'You get a coffee, and I'll see if Taylor's been given another brew. It'll do his nerves good to wait around a bit.'

'Does he have a brief with him?'

'He hadn't the last I heard. Why? Are you hoping to see the boyfriend?'

The boyfriend? Her love life, or lack thereof, was the last thing on her mind right now.

'No.' She refused to rise to it. There was no need to tell him that Scott was in the States . . .

Her second coffee helped, and she gazed at the photographs they'd been given of James Murphy. She didn't need photographs, she knew him too well, but they interested her. Unlike Martin Hayden, there was nothing posed about James. One photo showed him standing by his father's car pointing to the L-plates. It had been taken three months ago on his seventeenth birthday. He hadn't got the looks of Martin Hayden, but he was an attractive boy all the same. Tall, and dark-haired. He might appeal to Geoff Morrison, and he was good at sport. He was in the school's football team.

She knew he was a typical seventeen-year-old. He was destined for university, but did only the minimum to get there. He was planning on a gap year first.

He didn't have the same teachers as Martin Hayden. Apart from Bill Hicks who taught Maths, Donna Lord who

126

taught English, and Geoff Morrison who looked after the football team, their teachers were different.

He played the guitar which was interesting. Apparently, he'd taught himself from an early age and he'd just formed a band with three other schoolboys. At least it was some sort of link. It wasn't a great one, as dozens of boys played the guitar, but it was a link. It was the best they had so far.

George and Andy Hayden both had watertight alibis. But Jill, like everyone else on the force, had seen watertight alibis before. Those alibis were being checked, double-checked and checked again.

Was the answer at the farm? At times, she was convinced it was.

She'd been wrong before, though. Rodney Hill had reminded her of that when he'd been found hanged in his prison cell . . .

Brian Taylor had been given bacon sandwiches and cups of tea, and was chain-smoking when Jill and Max arrived to interview him. Having been assured that he wasn't being charged as yet, he had waived his rights to a lawyer.

He looked shaken and very nervous. Nervous because he had something to hide? Or nervous because he'd been waiting for hours in this interview room?

He'd emptied one packet of cigarettes and went to his pocket for another while Max went through the necessary procedures and made sure the tapes were running.

'Sorry, do you mind if I smoke?' he asked, addressing Jill.

'Not at all.' Being stuck in a smoke-filled room always reminded her of home. Her mother might have quit smoking recently, but all Jill's memories of her mother included the obligatory cigarette in her mouth. Which was why she'd just had an operation on her lung.

'Yesterday morning, Mr Taylor, can you tell us where you were?' Max began.

'Yesterday? Well –' he took a huge drag on his cigarette – 'I was talking to you, wasn't I?'

'Before that,' Max said patiently.

'At home. My flight landed just after eight o'clock the night before, as you know. I drove straight home and I was there until you arrived to see me.'

'You didn't go anywhere before I called?' Max asked.

'No. Why?'

Max ignored that. 'So you've no witnesses?'

'None. Oh, the postman delivered a letter I had to sign for. He might remember. Well, whether he remembers or not, my signature and the time will be on the form at the post office. That was about eight thirty.'

'You hadn't seen or spoken to Mrs Hayden since you returned to England?' Max asked.

'No.' He stubbed out his cigarette with hands that were shaking. 'I filled the car with diesel when I got off the plane,' he said. 'I've got a fuel card so have to provide the current mileage figure when I fill up. If you check that, you'll see that I drove home and haven't used up any more miles.'

'We'll check it.'

'Look,' Taylor said, 'I know it looks a bit coincidental, me trying to see Martin and then this happening, but I didn't do anything. Why would I? I wanted to see him, that's all. Why would I kill him? My own son?'

'It is very coincidental,' Max agreed. 'You remain silent for seventeen years and within a short time of you contacting the boy's mother, he's brutally murdered.'

'It has nothing to do with me. I swear it.' He frowned. 'And why do you care what I was doing yesterday morning?'

'Mrs Hayden was murdered,' Max said simply.

Either Brian Taylor was an actor worthy of an Oscar, Jill thought, or he hadn't known that.

'Murdered?' He fumbled for another cigarette. 'I had no idea.'

Jill and Max watched him.

'Really,' he said, squirming. 'I honestly didn't know.'

'Are you sure you don't want a lawyer?' Max asked him.

He considered it for a moment.

'Well, no. I mean, if it happened yesterday morning, I've got proof that I was at home. All you need to do is check with the post office and check my car's mileage. What time did you arrive? I was on the phone to Sue in the office. The time of the call will be on my mobile. And I sent some faxes and emails,' he added, talking quickly, 'so the time will be on those. I spoke to a lot of people.'

Jill and Max said nothing.

'What happened?' he asked. 'How did she die? Oh, I suppose you can't say.' Brian Taylor shook his head. He looked dazed, confused and frightened. Jill, however, had seen killers look like that before. Just as she'd seen water-tight alibis.

'Mr Taylor,' she began, 'tell me about your affair with Mrs Hayden.'

He sat back in his seat slightly, sweat on his brow and his fingers hanging on to his cigarette like grim death.

'I was a salesman – I still am – covering the Lancashire area,' he explained, 'and I was taking a short-cut home one day when my car broke down. I walked about half a mile and came to the farm. I called and asked if I might use their phone to call the AA.'

'Mrs Hayden was alone?'

'Yes. She made me a cup of tea while I waited for the breakdown man to appear and we chatted.'

'About what?' Jill asked.

'Just trivia, I seem to recall. The weather, the farm, parking in Harrington, her family, my family – that sort of thing.'

'You were married to your first wife at the time, yes?'

'Yes.'

'Was it a happy marriage?'

'Not really, no. To be honest, we'd talked about a divorce.'

'And then what happened? The AA arrived?'

'Yes. The chap couldn't fix the car, so he took me home and dropped the car off at a garage.'

'And when did you next see Mrs Hayden?'

'A week or so later,' he explained. 'I was doing the same short-cut and stopped off at the farm to thank her.'

And he just happened to have red roses in the car? No. He was lying.

'A spur of the moment thing?'

'Yes.'

'You took her flowers, I believe? Do you always drive around with flowers in your car?'

He frowned for a moment. 'Did I take her flowers? I honestly don't remember that.'

'Red roses and white gypsophila,' Jill told him. 'Strange that she could remember and you can't.'

'Then I must have stopped somewhere to buy them,' he said. 'It's a long time ago,' he added.

'So – with or without flowers – you called at the farm to thank her. Then what?'

'We chatted. I suggested we meet in town one day. She was quite eager, I recall, although terrified of her husband finding out. A week or so after that, I phoned her and we met in town.'

'Where?'

'At the Harrington Hotel. I booked a room so that she'd feel safer.'

'You made love?'

He nodded, which would mean nothing to people listening to the tape afterwards.

'Was that a yes?'

'Yes.'

'Was she in love with you?' Jill asked.

'She said she was, but . . .' He shook his head. 'I think she was more in love with my lifestyle. I travelled around a bit, went to parties, socialized – she was stuck on the farm with a man who seemed to ignore her for the most part.'

'What happened when you realized she was pregnant?'

He had the grace to look ashamed.

'I'm afraid I was angry,' he admitted. 'I thought she was lying. We'd been so careful, you see. I thought she wanted me to leave my wife and set up home with her. I didn't believe her.'

'How did she take that?'

'I don't know,' he admitted. 'We were at the hotel. We had a row, and I stormed off.'

'So how did you know the child was yours?'

'I saw her in town about eighteen months later,' he explained. 'She had the boy in a pushchair. Even at that age, he was the image of me.' His hands were shaking even more now. 'She was different – proud and angry. She'd always been a quiet thing, but she was angry. She went her way, and I went mine.'

'How did you feel, knowing you had a child of your own?'

'Strange,' he admitted. 'I kept thinking I should do something about it – financially, if nothing else. But I didn't want to wreck the boy's home life. And if I'm honest, I didn't want to get involved with Josie – Mrs Hayden. She was fun for a while, but I'm afraid that's all she meant to me.'

Jill gave him a pleasant smile. 'Do you have any more children scattered across the country?'

'No.'

'Just Martin?'

'Yes.'

'How often did you see him?'

'I told you.' He frowned. 'I didn't.'

'What? You're telling me that you weren't curious about him? You didn't hang around his school, watching out for him? Come on, I'm sure you did. You will have parked opposite the gates, waiting for him to walk down the drive, watching to see if he still looked like you, to see if he was a handsome boy.'

'I might have seen him a couple of times,' he admitted at last.

'A couple? Is that twice?'

'Maybe a few more times.'

131

'So is that what you did? Hung around the school gates waiting for him to appear?'

'Yes.'

'He was a good-looking boy, wasn't he? You must have been proud of him.'

'I wouldn't say proud,' he answered. 'Apart from giving him his looks, I never did anything for him.'

'Were you spotted when you hung around outside the school? Did any of the other children see you? Anyone ask you what you were doing?'

'No. I wasn't there that often.'

'Are you sure? You must have been easy enough to spot. Wouldn't some of Martin's friends be curious about the man who looked just like him?'

'I don't believe anyone ever noticed me,' he insisted. 'If they did, they didn't say anything to me.'

'Did you try to talk to him?' Jill asked.

'Never.'

'Why not? He was your son. Your own flesh and blood. Didn't you want to hear the sound of his voice? Didn't you want to know all about him?'

'Not enough to confront him,' he said grimly. 'Yes, I did want to get to know him, but I wouldn't have done it without going through Josie. I owed her that much at least.'

'And she said no, didn't she?'

'At first, yes. But she was coming round to it. She just didn't want her husband to find out.'

'And how would she prevent that?' Jill asked. 'Surely, if you'd met Martin, he would have gone straight to his father – the man he'd thought of as his father for the last seventeen years.'

'I don't know,' he said.

No way would Josie have let him near Martin. No way!

'I don't believe she was coming round to it, as you put it, at all,' Jill said frankly. 'I think she would have said no, and kept on saying no. Let's face it, you weren't going to pick up the pieces when her husband found out, were you?

132

No, you'd be going back to your lovely wife and your lovely home.'

He looked Jill straight in the eye.

'We'll never know, will we?'

He was more calm now. Why? Because he knew they had nothing they could pin on him?

'What did you and Josie talk about?' she asked. 'I know you spent most of your time in bed – hotel rooms don't come cheap, do they? – but you must have talked of something. You must have got to know each other a little. What about Josie's past? What did she say about that?'

His expression changed, became very thoughtful.

'She wouldn't talk about it,' he said. 'As soon as I mentioned her life before she married, she'd clam up. I always had the impression that she'd had a bad childhood. I don't know. As I said, she refused to talk about it. She'd clam up and get quite edgy about it.'

'She wouldn't even tell you?' Jill scoffed. 'But she loved you. She would have told you anything.'

'She wouldn't tell me about her past,' he said firmly. 'And to be honest, I was never interested enough to pry.'

Jill's head was still aching. Now, she wasn't sure if that was the alcohol or her frustration at getting nowhere with Brian Taylor.

Max asked him more questions, but they drew a blank. There was nothing with which to charge him.

Yet.

Chapter Twenty

It was just before three o'clock that afternoon when Max drove them to the school.

'Are we sure about George and Andy Hayden?' Jill asked, frowning. 'Are their alibis really as ironclad as they claim?'

'Seems like it,' Max said. 'Fletch and Grace have spent ages talking to them, but there's nothing odd about it. They were up in Cumbria at an auction. They even bought a couple of items.'

'What have you managed to find out about Josie's past?' she asked him.

'Not a lot. Mind you, we haven't put too much effort into it.'

'I think you should,' Jill murmured. 'If Brian Taylor is telling the truth, and something did happen in Josie's past, it will be worth finding out about.'

'Do you think he *is* telling the truth?'

'Yes, I think he is. A shame really, because I can't take to the bloke at all, but yes, I think he's telling the truth.' She gave him a curious glance. 'Don't you?'

Max sighed as he turned into the school's car park. 'I don't know what to think.'

The school had a sombre air about it and, without bothering to ask, Jill could see from empty seats in several classrooms that some pupils hadn't turned up. She wasn't surprised. If Phil Meredith was right about nothing else, he knew there would be panic in Harrington.

They spoke to a class filled with fellow pupils of James

Murphy. All said he was a good sort of boy. He was well liked by the other pupils. They were dazed, nervous.

It was depressing.

They then sought out Geoff Morrison.

'I'd like to bring him in,' Max said, 'but he'd be sure to want a brief there and it's not worth the effort. Besides, he's more likely to talk if he thinks he's helping us.'

'He won't talk,' Jill muttered. 'He's too well contained. A bit of a loner really. Oh, I know he lives with his boyfriend, but he's still a bit of a loner.'

There was a small room next to the school's gym. It contained a desk, half a dozen stacked plastic chairs, odd pieces of team kit, team jackets and the like. On a notice-board were fixtures lists for the school's various sports teams.

Geoff Morrison looked as uncomfortable as ever.

'The choice is yours,' Max told him pleasantly. 'We can either have an informal chat here, or you can come down to the station and we can talk there.'

'There's no point me wasting my time and yours by going to a police station,' Morrison told him. 'I've told you before that I can't help. I didn't know either boy very well.'

He spoke in the past tense, Jill noticed.

'What can you tell us about James Murphy?' she asked him.

'Good at sport,' Morrison said with a shrug, 'very confident, cheeky but only in fun. Nice-mannered, polite.'

'He's an only child, isn't he?' Jill mused.

'I believe he is, yes.'

'Are you an only child, Mr Morrison?'

'What?' He laughed in exasperation. 'As a matter of fact I am. What does that have to do with anything?'

'Just curious,' Jill told him. 'Having had siblings myself, I can't imagine what it's like. Is it OK?'

'I can't speak for Murphy, of course,' he answered, 'but I think you'll find that being an only child has many advantages. You never have to share, you get a room to yourself, you get your parents' undivided attention –'

135

'But no one to share confidences with, no one to laugh and have fun with, no one to learn about life – girls, boys, sex, relationships and stuff like that.'

'Nonsense. What about friends?'

'Friends tend to brag about their sexual conquests. Siblings are honest.'

'I never had problems.'

'Martin Hayden used to swim with an erection,' Jill remarked, smiling amiably. 'I suppose you noticed?'

'He did what? Oh, for God's sake. No, I didn't notice!'

'He told his sister you were a pervert,' she added.

'I'm not. I'm homosexual and I can't see that that is any-one's business but my own. You, Ms Kennedy, are pre-sumably into men. Men, that is. Not boys. Just because I also have relationships with men, doesn't mean that I'm different, that I like mine younger.'

'Fair point.' She didn't want to anger him unnecessarily.

'I thought the police force these days was anti gay-bashing, anti racism and all the rest of it,' he muttered.

'It is,' Max agreed. 'We've plenty of gays on the force.'

'Especially in the uniforms,' Jill said casually. 'A uniform attracts both sexes, I suppose. I'll bet,' she added, 'that if you and I watched Richard Gere in *An Officer and a Gentleman*, we'd both want to sleep with him. I'm not particularly fond of uniforms, but hey, Richard Gere must have done wonders for the recruitment. Am I right?'

'Probably,' he agreed, the ghost of a smile touching his face.

'And DCI Trentham here, I'm sure he's partial to uniforms – police uniforms, nurses' uniforms, school uni-forms.' She looked Morrison straight in the eye. 'Do you like school uniforms?'

'I'm sure Richard Gere would look good in one,' he retorted, 'but young boys in uniform aren't particularly appealing, are they?'

'Martin Hayden was. James Murphy is a good-looking boy, too. And at seventeen, well, he's as near a man as makes no odds, isn't he?'

'Ms Kennedy,' he said, speaking with exaggerated patience, 'I take exception to this line of questioning. I'm more than willing to help the police, as I've said many times, and I certainly have nothing to hide. I do, however, have a good, loving relationship and am not looking for anything else – not a lover, a friend, a confidant or fun. I get all that from my relationship.'

'And how long have you been in that relationship?'

'Three years.'

'Some people like the steady relationship *and* the illicit affairs,' Jill pointed out.

'Some do. I don't.' He turned his attention to Max, and spoke directly to him. 'Look, I know why you're centring attention on me and I can understand it. I've had two boys think – wrongly – that I'm up to no good. And shit sticks, right? But please believe me, you're wasting your time. While you're talking to me, the killer of Martin Hayden and his mother is on the loose. Can you have that on your conscience?'

'I'll have to live with it,' Max told him. 'Why did you tell me you drove a red car when, at the time in question, you drove a blue one?'

The sudden change of direction threw him momentarily, but he soon recovered.

'You asked what colour car I drove and I told you.'

'Where were you yesterday?' Max demanded.

They spent over an hour with Morrison but he stuck to his story.

'We may need you to come to the station at some point,' Max told him as they were leaving.

'Fine. But as I keep telling you, you really are wasting your time.'

It was late when they left the school, and all the pupils had long gone.

'Fancy a coffee?' Max asked, and Jill nodded.

He drove them to Mario's where they sat close to a radiator and thrashed out what little they had over cappuccinos and chocolate cake.

'Morrison's right,' Max said. 'We're wasting time with him.'

'Maybe, but don't let this gay-bashing crap get to you. Gay or not, we're entitled to grill him.'

'I know that.'

'Has anything of interest come from Martin Hayden's computer?'

'Nope. He wasn't into chat rooms or emailing loads of his mates. He used it mostly for schoolwork and looking at music sites. He's interested in guitarists, but that's as close a link as we can get to James Murphy.'

'Do we know where he got that coke from?'

'Nope.'

'I don't know if James Murphy is connected to this, Max,' Jill said thoughtfully, 'but if he is, it's not going to be good. The person who killed Josie was very angry indeed. She was hacked about a lot after she'd breathed her last, and that much anger stems from something very deep. As for Martin – if our killer felt that Martin's existence had ruined his life, he'd be very angry. Possibly more angry with Josie for bringing him into the world. Rejection could be another motive. Brian Taylor might kill Josie out of anger. Geoff Morrison could too if he'd been cruelly rejected. Any anger would be transferred to Josie simply because she'd given birth to Martin.'

Max drummed his fingers on the table. 'OK, but what about James Murphy? Why would our killer go for him?'

'We don't know for sure that he's met the same fate,' Jill pointed out.

Max pulled a face. 'We're both bloody clueless, aren't we?'

They were.

Perhaps there was someone else. Brian Taylor was a ghost from Josie's past. If he was innocent, and all evidence suggested that he was, there could be someone else from her past.

Just why had Josie been so reticent about her life?

Chapter Twenty-One

All Max wanted was to get home to his kids and his dogs. Normality. Few people would use that term to describe his lifestyle but, to Max, it was as normal as it was likely to be. He wouldn't have it any other way.

On the way, he stopped at the wine bar, Chameleon. It was usually filled with the town's misfits, and rumour had it that Geoff Morrison was occasionally seen there. Max wanted to see him with his boyfriend.

Some of the kids – young adults – from the school hung out there, too. That was a gem he'd picked up from Harry.

'They sometimes get free drinks,' Harry had said, adding a nonchalant, 'Some queer bloke owns it. This woman comes up from London to stay with him sometimes. Except the woman's really a bloke. Her name's Denise, and the queer bloke reckons he can't forget her name because all he has to think of is "de knees". He reckons that's funny.'

And Harry, thinking nothing amiss in the lifestyle of his fellow Harrington residents, had gone into the garden to kick a football around.

This evening, the Chameleon was quiet. The 'queer bloke' didn't put in an appearance and two young girls were busy serving drinks.

Max had a small glass of wine and stood by a tall table near the window to drink it.

Seeing nothing and no one of interest, he was about to leave when Donna Lord came in. Alone.

She walked up to the bar, shared a joke with one of the girls behind the bar and turned around holding a large glass of white wine.

When she spotted Max, she gave him a broad smile and walked over. Any other man, Max thought, would have been on his knees at such a smile. Max was glad he was immune. More or less immune, anyway.

At the school, she'd been wearing a short, tight black skirt, white striped blouse and high heels. She'd obviously been home to change and now wore white trousers and a chest-hugging black T-shirt that showed off plenty of cleavage and a stunning figure.

'Well, if it's not the famous detective,' she greeted him. 'Do you come here often?' she asked with a husky laugh.

'Hardly ever,' he told her, smiling. 'You?'

'Too often. It's handy for the gym,' she explained. The Chameleon was about a hundred yards away from Harrington's very expensive health and fitness centre. 'I work out most nights,' she explained, 'and a glass of chilled wine goes down well afterwards.'

He wasn't surprised to learn that she was a member of the fitness centre. She was proud of her body, rightly so, and it stood to reason that she'd take care of it.

'A glass of chilled wine goes down well most of the time.'

'True.'

She took a long, slow sip of her wine.

'Isn't it terrible about Mrs Hayden?' she said. 'My, she's suffered, hasn't she? It has to be the worst thing ever, doesn't it – losing a child, I mean?'

Max could think of nothing worse. It went against all laws of nature. Each generation was supposed to take care of the next, and anything that broke the chain upset the equilibrium.

'Awful,' he agreed.

'I only met her twice, at parents' evenings,' she went on, 'but she seemed a nice woman. A bit quiet perhaps but – well, fortunately, Martin wasn't a child who needed pushing. He was ambitious enough to do well. But now the poor woman's dead. Murdered. How awful for the family.'

'Tragic.'

'Sorry, I suppose that's shop talk as far as you're concerned. It's just that no one can think of anything else at the moment.' She brightened. 'I shouldn't be gloomy when you're trying to relax. We'll both forget about it.'

Forget about it? Max only wished he could forget it for more than sixty seconds at a stretch. Perhaps it was different if you didn't have to tell the family that their lovely boy had been brutally murdered, if you didn't have to look at the photos of his battered body, if you didn't have to live with the knowledge that, if you'd done something different, Martin Hayden and his mother might still be alive . . .

'Ah, you're one of those who doesn't forget about work,' she guessed. Her fingers went to the back of his neck, causing shivers to run down his spine. 'Thought so, you're very tense.'

Her eyes were alight with laughter as she realized the effect she was having on him. Her hand ran the length of his thigh and he shuddered. 'Tense thighs, too.' She tutted. 'You need a good massage.'

He needed a cold shower.

'You should relax more and have fun,' she told him. 'I'm serious. Stress is a killer.'

'I'll bear it in mind,' he promised.

The music was too loud so, when she suggested moving to the far side of the room, away from the speakers, he quickly agreed. Not that he intended staying long. There was a possibility she'd be able to tell him something of interest though and, besides, the scenery was stunning.

'Is this a meeting place for staff from Harrington High?' he asked.

'Hardly. Geoff Morrison comes in occasionally, and some of the sixth formers if they can afford it. That's about it.' She grinned. 'The staff at Harrington High are mostly too stuffy for this place. The men play their golf and the women are busy with their WI projects. Do you play golf, Max?'

'Nope, I'm with Mark Twain on that one. It's a good walk spoiled.'

She laughed. 'So how come you keep in such good shape?'

'Stress,' he whispered, and she laughed again, that incredible, husky, sexy laugh.

Max's mind was wandering. Instead of thinking of Geoff Morrison, he was mentally undressing Donna Lord as if he were a seventeen-year-old.

'I suppose Geoff Morrison is a member at the fitness centre,' he remarked, while wondering if he could still unfasten a bra with one hand.

'He is, yes.'

'You'd think he'd have enough of keeping fit at the school.'

'Ah, but exercise is addictive,' she told him. 'It releases all the happy hormones.' She thought for a moment. 'If all the staff at Harrington High kept fit, they might be a more cheerful bunch. Apart from Geoff, who's a good laugh once you get to know him, the rest of them tend to moan about the job. Teaching's not what it used to be, they keep saying. If they hate it so much, I don't know why they don't get out.'

'Are you and Geoff Morrison the only ones who enjoy your work?'

'We're the only ones who don't keep moaning about all the paperwork.'

Her glass was almost empty.

'Can I get you another?' Max asked.

'Please.' As he walked up to the bar, he couldn't help thinking what a tough job he had. Still, someone had to do it . . .

'Thanks,' she murmured, as he handed her a glass of white wine. 'Tell you what,' she went on, 'why don't you come along to the fitness centre one night this week? You can come as my guest. You don't have to do the weights or the machines, but a swim would do you good. It would get rid of some of that muscle tension. The pool's not too busy in the evening.'

Max had moved on from unfastening her bra and was now imagining her near-naked body in the water.

'I might just do that.'

'Might is no good,' she scolded. 'We'll make it tomorrow night. About seven? Who knows, we might even have the pool to ourselves. That would be fun.'

'OK,' he agreed, 'but if Geoff Morrison's there, I'm not attempting to keep up with him.'

'Don't worry. Geoff usually sticks to the machines. In any case, he's usually too busy with his boyfriend to notice anyone else.'

'Ah, yes.'

'You knew he was gay?'

'It cropped up, yes.'

'Each to their own, I say.'

'Indeed.'

Instead of thinking of her half-naked in a swimming pool, he should keep his mind on the case. It was difficult though.

'Do any of the kids from school go along?' he asked.

'Not that I've seen. You know what kids are like, though. They'll play games but they're happier sitting in front of computers. They're into internet chat rooms. For the most part that's harmless enough, and at least they're socializing.'

'And as the human race evolves, we'll be born with a mouse for a hand.'

'You don't approve?'

He shrugged. 'I'd rather see kids talking and having fun than sitting in front of a machine.'

'Is that what your two do? Ah yes, I suppose they do. Harry's mad keen on football, I hear.'

'He is.'

'He's in the team, isn't he? I've heard his name read out in assemblies.'

'Yes. He reckons it beats lessons.'

She smiled at that. 'What about Ben? What does he do?'

'Trains his dog,' Max said fondly. 'We've got two,' he added. 'One is an older dog that once belonged to . . .' he hesitated as he thought of Jim Brody who was currently pleasing Her Majesty, 'a friend. Ben has a young dog though, and he's training it. He's keen to get to Crufts one day.'

He could tell she wasn't impressed. Why should she be? She didn't know Ben, unless she'd seen him around the school, and there was nothing more boring than proud parents droning on about their kids. It was on a par with sitting through someone's holiday snaps.

'What about you?' he asked. 'Any family?'

'No husband and certainly no kids,' she told him, laughing at the thought. 'I have enough of kids all day. I'm the youngest of four – three brothers – so I have lots of nephews and nieces.'

'That's nice.'

'Yeah.' She nodded.

'I'd better be going,' he said, and he was surprised how reluctant he was to leave.

'Have a relaxing evening,' she instructed him, 'and forget work. It does you no good.'

'It's difficult to forget.' He didn't relish the task of telling James Murphy's parents that their son had met the same fate as Martin Hayden.

'There's not much you can do for poor Martin and his mother,' she pointed out, 'and James might be on his way home as we speak.'

'I hope so.'

'Sure to be,' she said. 'Either that or he's gone to seek his fortune busking in Venice.'

Max shook his head. 'He'd have sent a postcard.'

'If he's gone to Venice, he couldn't afford a postcard. Perhaps he's in London, busking on the underground. You know what kids are like.'

He didn't. He knew what *his* kids were like. They'd send a postcard. At least, he hoped they would.

'I hope you're right.'

'And don't forget our date tomorrow night,' she added, the promise of all sorts of delights dancing in her eyes. She ran her hand across his thigh again. 'A good swim will get that tension out of your legs.' She reached up to whisper in his ear. 'I'll wear my new costume for you.'

'You know how to tempt a man,' he said, resisting the urge to loosen his collar and tie.

She touched a long, perfectly manicured finger to his lips. 'You're worth tempting, Max.'

Phew. Max was almost grateful to get out in the fresh air.

Chapter Twenty-Two

Brian Taylor stopped his car, leapt out and managed to run to the grass verge before he was sick. Groaning, he took a handkerchief from his pocket and wiped his mouth. It was the third time he'd been sick today.

His first job had been to phone his boss and tell him he was too ill to work, and then he'd cancelled his appointments for the day.

Yesterday, being questioned by that detective and the shrink, had been hell. How he hadn't thrown up in that room, he had no idea.

But he had nothing to worry about. He reminded himself of that as he returned to his car and sat staring out of the windscreen.

Nothing to worry about.

That was the advantage of working in sales, of course. Everything he did came with a receipt. If he stopped for a coffee, he got a receipt. If he parked his car, he got a receipt. The fact that he had a fuel card and therefore a record of his mileage had worked in his favour, too. If nothing else, the fact that he could boast of having receipts made him *sound* innocent.

He'd had a lot of explaining to do to Beverley last night. On hearing that he'd had an affair – no matter that it had been years ago – and that he had a child, she'd stormed off to their bedroom and dragged the dressing table in front of the door to deny him entry. Sleeping in the spare room hadn't bothered him. In fact, he'd been relieved.

Beverley was the least of his problems right now.

He turned on the ignition, hit a button and watched the window whirr down. A good stiff drink was what he needed, but he settled for a cigarette. He'd smoked too many yesterday and his throat was scratchy today, but he didn't care. He needed something.

What a bloody nightmare!

His mind raced with worries and he didn't know what to do. He wished he was out of the country, away from it all.

They would find out he'd seen Martin. Or would they?

Even Martin didn't know him as Brian Taylor. If Martin had told anyone about meeting a bloke called Adam, no one would connect it with him. Martin had had no idea who he was so why the hell should anyone else make the connection?

All Brian had wanted was to talk to him. Nothing more. How the hell was he expected to know where it would end?

It had seemed simple enough.

He'd seen Martin at the school gates one afternoon and collided with him, knocking a bag off his shoulder. Brian had struck up a conversation and he'd offered Martin a lift home. Martin, his eyes on the BMW, had accepted readily enough.

The car. If anyone had noticed Martin getting into his car . . .

But they wouldn't. The only people around had been school kids, and they'd been intent on larking around or catching their buses.

As Brian had driven, Martin had asked all sorts of questions. He'd wanted to know everything about Brian. But that didn't matter. Even if Martin had talked, there must be dozens of blokes named Adam who owned a couple of properties that they rented out and who snorted a small amount of coke now and again. The coke had only come to light when Martin had been searching through the glovebox looking at Brian's CDs.

It was on their third meeting, when they'd walked along Harrington High Street, that Martin had seen the guitar in the shop window.

'I'll buy it for you,' Brian had offered.

'Why would you want to do that?'

'Why not? You can pay me back when you hit the big time, if you like.'

Martin had shrugged. 'Even if I had the guitar, I couldn't afford lessons. There's a bloke in Church Street who gives lessons, but they don't come cheap.'

Brian had smiled at the hint. Subtlety didn't exist in Martin's vocabulary.

So they struck an arrangement that suited both of them. Brian saw Martin once a week, and Martin had his guitar and lessons paid for . . .

Brian tossed his cigarette butt out of the window and leaned back in his seat. The bile rose in his throat but, just as he thought he was about to be sick again, it passed.

His son. Even now, having spent so much time with Martin and seeing his own face reflected back at him, it didn't sink in.

He'd always believed that a father must love his son. It was a law of nature. He'd truly thought that a bond would exist between them that was greater than anything he'd ever known.

He'd been wrong.

Martin wasn't easy to love. He loved himself, and that was all. He only thought of himself. It hadn't taken Brian long to realize that the only reason Martin had associated with him had been the money. Martin had believed he was well off. He was out for his own gain. Nothing more.

Martin had grown too greedy. He'd wanted more and more money and then, finally, he'd threatened to tell everyone about the 'weirdo' who kept giving him money.

'You've been trying to get me into the sack all this time, haven't you?' He grinned with the confidence of youth and Brian had been horrified.

'Don't be ridiculous!'

148

'That's what everyone would think. My parents, the police . . .'

The threat had been left unspoken.

Brian hadn't known what to do. In the end, he'd contacted Josie. If he could see Martin, with everyone knowing he was the boy's father, he'd thought it would make life easier. He'd thought everyone would realize why he'd tried to get close to Martin.

Josie, of course, would have none of it.

'George would kill me,' she said, over and over again.

'He'd come round,' Brian had insisted.

'No. He would kill me.'

Brian lit another cigarette. What in hell's name was he to do?

Had Martin blabbed to his family? His sister perhaps? That guitar teacher?

His stomach churned. He leapt out of the car and was sick again.

Chapter Twenty-Three

Jill had been dreading this. However, she rang the Murphys' doorbell and waited.

Gerald Murphy opened the door and, from the quick flash of disappointment that registered in his eyes, Jill guessed he'd seen too many visitors.

'Hello, Jill. Come in. Good to see you.'

Emma Murphy, a pale imitation of her usual self, gave Jill a quick hug. 'Thanks for coming, Jill.'

'This is an official visit,' Jill explained. 'I'm helping the police . . .'

Gerald and Emma were scared witless, with good reason, and they sat on the sofa together, usually holding hands and touching to reassure each other. It was warming to see them both giving so much to the other.

Their home was very different to Lower Crags Farm. This was a large house and it was a place that was loved. Emma's sense of style was evident in every room. The furniture was modern, expensive and had been chosen with care. The carpets were thick. Fresh flowers sat on tables and in windows.

Gerald Murphy was a successful architect and had his own large practice in Manchester. He was a busy man, yet he was here with his wife and Jill knew he wouldn't leave her alone until their boy was found safe and sound.

'If we've done anything wrong, Jill,' Emma said softly, 'we've spoilt him. He's an only child, and that makes it difficult. We waited a long time to have him, you see. It was a difficult birth with complications and we were told we couldn't have more. Not that we minded. We had James, and he's our life.'

'But we've brought him up to be independent,' Gerald put in, absently squeezing his wife's hand. 'He's not a mummy's boy. He's popular, has lots of friends. His friends are always made welcome here and he's never been afraid to bring them home.'

Jill nodded her understanding.

'I know this is an imposition,' she said, 'and I know the police have already seen his room and taken away his computer, but would you mind if I had a look? There might be something.' Jill prayed there was.

'Of course,' Emma said, getting to her feet. 'We've not touched anything,' she added. 'It's just as he left it.'

Emma walked up the stairs with her. Jill would have preferred to look alone, but Emma was talkative and she might say something useful. She wanted to help them. Both she and her husband were touchingly grateful for everything the police were trying to do.

'For a boy, he's quite tidy,' Emma murmured as she pushed open the door to James' bedroom.

It was a large room, painted in a dark orange. There was little of the walls to be seen as they were covered in huge posters, mostly of bands. On the double bed was a Manchester United FC duvet cover. There was a matching lampshade on the bedside light. A large bookcase sat against one wall, and it held a few books and hundreds of CDs.

'That's a good music collection,' Jill said.

'He loves his music. It drives you mad,' Emma said, and there was a catch in her voice. Jill knew Emma would love to be driven mad right now. 'He plays the same CD, sometimes the same song, over and over again at ear-splitting volume. His dad tells him it'll send him deaf but he takes no notice. Oh, God –' Emma covered her face with her hands.

Jill held her close for a few moments. 'We're doing all we can, Emma.'

'I know.' She took a shaky breath. 'Everyone's been so kind.'

Kelton Bridge was that sort of village. Kindness, however, wouldn't bring James home.

Jill looked at each of the books in turn. They were mostly horror fiction. Several were by Stephen King.

There was a desk in the corner and she saw that he'd been doing maths homework that had to be handed in by the end of the week.

'I don't know how he was getting on with that,' Emma said, spotting Jill's interest. 'He does it on his computer and the police have taken that. Not,' she added, 'that I think they'll find anything. He's not one for email or chat rooms. He uses his mobile phone to keep in touch with his friends.'

Jill looked through the pile of papers on his desk. It was all schoolwork.

'Would he struggle with maths homework?' Jill asked.

'Not enough to worry him,' Emma replied. 'He likes sport, chemistry and physics best, but he gets by in the other subjects.'

Two electric guitars sat on stands near the bed.

'Does he practise a lot?' Jill asked.

'Day in, day out,' Emma told her, smiling.

'He taught himself, didn't he?'

'Yes. He had a toy one for Christmas when he was – oh, he must have been four or five at the time. He loved it, and managed to get a good tune from it. We bought him a real one – and he's had several since. He's formed a band, you know.'

Jill smiled. 'I bet he loves that.'

'He does. Mind you, his father's told him that it's not to interfere with his schoolwork. If he wants to be the next U2, or whoever it is these days, he has to wait until he's finished his education.'

'Wise move,' Jill agreed.

'The trouble is,' Emma went on, 'people fill his head with nonsense. James, like the other band members, is a

152

talented musician, but there are plenty of those around. You have to have luck to make it to the top. Yet people keep telling them how good they are.'

'James sounds sensible enough not to take any risks.'

'Yes, yes he is.'

Was James as sensible as his parents made him sound? He was loved, that much was evident. He was worshipped even. But was he under pressure to perform well and achieve great things? Did he find the constraints here too much?

'What about family quarrels, Emma? Every family has them. What did James argue about? What turned him into the monster that teenagers are?'

Emma's arms were wrapped tight around herself. She walked to the window and gazed out at the back garden below. That, too, was immaculate. A table and chairs on the patio had been covered for winter. The foliage in the borders provided colour in warm reds and oranges.

'Teenagers have to rebel,' Jill went on softly. 'It's nature's way of preparing them for flying the nest.' She smiled. 'And the way they turn into monsters – well, that's nature's way of making sure the parents are happy for them to fly. What did James rebel against?'

Emma turned around, her face pale as she chewed on her lower lip.

'He got in with a bad crowd,' she confided at last, her voice halting. 'His father didn't approve. I expect you know the sort. They've left school and just seem to hang around the streets all day causing trouble.'

'Yes, I know the sort,' Jill assured her. 'I expect James finds them good company. Instead of doing boring school-work, they'll be having all kinds of fun.'

Emma nodded. 'He's argued with his father about it lately. Well, he's argued with me, too. He can't seem to understand that school will soon be behind him. All he thinks about is his music. Sometimes . . .' she paused briefly, 'he goes to his room straight after school and we don't see him again until the following morning.'

153

'But there was no argument before he went missing?' Jill asked.

'Nothing. In fact, he'd been a bit better for a few days. More settled, more like his old self.' She looked straight at Jill. 'I would love to think he's gone off with these so-called friends of his.' She shook her head sadly, and Jill could understand how she felt.

'Does the name Brian Taylor mean anything to you?' Jill asked, changing the subject.

Tears welled up in Emma's eyes. 'He's connected with Martin Hayden, the boy who was murdered, isn't he?'

'Yes,' Jill admitted.

'No. I'd never heard the name until Chief Inspector Trentham spoke of him.'

'And James never mentioned being friendly with Martin Hayden?'

'No. He knew him from school of course, but they didn't hang around together.'

Jill was on the point of leaving the bedroom when she spotted something on the floor. Lying there, beneath the blue electric guitar, was a small business card. She picked it up.

On the back, was a scribbled note: *Keep practising. Call me sometime.* On the front was the name: *Tobias Campbell, Private Music Tutor* and his address in Church Street.

Bingo! They had their link.

Chapter Twenty-Four

Jill was trying to give her mind a rest by studying the *Racing Post*. She'd had a successful day on the horses with Guitar Man romping home at twelve to one and Back on the Job winning by a short head at sixteen to one.

After leaving the Murphys' house, she'd spent her time looking through a mountain of paperwork for clues their killer had left. There were very few.

She had no doubt that their killer had chosen Martin and Josie Hayden, but there was something almost impulsive about the actual killings.

It was the rage that puzzled Jill most. Martin had been badly beaten but Josie . . . She shivered. The killer had been half out of his mind with anger when he'd cut Josie. It had been personal, too.

Jill was convinced their killer was someone close to Josie. So how did James Murphy fit in?

She returned her attention to the *Racing Post* . . .

Ten minutes later, just as she was about to put a pizza in the oven, her doorbell rang.

She guessed it was Max as he'd taken to calling in most evenings on his way home. Except it wasn't on his way. In fact, it was one hell of a detour. However, before she could shout to let him know it was open, he was inside.

'Great idea that, kiddo. Keeping the door unlocked, I mean. Makes it so much easier for killers to get in. Or did you forget we've got a maniac on the loose?'

He was right; she should be more careful. 'I doubt he's interested in me.'

'You said that about Valentine.'

She'd said exactly that, and her stomach flipped over as she remembered the way he'd had her pinned in her chair with a knife held to her throat . . .

'I did,' she agreed, having no witty retort for that. 'Drink?' she asked, ready to open a bottle of wine.

'Better not,' he said, taking her by surprise. 'I've got an appointment this evening.'

There was something different about him this evening. He always looked smart but, unless she was mistaken, he'd made a special effort. He seemed distracted, too.

'Oh? Business or pleasure?'

There was a slight hesitation before he said, 'Business.'

She didn't believe him. Why was that? Because she felt she could no longer trust him, or because he looked shifty? Did he look shifty? Yes, he did.

Not that it mattered to her what he did in his spare time, she reminded herself.

'Anything new?' she asked briskly.

'Not a lot. Toby Campbell's been in London all day. He's due back late tonight so we're bringing him in first thing in the morning. I'd like you there if you can make it.'

She nodded.

'What did you reckon to him?' he asked.

Jill thought back to their meeting.

'He didn't strike me as a killer if that's what you mean,' she answered thoughtfully. 'I'd bet he likes the company of young people, but lots of folk do.'

'True. It's one hell of a coincidence though, don't you think? Both boys having come into contact with him.'

'It is.' She couldn't argue with that, which is why she'd called Max the moment she left the Murphys' house. 'But I don't see him as your killer. He's too patient and con-trolled a person for such a brutal attack. Your killer is angry, someone verging on the edge.'

'He doesn't drive, either,' Max put in.

'Oh? Why not?'

'Dunno.' Max shrugged. 'Never bothered, I suppose. So

156

that alone almost puts him out of the running. It's a good walk out to where Martin Hayden was abducted. Having said that, he could have been in a taxi. We think Martin knew his killer and went off with him willingly.'

She tapped her foot on the kitchen floor.

'Brian Taylor is still top of my list. He had a hold over Josie. Love, I suppose. She really loved that man and she never did get over the way he abandoned her. Of course, that only works if James Murphy turns up safe and sound. There's definitely no connection between him and Brian Taylor, is there?'

'None that we can find. I asked the Murphys if they knew the name and they both looked blank.'

'I asked, too. And I certainly can't see Emma going off for an afternoon of passion with Taylor,' she said. 'She'd far rather spend her time in the house and garden, or at an art gallery.'

'We've checked everything we can – no, there's no connection there.'

'If Josie confronted Brian Taylor, if she guessed he'd killed Martin – then he might kill her too,' Jill pointed out. 'Or maybe he was simply angry with her.'

'I know, but it doesn't make sense. Unless James Murphy turns up safe and sound.' He looked at her. 'But he won't, will he? You know that and I know that. He might not be dead – might not – but he's being held against his will.'

'I imagine so, yes. Let's think of Morrison. If Josie knew something about Geoff Morrison and confronted him, well, that makes more sense. He's linked to both boys.'

'Yeah, I know, and we're watching him very, very closely.'

Max glanced at his watch for the third time in as many minutes.

'You'd better not keep your hot business appointment waiting,' she said, smiling sweetly at him.

He frowned at her tone. 'Mm. OK, I had better go. I'll see you tomorrow when we put Toby Campbell through the mill?'

'OK.' He wasn't going to tell her who his appointment was with, she noticed.

'By the way, how's your friend? Ella Gardner.'

'She's OK.' Finding Josie Hayden's butchered body would be a terrible shock for anyone but Ella was a practical, no-nonsense type. 'She told me how marvellous you were,' she added drily.

'Yeah?'

'And she told me that, although she'd been offered counselling, she thought she was a bit long in the tooth for that poppycock.'

'Poppycock?' He grinned at that.

'She's fine.'

'Good.' He checked his watch yet again. 'Right, must dash. I'll let you know if anything happens.'

'Fine. Enjoy your evening.'

'I will. See you.'

Yes, he definitely had something important lined up. So important that reminding her to keep her bloody door locked had completely slipped his mind.

Chapter Twenty-Five

As Max pulled into the fitness centre's car park, he was just in time to see Donna Lord striding towards the entrance with a bag slung over her shoulder. She glanced back, saw him, and was standing by his car when he parked.

'That's good timing,' he greeted her.

'Isn't it? I do like a man who's punctual.'

If Jill hadn't made him feel so uncomfortable, he would have stayed at Lilac Cottage a little longer. Punctuality had never been one of his strong points.

Donna shifted her bag to her other shoulder and Max, beginning to regret this already, grabbed his own bag from his back seat.

This wasn't business. Who was he trying to kid? And damn it, he'd far rather be at Jill's enjoying a glass of wine before he went home to the boys.

'You're looking more tense than ever,' she scolded as they walked into the club.

She, on the other hand, seemed very relaxed. It was the first time he'd seen her without make-up, and it came as a painful reminder that she was far too young for him.

As she signed them in, Max looked around him.

The man sitting at the reception desk clearly worked out in every spare minute. A couple of young women, both wearing black dresses which he assumed was the club's uniform, walked across the reception area and through a door marked *Pool*.

When Donna had finished flirting with Mr Muscles at

the desk, she slipped her arm through Max's and nudged him towards that same door.

'See you in the pool in five minutes,' she murmured. 'Oh, and here's the key for your locker.'

Max went to the appropriate changing room and found the appropriate locker. He must be mad; he hadn't been swimming, other than a splash around in the sea, for years. He didn't particularly like swimming.

However, he was changed in well under five minutes and he walked out to the pool. It was massive, and he had to admit that the water, shimmering against blue tiles, did look inviting. There were four people in the water, all of them swimming determined lengths. And this was supposed to be fun?

It was a good ten minutes before Donna appeared. She was wearing a black one-piece with a vivid slash of purple across her left breast. The effect was stunning. Her legs really did go on forever.

She stood by the side of the pool, gazed at the water for a moment, then, giving him that broad smile, called out to him, 'Frightened it might be cold?'

'Yes.'

She laughed, a laugh that started at red-painted toenails and ended with a toss of blonde hair.

Shaking his head, Max walked to the deep end and dived in.

She'd lied, he realized immediately. The water was freezing. It might clear his head, but it wouldn't do much for the rest of him.

He'd completed half a length in an effort to fight off the shivers when she appeared at his side, laughed, and overtook him. OK, so she'd had plenty of practice. Max put in more effort and caught her midway down the second length.

He stopped at the shallow end and brushed the water from his eyes with his hands. She stopped, too, and stood very close to him, shaking the water from her hair very much like his dogs did. With wet hair clinging to her face and her skin shining with vitality, she looked better than ever. She knew it, of course.

'Not bad,' she teased him.

'For someone so out of condition?'

'I couldn't possibly comment on that,' she said, spluttering with laughter. 'And I never said you were out of condition. Just the opposite, in fact. I merely said you were tense.'

'True.'

The next thing he felt was her foot running along the back of his calf muscle, and suddenly he was breathing harder.

'Come on, lazy bones,' she said, and she set off to do another length.

As Max swam, she was all over him. One moment she was by his side, the next she'd dived underneath him.

By the time they decided to call it a day, Max was knackered. She wasn't even breathing hard.

'Well?' she asked. 'Feel better for that?'

'Actually, I do,' he admitted. He was knackered, but he felt good.

'I'll see you in five minutes then.' She patted him on wet buttocks and strode off towards the ladies' changing room.

As Max showered, and dressed, he asked himself what in hell's name he was doing. One minute he was fantasizing about Donna's naked body next to his, and the next he was wishing he was at home with his kids. One thing was certain, he was too old to be chasing leggy young blondes . . .

They met up in the reception area.

'Drink?' she suggested. 'I think we've earned one.'

It was tempting. But he really was too old.

'I can't,' he said.

'What? Not even one drink?'

'Sorry. I have things to do.'

'What sort of things?' she demanded. 'You can't be working, surely? You need to have some fun, detective.'

He did, but not with Donna. She was everything a man could want, and he was flattered, but he'd been there, done that, and had the wrecked relationship to prove it.

'Some other time maybe,' he said.

'OK. Some other time,' she said, and although the smile was still in place, her manner had changed. She wasn't used to being turned down, he realized. Not that it surprised him.

He must be mad.

'I'm sorry, Donna, really. I've enjoyed this evening very much. It's just that – well, I've got a couple of kids at home. I need to spend some time with them.' She didn't look convinced. 'There's someone else,' he tried to explain, 'and I don't want to mess that up.'

'And who's the lucky lady?'

'No one you know.'

'Ah, you're trying to get back with your psychiatrist.' She smiled. 'OK, Max. Don't worry, I won't embarrass either of us by asking again.'

With that, she dropped a quick kiss on his cheek, and strode off. Max stood watching as she threw her bag on the front seat of her car, climbed in and drove out of the car park.

He regretted his decision the second she was out of sight.

Jill was probably enjoying rampant sex at that very moment. What did she care whether he jumped in the sack with Donna Lord or anyone else? She didn't. She had the nation's favourite defence lawyer to keep her warm.

Besides, Donna had only suggested a drink. What harm would that have done? She must think him mad.

She wasn't far wrong, he decided.

Chapter Twenty-Six

Jill's first thought when she walked into Max's office the following morning was that he looked rattled. He was glancing at papers on his desk before screwing them into balls and tossing them at the wastepaper basket. Most of them missed.

'Good time last night?' she asked casually.

'OK, thanks.' He didn't look at her; he threw another ball of paper at the wastepaper bin.

Why wasn't he going to tell her about last night? Because it wasn't important? Or because it was?

The remaining sheets of paper were barely glanced at before being crumpled and thrown at the bin.

'Right,' he said, getting to his feet. 'Let's see what Toby Campbell has to say for himself.'

Plenty, Jill hoped. It was exactly a week since they'd been to his house, and they were no further forward.

'He doesn't want a brief,' Max said as they walked to the interview room.

Five minutes later, they were sitting opposite Toby Campbell. The tapes were running and Max had introduced those present.

'What can you tell us about James Murphy?' Max asked.

The question took Toby Campbell completely by surprise. 'James Murphy? The boy that's missing?'

'Yes.'

'Well, nothing. How do you mean? I don't know him.'

'You've never spoken to him?' Max asked.

'Never. All I know is what I've heard on the TV or radio.'

'So can you explain what this card was doing in his bedroom?' Max passed the small business card across the table.

'No, I can't,' he said, 'but I can tell you who I gave it to. Well, not his name, but he's a young chap in a band called Watershed. He plays the bass guitar very well. He's a short, chubby boy with ginger hair and a mass of freckles.' He looked from Max to Jill. 'The missing boy,' he said thoughtfully. 'Do you have a recent photo? I haven't paid much attention to the picture that's been on the TV.'

Max looked in his file, found one and passed it across the table.

'I'm not sure,' Toby Campbell murmured, 'but it could just be that this boy, James Murphy, plays lead guitar in the same band. On stage, his hair is – well, it's stuck up like a hedgehog's. He wears a hat, too.'

'He plays in the same band,' Max confirmed. 'And you claim that you gave that card to the other boy?'

'I did. He's talented and I know of a band who are looking for a good bassist. How James Murphy got hold of it, I can't explain.'

Max leaned back in his seat. 'I hope you can appreciate my problem,' he said slowly. 'Two boys from the same school go missing. One turns up dead. A common link? You. Guitars and you.'

Toby Campbell wasn't as cool as he was trying to appear. Jill noticed the way he flinched as Max had said 'One turns up dead.'

'Martin Hayden,' she said. 'How did you feel when you heard he'd been murdered?'

'Very sad, of course.'

'Define sad. Tell us what you did when you heard about it. Did you think, Oh dear, what a shame, did you have a good cry, did you contemplate suicide?'

'I did cry, yes,' he admitted softly. 'For all his faults, he was a lovely boy.'

'You don't have children, do you?' she said.

'No. I've never married.'

'Do you regret that? Did you want children of your own?'

'I think most people do,' he answered frankly. 'If they didn't, the IVF clinics wouldn't have such a workload.'

'But Martin was special, yes?'

'To me, I suppose he was. Yes.'

'He was special. You cried.' She watched him carefully. 'You loved him, didn't you?'

His answer was barely audible.

'Was that a yes?' she prompted.

'Yes.' He reached into his trouser pocket and pulled out a colourful handkerchief. 'Yes, I did. He was beautiful, confident, ambitious – everything I ever wanted to be.'

'Martin teased you about that, didn't he?'

'Martin never knew how I felt.'

'Of course he did,' Jill scoffed. 'He was a bright boy. He'd know how you felt.'

'Maybe,' Campbell replied, 'but, if he did, he never said anything.'

'I think he teased you,' she said. 'He would have enjoyed that. He'd have taunted you. Flaunted himself. Reminded you at every opportunity that you couldn't have him.'

'No.'

'That hurt you, didn't it? It made you angry.'

'No. I told you, he never said anything.'

'You told him how you felt. He laughed in your face. You decided to teach him a lesson. A lesson he'd never forget. He'd never taunt you again, would he?'

'No, no, no. You've got it all wrong. He never knew how I felt. I swear to God.' He threw out his hands. 'I'm not stupid. Martin was a bright young thing. What interest would he have in an old has-been like me? None. None whatsoever. Yes, I loved him. I admired him from afar. I was never stupid enough to let him know how I felt.'

Jill didn't know why she was bothering. Toby Campbell couldn't tell them anything.

Max must have thought the same because he rose to his feet.

165

'OK, thanks for your time, Mr Campbell. We'll get an officer to take you home.'

Blowing his nose again, Toby Campbell nodded. 'Thank you.'

Jill and Max left the room, walked out into the corridor and stopped by the coffee machine.

'Well?' Jill asked as Max hunted in his pockets for change.

'We're not going to get anything out of him, but I'm sure he knows something.'

'I'm not.'

'He's the one firm link to the two boys – yes, yes, I haven't forgotten Geoff Morrison –'

'Whose boyfriend sings in a band,' she reminded him.

'I know, but Campbell's admitted to being in love with the boy, for God's sake. What sort of weirdo is he?'

'He's a sad, pathetic, lonely sort of weirdo, and yes, he might even have tried it on with Martin Hayden, but he's not your man. Think about it logically, Max. Apart from anything else, he doesn't drive and never has. He could have taken a taxi out to Lower Crags Farm – but why not wait until Martin arrived for his guitar lesson?'

'Because Martin had no intention of going back for a guitar lesson.'

'OK, so he gets a taxi to the farm, leaps out of the bushes and bludgeons Martin to death. Except he wouldn't because he loved the boy. But then what? Does he carry the body into Harrington town centre and throw it in the canal?'

'You're a psychologist, Jill.' Max handed her a coffee.

'Oh, yes, silly me. You're the mighty detective and I'm the idiot who does the – what is it? – oh yes, the psychology bollocks. Forgive me, oh wise one, I was forgetting my place for the moment.'

'There's no need to get bloody sarky with me!'

'None at all,' she agreed sweetly. 'There's no need for me to waste my time thinking about Toby Campbell, either. It's Josie Hayden we need to concentrate on. I'll see you later.'

Toby Campbell wasn't their man, Jill was sure of it. Geoff Morrison wasn't, either.

She'd go and find someone else on the case, Grace possibly, and see what they had on Brian Taylor . . .

Grace, however, had problems of her own.

'What sort of mood is he in?' she asked Jill.

'Max? The usual. Why?'

'He won't be when I've told him the latest.' She was already striding off toward Max's office. 'Another kid from Harrington High has gone AWOL.'

'No!' Jill quickly caught up with her. 'When? And who?'

'Keane. Jason Keane. Vanished into thin air this morning.'

Chapter Twenty-Seven

The curtains needed pulling across, but Toby Campbell couldn't summon enough energy. Let passers-by see him sitting in his armchair with an untouched cup of tea at his side and tears pouring down his face. He no longer cared.

Everyone thought he was odd anyway. He may as well give them more reasons to think so.

To hell with them. He switched off the table lamp and sat in the dark so they couldn't see inside.

If Emily had married him, he wouldn't have been in this mess. He would have been teaching, providing for the family he'd longed for.

They had met at university in the early sixties, when Emily had been studying European literature and he'd been studying music. For Toby, it had been love at first sight. He could see her now; tall, willowy, always laughing, untidy blonde hair flying around her face, enthusing over her best-loved poets, hugging her favourite novels to her chest, a long scarf wrapped around her neck . . .

They had shared a flat. And a bed.

Emily, however, had refused to share his life.

'Me? Settle down?' She'd laughed at the very idea. 'Hell's teeth, Toby, it's not me, is it? Can you see me as the adoring wife putting your slippers to warm and your dinner on the table?'

Oh, how she'd laughed.

That was the problem, of course. Toby *could* see her as the adoring wife. He hadn't wanted his slippers warmed or his dinner on the table, but he had wanted Emily in his life. Had needed her in his life. They had been ideally suited, or so he'd thought. She had her books and he had his music. More importantly, they'd had each other.

When those idyllic days came to an end, Emily had gone to Venice. Toby would have gone with her, or followed her.

'Don't talk daft, Toby,' she'd scoffed. 'Look, it's been fun, huge fun, but we have our own lives to live now. I want to travel and have fun. I want to see Venice and Rome, Barcelona, Russia – I want to see the world.'

'Let me see it with you,' he'd pleaded.

'No. Please don't make this difficult.' A rare frown had creased her brow. 'Please set me free.'

'At least promise me that you'll keep in touch.'

'OK. I can promise that.' The smile had been back. 'I'll send you postcards. Dozens of them,' she'd vowed, laughing happily.

So Toby had set her free.

He had taken a job teaching. Without Emily, though, life had been meaningless. And those promised postcards had never arrived . . .

When his parents died, leaving him a sum of money, he was finally able to give up teaching. He had enough to live on. Teaching music privately was more to keep his mind occupied than for financial gain. Mostly, he'd taught young girls to play the piano. Occasionally, if he were lucky, he'd teach the guitar or violin.

Then, one day, Martin Hayden arrived on his doorstep.

His blond hair had been blown into his face and a long scarf had been wrapped around his neck. He had reminded Toby of Emily . . .

In Martin Hayden, Toby had seen the young man he had always wanted to be, the young man with whom Emily would have shared her life.

Martin had been rash, a risk taker. Just like Emily, he'd been ambitious and greedy. No way would he have allowed something or someone he wanted to walk out of his life.

'What would you know about life, old man?' he'd asked once.

It was the sort of thing Emily would have said, he realized. Looking back, it was easy to see how she had used him. It had suited her to share his flat while she was at university. There had been no one else in her life, as far as Toby knew, so sharing his bed had been easy repayment.

For years, he had longed to see her again. That was impossible, of course. He had no idea which country she was in. In his more bitter moments, he hoped she'd fallen on hard times. He hoped that someone had used her, hurt her like she had once hurt him. He would have liked to talk to her again, to let her know just how much the memory of their affair, if it could be called an affair, angered him.

Instead, he'd had to settle for a new love in his life, Martin Hayden. And now Martin was dead.

In a strange way, it was like losing Emily all over again . . .

His ginger cat wandered into the dark room.

'I suppose you want feeding, Marmalade? Hmm?'

Toby dried his face on his hands, switched on the lamp, rose to his feet and pulled the curtains across.

His cat needed feeding. Life went on.

Chapter Twenty-Eight

'And anyway,' Jill's mum was saying, 'they've got four little girls now. How daft is that? He's a bone idle, work-shy bugger and she's fit for nothing but letting the kids run around screaming while she sits on her fat arse watching telly.'

Jill had to smile. There was nothing like hearing the gossip from River View estate.

Little input was required so Jill had switched on the speakerphone and was doing other things. She'd already cleaned the inside of the kitchen window and now she was eating toast before Max arrived.

'That's good then, Mum,' she said, taking a bite of toast. 'It's reassuring to know you've got such nice neighbours.'

'Ha! And you'll remember young Freda Tomms. She'd be about the same age as you, wouldn't she? Yes, I remember her going to school with you. Well, she's expecting again. That'll be four kids with four different fathers.'

Jill thought her mum was wrong. The name Freda Tomms meant nothing to her. But she wasn't going to argue.

'The first was with that Gerry. Remember him? He wasn't a bad bloke really . . .'

While Mum recited the Tomms children's family tree, Jill saw Max's car pull up outside. She held the door open for him and gave a helpless shrug as she nodded at the phone.

'That Gerry was the best of a bad bunch,' Mum went on. 'Oh, and you'll never guess what I found yesterday.

171

Remember those photos your dad took when you and Max came for the day? When your dad and Max were trying to get the barbecue going?'

'Yes.' Jill felt a rush of colour invade her face. 'Look, Mum –'

'I found those,' Mum said fondly. 'Ah, happy days. Max was a wonder with that barbecue, wasn't he?'

It must have been a couple of years ago now, but Jill could remember that day as clearly as if it had been yesterday. She and Max had been living together and the boys had been spending the weekend on a camping trip. It was the first time Max had met her parents, and she could remember that they'd been anxious at the prospect of meeting her 'fancy friend'.

After days of rain, the sun had shone and her dad and Max had been hell-bent on having a barbecue. They'd had to find the thing first, and then clean it. That they had escaped without food poisoning never failed to amaze Jill.

It had been a good day, though. They'd eventually eaten burnt sausages with salad, and then sat in the sunshine. She'd been drinking wine. Max had been driving so he'd stuck to her mum's home-made cordial . . .

'Yes. Anyway, I have to dash, Mum,' she said, pushing the memories aside, and unable to look at Max. 'Life's very hectic here at the moment, but as soon as everything calms down, I'll drive over and visit. Give my love to Dad . . .'

Jill cut the connection and grabbed her bag. She still couldn't look at Max. 'Right,' she murmured, face burning, 'I'm ready.'

'Your mum's well, I take it?' he said as she locked up her cottage.

'Fine, thanks.' She strode over to his car, asking over her shoulder, 'Anything new?'

'Nah, I'm still a wonder with a barbecue,' he said softly.

Damn him!

She refused to get wound up in memories. Other people managed to work with ex-lovers; she could, too.

172

'Let's get going then,' she said briskly. 'There are plenty of other ways I could be spending my Saturday.'

'Me, too,' he replied with a sigh, flicking the remote to unlock his car.

She wasn't even going to think about what he meant by that . . .

It was a cold, damp morning but at least his car was warm. As he drove, she forced her mind to concentrate on Martin Hayden, James Murphy and Jason Keane.

She was sure the answer was at Lower Crags Farm. But what if she was wrong?

Martin Hayden and James Murphy couldn't have been more different. Martin believed himself to be special; James believed himself to be the same as hundreds of other boys at Harrington High School. Martin was ambitious and chose friends who might benefit him; James chose friends that he could confide in and have fun with. Martin had made enemies; James appeared to have no enemies. Martin came from a private family who kept its feelings hidden; James came from a loving, close family that didn't care if the world saw its terror. Martin was out to make an impression; James was out to enjoy life. Martin had siblings; James was an only child.

Jason Keane was different again, yet he had been Martin's best friend. He'd known about Toby Campbell. In fact, it was Jason who'd put them on to him.

No, there had to be something else, something they had overlooked.

Unlike Max, she didn't believe Campbell was their link. His coming into contact with two of the boys was merely coincidence. As they lived in the same area, attended the same school and had only a year between their ages, it was natural that they would come into contact with the same people.

There was something else. There had to be.

'Isn't this the most dismal place in the world?' she said, as Max turned the steering wheel to avoid the deep pot-holes in the track leading to Lower Crags Farm.

'The house of bloody death,' he muttered grimly.

After bumping their way up to the farmhouse, Max parked alongside a police car and killed the engine.

'Look.' Jill pointed to a low stone wall at the side of the old barn where George Hayden was sitting. 'You go inside and I'll have a word with him there. He might be more accommodating away from everyone.'

'OK.'

Max walked off and Jill approached George Hayden.

All she could think about was the killer's anger. The answer to this nightmare had to be hidden in Josie Hayden's past.

If the killer had been connected to Josie from the start, maybe he'd killed Martin to make her suffer. Surely, far worse than death, was for a mother to lose her child in such a brutal way. Then, the killer must have thought she hadn't suffered enough.

Max, of course, thought she was talking nonsense and she had to admit that her theory didn't make allowances for James Murphy or Jason Keane. How were they connected? Connected they must be . . .

As if aware he had company, George Hayden looked up. 'Good morning,' he called out.

She had only seen him once since Josie had been murdered, and then only briefly, and she was amazed by the change in him. All his bluff, domineering manner was missing. He was as meek as a lamb. It was as if Josie had taken all his anger, his arrogance, his pigheadedness, his rudeness – as if she'd taken it all with her.

'Good morning, Mr Hayden. I hope I'm not intruding.'

'I was just taking a breather. Thinking about things.'

'How are you managing?' She sat on the wall beside him.

'We're managing,' he said abruptly. 'We don't have no choice, do we?'

No, they had no choice.

'I wondered if I might talk to you about your wife,' she began. 'I don't want to intrude into your grief, but I was

174

thinking about her past – family, relationships, that sort of thing.'

'Family?' He spat out the word. 'Pah! Her mother paid her no attention at all, and she never did know who her father were. She never spoke about her childhood, but I don't reckon the memories were pleasant.'

Brian Taylor had said something similar.

'How did you meet her?'

'It were at a dance,' he told her. 'An old pal of mine were getting married, and a gang of us had gone along to this dance. There were no stag night or anything like that, we were just going to have a few drinks and chat up the girls.'

'And you chatted up Josie?' she guessed.

'She were different to the others,' he explained, his thoughts miles away. 'She'd had too much to drink, like everyone else, but you could tell she weren't used to it. She were a shy little thing. She looked out of place and, to be honest, I felt sorry for her.'

Poor Josie. A woman wanted to feel desired, attractive and special. She didn't want members of the opposite sex feeling sorry for her.

'We had a couple of dances but neither of us were natural dancers and we both felt out of place. Then we – I took her out to my car for, well, you know.'

'I can imagine,' Jill said, struggling to keep the shock from her voice.

'Aye, well, as I said, we'd both had too much to drink.' He was clearly embarrassed, and she was surprised by such honesty from him. She would have expected him to keep such personal memories to himself.

'How old was she then?'

He thought for a moment. 'Eighteen or nineteen. I can't rightly remember.'

He took a grubby handkerchief from his pocket and blew his nose. His eyes were moist, Jill noticed.

'So she wasn't as shy as you thought,' Jill said lightly. 'She must have been strongly attracted to you to make love on a first date.'

175

'Nah, she were drunk. We both were.'

'I hate to ask such personal questions, Mr Hayden, but we do need to find out as much as we can.'

He nodded. Jill preferred it when he was his usual belligerent self. Now, he looked weak and broken. Two murders in the family would break anyone, though. Anyone except a man who had killed before, who had engineered his brother's death . . .

'Was she a virgin?'

'No.' He clearly didn't like talking about such personal matters, and Jill didn't blame him. 'I don't think she liked – well, you know. If she hadn't been drunk, she wouldn't have let me touch her.'

'What makes you say that? That she didn't like sex?'

He shrugged, growing more and more uncomfortable by the second.

'That first time, she were – well, it were as if she felt she should do what I said.' His face was scarlet. 'Perhaps I were a bit too forceful.'

Was he talking rape?

'Like I said, I were drunk.'

'How forceful were you?'

'I didn't use force,' he said immediately, 'but I were a bit persuasive. Only talking, you know.'

'And afterwards?' Jill asked curiously. 'How did she react afterwards?'

'She wanted nothing to do with me. I phoned her at her home, and she gave me the brush-off. It were a while later that she phoned me asking to meet. She were pregnant with our Andy.'

Jill knew they had both felt duty bound to get married, and she knew that Josie had been grateful.

'I did the right thing by her and asked her to marry me,' George said, some of his gruffness returning. 'I don't suppose she were any happier about it than I were, but we got by.'

'You did,' Jill agreed. 'For a long time, too. Did she ever

176

mention past boyfriends? You said she wasn't a virgin. Was there anyone special in her life before you?'

'Not that I know of.'

There must have been. She wasn't into having sex on first dates, yet she'd clearly been with someone before meeting George.

What a sad life she'd had. No wonder Brian Taylor had charmed her so easily.

'Is that it?' he asked, standing up. 'I've got work to do.'

'Yes, that's about it.'

George Hayden was too private to give much away.

'If you think of anything, Mr Hayden, about any names she mentioned from the past, let us know, will you?'

'I will at that. I want this bugger caught,' he assured her fiercely.

His sudden intensity surprised her.

'I'm sick to death of the guilt that goes with it,' he went on, eyes alight with anger. 'First it were me brother, then me son – well, the lad I thought were me son, then me wife.'

'Guilt?' she queried.

'Aye, bloody guilt. When me brother died, it were a stupid accident but, all these years later, I still wonder if I could have done summat different. I'm sick of it!'

With that, he stomped off.

When he was about ten yards from her, he once again took that grubby handkerchief from his pocket and blew his nose loudly. Was he shedding tears for Josie? Or for his brother? Or for himself?

Given that unexpected and rare display of emotion, Jill supposed he was innocent of his brother's death after all. And of Martin's and Josie's . . .

Brian Taylor had said Josie was naive when it came to sex. George had claimed she hadn't liked it. So who had made her that way? Who had given her that first disappointing – or possibly worse – experience of sex?

Clouds danced across the sky, blotting out the watery sun, and the temperature dropped dramatically.

Had Josie enjoyed sex with Brian Taylor? She had loved him, yes, but had she enjoyed the sex or had she been passive, letting him do as he wanted just to please him? She would have done anything to please that man.

Jill still had no answers when Max was driving them away from the farm.

'There's someone from Josie's past, someone important,' she told him. 'She may even have been raped.'

He gave her a quick glance. 'Who said that?'

'She was a shy thing when George met her, yet she had sex with him on their first meeting. That was unlike her. He said she didn't like sex particularly, yet she wasn't a virgin. Someone must have put her off sex, Max. She may even have been raped. Or she may just have been disappointed, I suppose. Perhaps there was someone special in her life and the sex wasn't very good. She was young – perhaps the man in question was young. We need to find out who that person was.'

'You're on the wrong track, Jill,' Max said. 'It's wasting time. No matter what happened to Josie Hayden, she had no ties with James Murphy or Jason Keane. None whatsoever.'

He was right; she knew that. All the same, she was convinced this revolved around Josie.

'So what's your theory?'

'Ha!' He drummed his fingers on the steering wheel. 'If only I had a theory. One schoolboy has been murdered. Possibly three. Schoolboys. So where in hell does Josie Hayden come into it?'

Jill wished she knew.

'On the other hand,' he went on, 'forty per cent of the Hayden family has been wiped out. So where in hell do James Murphy and Jason Keane come into that?'

'What a bloody mess!'

He smiled at that. 'That's what I love about you, kiddo. The queen of the understatement.'

The traffic in Harrington's centre was going nowhere

fast. People were doing their Christmas shopping. Jill hadn't even started hers . . .

'What do we know about Josie's past?' she asked.

'Not a lot. Let's see, her mother's suffering from Alzheimer's. She's in Blue Lodge. They didn't have much to do with each other, though. Her mother attended her wedding to George, but that was about it. Josie was an only child and her father vanished before she was born.'

'But what about boyfriends? There was someone before George so she would have been living with her mother then.'

'No one's mentioned any boyfriend.'

'Perhaps it wasn't a boyfriend. Perhaps she was attacked – raped.'

'And the link to James Murphy or Jason Keane?'

'I don't know,' she admitted, 'but I'd like to talk to her mother.'

'Sadly, nothing she said would be admissible.' Max pulled a face. 'She's gaga. She doesn't know where she is half the time and she talks to dead people the rest of the time. There's no point.'

'I'd still like to talk to her.'

Max looked at her long and hard. She could see that he wanted to argue, but he didn't have anything else to go on. He was quite right, of course. There was probably no point whatsoever in talking to Josie's mother. On the other hand, they had to clutch at any straw offered.

'How gaga is she?' she asked.

'Totally!'

Chapter Twenty-Nine

It was early evening when, after a lot of arguing, Jill and Max arrived at the Blue Lodge Care Home.

Blue Lodge was a luxurious home offering respite, residential and full nursing care, and was only for those who could afford it. A large, stone building, it was set well back from the road and hidden by tall trees.

It made Jill shudder and she prayed that she never ended up in such a place. Like most people, she supposed, she hoped that a simple, quick heart attack would finish her off. Although not for some time, obviously.

'Home of the living dead,' Max said on a sigh. 'If I ever ended up in a place like this –' He broke off, and continued more cheerfully, 'But I won't. At the slightest hint that I might be coming here, I'll put a few bullets in myself.'

'I think I will, too.' Another thought struck Jill. 'Who's paying for all this?'

'Her parents' house sale,' Max replied. 'They lived in a big terraced place for most of their lives. Rose lived on the Brook estate, but her parents' place fetched a good sum. She inherited it five years ago. Mind you, it wasn't a fortune, so I don't know what happens if the money runs out and she's still alive.'

Max parked the car in a bay marked *Emergency Vehicles Only* and they climbed out.

'This place doesn't come cheap,' he murmured.

Wide steps led to a huge blue front door. Beneath a bell set into the wall was a small plaque: *Please ring the bell before entering.* They did so.

On the right-hand side of a large hallway was a reception desk.

'Detective Chief Inspector Max Trentham and Jill Kennedy, Harrington CID,' Max introduced them, showing his ID to the girl behind the desk. 'We've come to talk to Mrs Rose Dee.'

'Ah, yes. If you can just hang on a second, I'll give Julie a buzz. She's expecting you. She can tell you how Mrs Dee is today.'

Literally seconds later, Julie burst into reception. She was in her mid to late forties, one of the 'jolly hockey sticks' types whose energy and *joie de vivre* would soon have driven Jill mad. She could imagine Julie persuading the residents to sing 'Pack Up Your Troubles'. Or perhaps the elderly sang Status Quo's 'Rocking All Over The World' these days.

'Rose has been quite lucid today,' she informed them, beaming at them. 'She recognized me and she talked of her garden.'

'That's encouraging then,' Jill responded, not very encouraged. 'How long do her lucid periods last?'

'It depends. Some days, she doesn't have any. Yesterday, for example, she was quite agitated because she thought we were letting rabbits into her room. Heaven knows what put the idea of rabbits in her head, but there, we don't know, do we?'

She looked to them both for an answer.

'No,' Max said.

'She's in the conservatory,' Julie told them, 'and she's quite alone, so perhaps you'd like to talk to her there? Yes?'

'Fine,' Max said, smiling.

'As you know,' Julie said in a whisper as she led the way to the conservatory, 'we did tell her about her daughter, but I don't think it sunk in. We don't know, do we?'

'No,' Jill said to save Max the bother.

The conservatory was a huge, Victorian affair, filled with tall ferns and cane furniture, and lit by stark, fluorescent tubes. It was a cold place.

'Rose,' Julie boomed out, 'you have visitors. Do you remember I told you they were coming?'

Rose looked up with blank eyes.

'You didn't tell me,' she argued. 'Who are they? I don't want to talk to anyone.'

'Yes, you do,' Julie scolded with a teasing laugh. 'You're always complaining that you don't get visitors. Now, you talk to these nice people and I'll go and make you all a lovely pot of tea. How's that?'

'Hurry up about it,' Rose told her. 'You know I have to be at work soon. What time is it now?'

'A quarter to six,' Julie answered, 'and you don't go to work any more. You've retired now, don't you remember?'

'Of course I remember,' Rose said, rolling her eyes at such stupidity.

She looked a little like her daughter, Jill thought, surprised, but Rose, she suspected, was a far stronger character. Her hair was long and white, and it had been combed neatly and tied back. Her hands were thin and the skin almost translucent. She was wearing a black skirt and a pink cardigan over a white blouse.

Jill pulled up a chair opposite her.

'I'm Jill,' she explained, while Max got his own chair, 'and we've come to ask you a few questions. Is that all right, Rose? May I call you Rose?'

'You can call me what you like. But I'll need to get Robbie's tea on soon. He gets mad if his tea's not on the table when he gets in.'

'Robbie? Who's Robbie?'

'Pork chops are his favourite. He won't eat them without apple sauce though. Mind, he won't eat lamb without mint jelly, either. Mint sauce is no good. It has to be jelly. I buy that from the shop. He don't know if I make it or not.'

'Does Robbie work?'

'What time is it? I've got to be at work soon.'

Jill's spirits sank. They'd be lucky to get anything useful out of Rose.

182

But at least they had a name. Robbie could be Josie's father. On the other hand, he could be a figment of Rose's imagination.

'What time does Robbie come home, Rose?' she asked.

Rose leaned toward her and her voice rasped in Jill's ear. 'Don't drink the tea when she brings it. She's trying to poison me.'

'I'm sure she isn't. Why would she do that?'

'She sent him away, you know,' Rose confided.

'Sent who away?' Jill asked.

Rose stared out through the glass to the darkness beyond.

'Who did she send away, Rose? Was it Robbie? Did she send him away?'

'She didn't know Robbie. I made sure of that.'

The door opened and Julie appeared with a pot of tea and a plate of biscuits.

'There we are, Rose. Isn't this nice? You like visitors, don't you?'

Rose's hand, painfully thin, shot out and took a biscuit. She was like a starved cat, grabbing food before someone took it away. At least she didn't think the biscuits were poisoned.

Julie beamed at Jill. 'Shall I let you be mother?'

'Yes.' Be mother indeed. Max was right; the best option was a quick bullet.

When the tea was poured and Rose had eaten all the biscuits, Jill tried to talk to her again.

'Did they tell you about Josie?' she asked gently.

'Josie?' She looked blank, as if she'd never heard the name before.

'Your daughter,' Jill prompted her. 'You remember Josie, don't you?'

Rose ignored that. She looked at Max, and then grinned at Jill. 'Is he your fella?'

'No.' Bloody hell! Rose didn't know what day it was, but she automatically assumed that she and Max were an item.

'Was Josie a good daughter, Rose?' she persisted.

183

'Daughter? I don't know any daughters.' Rose thought for a moment. 'Are you muddling her up with the one that married the farmer?'

Jill heard Max sigh. He'd been right, and he knew it. Even if Rose gave them a wealth of information, they wouldn't know if it was real or imaginary.

But Josie was the key. Jill was convinced of it.

'Yes,' she said. 'Josie married George, the farmer. She had three children, didn't she? Did you see them? There was Andy, Sarah and Martin.'

'She married a farmer.'

'That's right,' Jill agreed.

'She didn't know Robbie, I made sure of that. It was because she sent him away.'

'If she didn't know Robbie, how could she send him away, Rose?'

'Not Robbie. She didn't send *him* away.'

'Who *did* she send away?'

'She told lies about him.'

'What sort of lies?'

'That's why I had to send her away,' Rose said.

'Josie? Where did you send Josie?'

'She married the farmer, you know.'

'Yes, that's right.'

Rose looked at her right wrist. 'My watch! It's gone! Who's stolen my watch?'

Max patted her other arm. 'It's on this hand.'

'Oh, yes.' She began humming to herself as she rocked in her chair. 'I've got to go now. I need to be at work soon. What time do I have to be there, do you know?'

'You don't work now, Rose,' Max reminded her. 'You've retired. You're lucky, aren't you? I wish I was retired.'

She looked at him for a moment. 'Why aren't you her fella?'

'I'm working on it,' Max told her in a whisper. 'What about your fella, Rose? Is his name Robbie?'

'I've got to go to work now,' she said vaguely.

184

For the next half-hour, they talked to Rose. Her answer was always the same. She had to go to work.

In the end, they said their goodbyes and left her in Julie's capable hands.

'Come again soon,' Julie called as they were leaving.

It was a relief to drive away from Blue Lodge, but Jill could still smell the place.

'OK, you win,' she said on a sigh. 'It was worth a try, though. And I still think it would be worth finding out who this Robbie is or was and –'

'Robbie Williams probably.'

'It could be,' she admitted, 'but perhaps Josie did send someone away. Who could that be? Perhaps Rose had a boyfriend and Josie, used to having her mum to herself, was difficult. This man – if indeed there was a man – might have thought better of it and done a runner. Robbie might have been another boyfriend – one she didn't tell Josie about in case she started behaving badly.'

'Or it might be the ravings of an old, sick woman,' Max pointed out.

'That's what I love about you, Max. You're such an optimist.'

'Tsk! And I thought it was my skill with a barbecue.'

Chapter Thirty

On Monday, Jill was at the station early and she went straight to Max's office.

'I've been thinking.' She'd been doing little else and she'd hardly slept at all last night. 'I'd like to talk to some of Josie Hayden's old neighbours.' She knew he'd argue, say it was a waste of time. Perhaps he was right. 'I know she hadn't lived there for years, and I know her mother has Alzheimer's and isn't reliable, but there might be something.'

Max gathered up papers off his desk, gave them a scathing glance and put them on the pile that was already teetering in his in-tray.

'If we can find out about this Robbie,' she said, 'it might lead us to –'

'He probably doesn't exist. Rose was getting ready to go to work at God knows where. She didn't even know who her daughter was so this Robbie . . .' He shrugged.

He had a point. On the other hand, they had nothing to work with, nothing at all, so anything would be a bonus. She'd had enough sarcastic comments from Meredith about her inability to build a profile.

A profile? Ha. She had nothing to go on. Nothing. Only the fact that their killer was half out of his mind with anger. More angry with Josie than with Martin? Yes.

'What do you want to do?' he asked.

At least he was prepared to discuss it.

'Josie grew up on the Brook estate,' she said, 'and if it's anything like River View, and they seem much the same, someone will know something. I have my mum on the phone on a daily basis telling me the goings-on at River View. Everyone knows everyone else's business.'

'They might know it,' Max muttered, 'but they won't talk, and certainly not to us. They stick together on the Brook.'

That was true. The residents were born with a loathing of the police.

'It's worth a try, Max.'

He leaned back in his chair and tapped his pen against his desk. 'It'll cost you,' he said at last.

'What?'

'Dinner tonight. It's Kate's birthday and she'd love it if you came along.'

She'd planned to call on his mother-in-law on her way home to hand over the card and present she'd bought, but it would be good to be part of the celebration.

'Who else is going?' she asked.

'Only me, Kate and the boys. Why?'

'Just curious.'

He was frowning at her, trying to read her mind.

'I thought your favourite teacher might have made her move by now,' she said casually.

That was something else that had kept her awake. She'd convinced herself, rightly or wrongly, that his 'business appointment' on Thursday night had been with her.

'Donna Lord?' He sounded as if he'd never heard the name, yet he looked shifty. 'What makes you think she's planning a move?'

She could tell from the way he couldn't meet her gaze that she already had.

'Oh, just a hunch. Must have been something to do with the way she was all over you like a rash.'

A smug smile touched his lips at that. 'Was she?'

'Yeah, it's a copper thing,' she told him, hoping to dent his ego. 'The macho testosterone-fuelled bloke who's keeping our streets safe is always a turn-on. Except in this case, of course, he's not keeping our streets safe.' She needed to

187

get out of his office before she threw something at him. 'So I can go to the Brook estate?'

'You'll come along this evening?'

She nodded.

'OK,' he said, resigned. 'Tell you what, take Grace with you.'

'Right.'

She was at the door, and almost had it open when he spoke.

'I turned her down.'

She didn't look back at him. 'You do surprise me. Too young for you, I suppose? Afraid you wouldn't be able to keep up with her?'

Before he could see the smile that insisted on curving her mouth, she walked out of his office, closing the door quietly behind her.

Why had he turned down Donna Lord? Much as Jill hated to admit it, Ms Lord had everything going for her. She was stunning to look at with her envious figure and her neatly trimmed, natural blonde hair. She was also young and clever, of course.

Jill caught sight of herself as she approached the glass doors in the corridor. Her hair was naturally blonde, but it was a mess today. Still, wasn't the messed-up look in fashion? Her jeans were clean, as was her shirt. True, her shirt could have done with a good iron . . .

What the hell? Max had turned down Donna Lord and it was she who'd be with him for Kate's birthday celebration.

Without wasting time on analysing why that made her feel so good, she put her mind to the more important matter of brutal murders and went in search of Grace.

The Brook estate was rough. As soon as Grace turned the car into Byron Way, Jill's spirits sank. Gardens were overgrown and crammed with rusting junk. Children's toys lay abandoned with grass growing around them.

Scruffy cars littered drives and the road. Despite this, almost every house boasted garish Christmas decorations. Giant inflatable snowmen swayed in gardens. Santas climbed the walls.

'It's just like going home,' she quipped to Grace.

'Yeah, me, too.' Grace looked up and down the road. 'Where shall we start?'

'Keats Avenue. Josie grew up at number eleven.'

'The boss thinks you're wasting time.'

Jill had to smile. 'The annoying thing is that he's probably right.'

Grace parked the car and they were soon knocking on doors. Most people were out, or ignoring them, but the girl at number nineteen, the first to answer the door, invited them inside. The carpets and walls were filthy but at least a thousand pounds' worth of television sat in one corner of the lounge. In front of the window and totally obscuring the view was a huge plastic Christmas tree adorned with flashing, musical lights.

The girl's name was Sally and she looked as if she hadn't combed her hair in days.

'We're trying to find anyone who knows anything about a Mrs Josie Hayden,' Jill explained.

'The one who were done in?' Sally clearly relished being, as she saw it, part of a real-life drama. She wasn't even dressed yet and Jill suspected her life was a mundane round of daytime television.

'Yes. When she lived round here, she was Miss Dee, Josie Dee.'

The girl looked blank. 'I know Rose Dee. A strange old cow she were. She's in a home now.'

'That's the woman's mother,' Jill explained. 'How well do you know her, Sally?'

'It's not me. Me aunt were friendly with her. Not friendly perhaps, but they worked at Reno's. It weren't called Reno's then, it were Rockafella's.'

'Rose Dee worked at Rockafella's?'

'Yeah.'

189

'Doing what?' Jill was amazed. Reno's, or Rockafella's as it once was, was Harrington's trendiest nightclub.

'They worked behind the bar,' Sally told her. 'I don't know about Rose Dee, but my aunt thought it were great. All the blokes bought 'em drinks – not that they had the drinks, of course, but they put the money aside.'

'Where does your aunt live?'

'She died a couple of years ago,' Sally said. 'Breast cancer, it were. I keep checking for lumps, I can tell you. I don't want to go like her. I reckon it runs in our family because me cousin had it an' all. She's all right now, though.'

'Make sure your doctor checks you out,' Jill said, getting ready to leave.

'They're not interested.' Sally dismissed the medical profession and reached for a cigarette.

Once outside, Jill wasn't sure where to go next. Did they carry on along the estate, or did they head for Reno's? The estate was the best bet. It was unlikely that anyone working at Reno's these days had any recollection of Rose.

She might not be sure where to go, but she did feel they were getting somewhere. Unfortunately, Grace didn't share her views.

'So Josie Hayden's mother was a bit of a goer,' she said. 'It means nothing, Jill. Josie had lived on that farm for twenty years. Digging around here won't find our man.'

'You've been working with Max too long . . .'

She was probably right, though. Perhaps Jill was on the wrong track. Perhaps Martin Hayden's murder had been –

No, the answer lay with Josie, she was sure of it, and to find out about Josie, they had to talk to people who had known her.

They carried on knocking on doors and trying to talk to people who'd known Josie and her mother.

Slowly, Jill began to piece together a picture.

Josie's father, as they knew, hadn't been named on the birth certificate. From what people said, it was unlikely that Rose had known who he was. By all accounts, Rose

190

had had more boyfriends than most people had Sunday lunches.

'She was a looker,' they'd been told, 'and she knew how to flirt.'

Josie, on the other hand, might not have existed.

'A quiet thing,' a few said.

Most people had forgotten that Rose had a daughter, and no one had connected the murdered farmer's wife, Josie Hayden, with her.

Grace was all for calling it a day.

'Let's just try Brenda Daley's place again,' Jill said. 'She worked at Rockafella's with Rose, too, so she might be able to tell us something.'

'Like what? That Rose flirted with all the blokes then dragged them off to her bed? I think we've got the picture by now.'

'We may as well knock on her door again on the way back . . .'

Brenda Daley had moved off the Brook estate to Jubilee Crescent where she lived in a semi-detached bungalow on a quiet road.

A blue Fiat sat on the drive when they pulled up. An encouraging sign.

Jill spotted the resigned expression on Grace's face and grinned. 'This is a nice neighbourhood, Grace. Who knows, we might even get a cup of tea out of a clean cup.'

'I'd rather be at home making my own tea,' Grace grumbled.

Jill rang the doorbell for the second time that day and, for the second time that day, caused a dog to start yapping for all it was worth.

There was a movement behind the glass panel and then a woman in her early sixties opened the door to them.

'Mrs Daley?' Grace asked.

'Yes.'

Grace introduced them, and showed her ID. 'We'd like to talk to you about Rose Dee.'

'You'd better come in.' Brenda Daley's first priority was stopping her dog, a small Yorkshire terrier, escaping.

'I'll tell you what I can, but it won't be much, I'm afraid,' she said, once they were inside. 'I haven't seen her for years. I haven't even thought about her until recently – it was when I saw that her daughter had been murdered. How awful. That poor kid – well, a woman now, of course – didn't have much of a life.'

Brenda was the first person who had realized that Josie had been Rose's daughter. Progress perhaps?

'Can I get you a cup of tea?' Brenda asked. 'The kettle's just boiled.'

'Two sugars for me, please,' Grace said immediately.

'No sugar for me, thanks,' Jill told her.

The dog, Susie, had stopped yapping and was curled up on what was, judging by the pet blanket and dog toys crammed on it, her personal armchair. While Brenda made the tea, they had to hear how Susie was a rescue dog, how Brenda had only had her four years, and how she didn't know how she'd cope without her.

'What can you tell us about Rose Dee?' Jill managed to ask at last.

'What do you want to know?'

At least she was willing to talk. Unlike the residents of the Brook estate, she didn't clam up and eye them both with suspicion.

'Anything,' Jill told her. 'We know you worked together for a while at Rockafella's. How did you get on with her? Were you close?'

Brenda thought about that for a moment.

'We worked together three, sometimes four nights a week,' she said, 'but no, we weren't close. For all that, I knew her business. She talked non-stop. She went on and on about the men she was seeing. Sometimes, she had two or three on the go at once. I can't say I liked her and, to be honest, I thought she was a fool. They were only after a good time, but she couldn't see that. "He's the one, Brenda," she'd say. They weren't interested, though. Half of them were married anyway. Even if they weren't married, they didn't fancy the idea of taking on another man's kid.'

'Josie?'

Brenda nodded. 'Most of them didn't know about her – Rose kept quiet – but as soon as they found out, she didn't see them for dust.'

'Did you know Josie?' Jill asked.

'I saw her a few times,' Brenda told her, and there was a touching wistfulness to her voice. 'I used to buy small presents for her on her birthday and at Christmas. I felt sorry for the kid. Half the time, Rose would come to work and leave her in the house alone. She was only about twelve then. Poor kid.'

She broke off and took a sip of her tea.

'There was one bloke who wasn't put off by Josie,' she said thoughtfully. 'I can't remember his name now, but he'd often stay and babysit while Rose came to work. I thought he had to be a decent bloke. Of course, he had no idea that Rose was busy flirting with other men while he sat at the house with Josie.'

'Are you sure you can't remember his name?'

Brenda shook her head apologetically. 'There were so many, you see.'

'Did you see Rose or Josie after you left Rockafella's?'

'I didn't,' Brenda said. 'I left when I got married. Bob, that's my husband, died five years ago.'

'I'm sorry.'

'Thank you.'

There was a brief, respectful silence for the absent Bob's benefit.

'How long did you work with Rose?' Jill asked, bringing the conversation back to Rockafella's.

'About four years,' she replied. 'Yes, four years, almost to the day. I left the day after Josie's fourteenth birthday. Funny how you remember things like that, isn't it?'

'It is.' Jill wished Brenda could remember the man's name.

'Another funny thing,' she went on suddenly. 'I went back two weeks later because they owed me some money and I was amazed to hear that Rose had left, too. She just hadn't turned up one night. No notice, no nothing. She left them in a right pickle, I can tell you. Mind, that was typical of Rose. She had no consideration for others. But no, I never saw her again.'

'Did she ever mention anyone called Robbie?' Jill asked, holding her breath.

'She may have, but I don't remember the name. Why do you ask?'

'Something she said,' Jill explained. 'She's quite ill at the moment, and inclined to lose touch with reality, but she mentioned having to get Robbie's tea on the table. I wondered if you knew anyone called Robbie.'

'No. I'm sorry, but the name means nothing to me.'

Brenda made them another cup of tea, but was unable to tell them much else and they were soon leaving.

'Will you give us a call if you think of anything else?' Grace asked, handing her a card with the phone number on it.

'I will.'

They were at the car when Brenda suddenly called out. 'Terry! The one who used to babysit, I reckon his name were Terry or something like that.'

Chapter Thirty-One

It was good to spend the evening with Kate and the boys. Max too, if Jill was honest with herself. She couldn't help wondering, though, if she was so pleased about his turning down Donna Lord and asking her to accompany them this evening simply because she wanted him to want her. And why? So that she could have the satisfaction of turning *him* down, and proving to him that she liked her life without him? The trouble was that, although she did enjoy her life, she missed him and the boys terribly. Evenings like this were simply a reminder of how good things had been between them. Why was it so easy to remember the good times? And why was it so easy to ignore the bad memories – the fighting, Max's drinking, his betrayal?

They were having a pub meal before Kate returned to her flat for a small party with her friends.

'I might win another rosette on Sunday,' Ben was telling Jill.

'What for?' Harry scoffed with a guffaw of laughter. 'Sitting down when you're told to?'

'OK, so Fly might win one,' Ben muttered, used to his brother's teasing.

'Is it a show?' Jill asked.

'Yeah, at the leisure centre. It starts at ten,' he added, looking hopeful, 'but Fly doesn't go into the ring till two.'

'Can I come and watch,' Jill asked, 'or will that put you off?'

'You can come,' he told her.

'I'll be there then.'

The unconcealed pleasure on his face at that statement brought tears to her eyes and she had to blink them back. Max was looking at her. He saw. He knew.

'So what does sixty-two feel like, Kate?' she asked, changing the subject.

'Old!'

Jill laughed. 'Don't talk silly.'

Kate pulled a face. 'You wait.'

It didn't seem like two years since they'd celebrated Kate's sixtieth. She'd insisted she didn't want any fuss, yet Jill and Max had organized a surprise party and she'd loved every second of it.

The thought of birthdays dragged her mind back to what Brenda Daley had said about leaving Rockafella's the day after Josie's fourteenth birthday. Why had Rose left at the same time, and why leave so suddenly?

Had she met someone new? Had she had trouble from a boyfriend? Perhaps an irate wife had been after her.

It sounded as if she'd loved that job so what had made her leave? Something important must have happened.

She glanced across at Max and she could see that, although he was laughing and joking, his mind was on the case. That didn't surprise her. They were all on edge as they tried to race against time. They had two boys missing, and it was Max who would have to break the news to their parents if they ran out of time.

It was possible, of course, that James Murphy and Jason Keane were already dead. So how did they fit in?

She was convinced, rightly or wrongly, that Josie Hayden's past was responsible for her murder and that of her son. But what about the two missing boys?

'Come on, you two,' Kate said to the boys, 'let's go and put some money in the machines.' She shook her head at Jill and Max. 'You two are miles away,' she scolded.

Jill watched them wander off.

'Anything new?' she asked Max.

'No. Apart from a few dozen more loose ends,' he said grimly, 'and another couple of dozen possible sightings of

196

James Murphy and Jason Keane. Murphy's been spotted hitching a lift near the M62 junction at Milnrow, going into a cafe in Blackpool, and eating a sandwich in Carlisle.'

Like Max, Jill wouldn't get excited. When someone was reported missing, so-called sightings came in from all over the country.

'And you still haven't found a link with the Haydens?'

'Only Toby Campbell,' Max told her, 'and he checks out. He couldn't have killed Josie.'

'I know.' She signalled for the waiter and asked for another coffee.

'Geoff Morrison's hiding something,' Max said, 'and so is that boyfriend of his.'

'Like what?'

'I don't know,' he admitted, 'but there's something. When Martin Hayden was taken, they claim they were together. I don't believe them.'

'And when Josie was murdered?'

He sighed. 'Geoff Morrison was at the school entertaining a visiting football team with a very convenient shed load of witnesses.'

'And the boyfriend?' Jill asked.

'In a recording studio in London,' Max told her, 'and yeah, it checks out. There's no way he could have killed Josie.'

'We're assuming that Martin and Josie were killed by the same person. Perhaps we're wrong.'

'We're assuming that,' he agreed, 'but we're looking at every possibility. We're questioning everyone in Harrington, we've checked out everyone at Harrington High – clerical staff, cleaners, teachers, canteen staff, the groundsman . . .' He sighed again.

Jill finished her coffee.

'Come on, let's find Kate and the boys, throw some money in the machines and put it from our minds for a while.'

'Good idea. You go ahead and I'll settle the bill.'

The boys were on a winning streak, but it didn't last long.

Half an hour later, they all headed back to Max's place. Kate went straight to her self-contained flat to get ready for her guests. Jill and Max had coffee while Ben showed them how Fly's training was coming along. Ben took it very seriously; Fly thought it was great fun.

'I'm impressed,' Jill said, hugging Ben to her. 'I'll be at that show on Sunday to watch Fly win that rosette.'

'You'll have to be quick,' Harry grinned. 'Fly will eat it . . .'

Jill was about to leave when Max's phone rang.

'Yes, Fletch?'

Jill watched him. His gaze darted from Harry to her, and it rested on her, unnerving her, as he spoke. Something awful had happened; she could see it in the tension in his jaw and the hard anger blazing in his eyes.

Had a body been found?

The house was warm, but Jill was shivering. She turned on the gas fire.

Max finished his call.

'Right, you two, time you were in bed,' he said, and there was something in his voice that chilled Jill even more . . .

Half an hour later, the boys were in bed.

'What's happened?' she asked.

They were in the kitchen. Max was reaching for glasses.

'A text message – a fucking text message, for God's sake – has been received at the nick. It was sent from Jason's Keane's mobile.'

'Jason sent it?'

'I didn't say that.'

Without asking, he half filled two glasses with whisky and handed one to her.

She tried to remind him that she was driving, that her car was parked on his drive and that she needed to go home. She couldn't. Her hand trembled as she took the glass.

'What did it say, Max?'

He looked at her long and hard. 'Tell DCI Trentham that Harry is next.'

Chapter Thirty-Two

Max sat in the armchair, a glass of Scotch in his hand and the bottle on the table at his elbow. He felt sick.

Jill was curled up on the sofa, a glass beside her. She'd planned to drive back to her cottage after the birthday meal but, if she left now, she'd have to get a taxi. Apart from the fact that they'd both been drinking, she didn't look capable of walking across the room let alone driving.

'You OK, Jill?'

'Not really. You?'

Of course he wasn't.

'What are you going to do, Max?'

He'd been asking himself that same question and, other than find this sick bastard and blow his brains out, he had no answers. Who the fuck was he dealing with? Someone he'd leaned on? Geoff Morrison? Toby Campbell? Brian Taylor?

'I don't know.' For her sake, he had to at least give the appearance of being calm. 'It's tempting to pack the boys off to a safe place in Scotland or somewhere, but I can't do that. Whether I like it or not, they have to be at that bloody school tomorrow.'

She nodded, and he saw a shimmer of moisture in her eyes.

'Hey, nothing's going to happen to Harry,' he promised.

She nodded again, as if she hadn't doubted it for a second.

Nothing's going to happen to Harry. Who the hell was he to say that? The great detective who had no idea what the fuck was happening? The great detective who already had two, and possibly four, bodies on his hands?

He felt sick. Physically sick. A mixture of fear and fury was churning away inside him, fear that he might not be able to protect Harry and fury that some sick bastard thought he could fuck with him!

'As a rule,' he said, 'Kate takes them to school, but sometimes, I take them. Starting tomorrow, I'll take them every day and bring them home. We'll get someone at the school watching them – classrooms will need painting or the electrics will need checking.' He drained his glass. 'Half of Harrington Constabulary will be at the school watching Harry and Ben, and if Meredith even thinks the word shoestring, I'll bloody deck him.' He sloshed more whisky into his glass. 'Do you want another?'

She looked at her glass, seemed surprised to find it was almost empty, and nodded. She stood up, helped herself, then sat on the floor, close to his chair, gazing at the fireplace.

'Have I had this wrong from the start?' she said shakily. 'I've convinced myself this is all to do with Josie, but perhaps she simply knew too much.' She kicked off her shoes and rested her feet on the hearth. 'This maniac may not be directly linked with the school,' she went on, 'but if it's someone who likes young boys, it's the most convenient place to hang out.'

'Agreed.'

'But if it *is* someone with an unhealthy interest in boys, and we'll forget Josie for the moment, then Harry doesn't fit, Max. Our man likes them sixteen or seventeen years old. Young adults. Harry's too young.'

She stood up again, walked over to the bureau and hunted round for a pen and paper.

'Let's start with Harry and work backwards,' she suggested, resuming her place on the floor. 'If we work on the assumption that Harry has been chosen because of you, and we have to assume that because no one else has had a warning, we need to think –'

'About someone I've spoken to,' he finished for her.

She sighed. 'Or someone you *haven't* spoken to. You're the face on TV, Max. The face everyone associates with this case. This could be a cry for help. Our killer might want to be caught.'

They talked, argued and made notes for three hours. And they were still in the dark.

'What about the teachers?' Jill murmured. 'Philip McKay's too worried about the school's reputation to be of much help, but the other teachers must know something. They must. It'll be something they've dismissed as unimportant, but the kids must have mentioned someone –'

'We've questioned every last one of them.'

'Donna Lord's your best bet. She's worked at the school for two years, yes? She's bright and clever, and, more important, she gets on well with the kids. Yes, yes, I know you've spoken to her, but perhaps it's worth having a good long chat, off the record, to see if she can come up with something. Someone has been behaving out of the ordinary. Someone must have aroused the kids' interest. She's on the same wavelength as her pupils, Max.'

'It's worth a try, I suppose.'

'It'll be a terrible hardship for you, I know,' she said sarcastically.

He let that go. 'We're missing something here, Jill.' He'd felt that all along. There was something vital they'd overlooked.

'Like the killer's identity?'

Yes, that would be a help . . .

It was four in the morning. Max couldn't decide if it was worth trying to sleep for a couple of hours or not. Probably not.

Chapter Thirty-Three

Max wouldn't be surprised if Donna Lord stood him up. He wouldn't be too bothered, either. He'd had one hell of a day.

Credit where it was due, though, Phil Meredith had been a star. Apart from muttering about pulling Max off the case because it had become personal – hell, it was *always* personal with Max – he'd been great. He hadn't so much as hinted at the word shoestring. The force might never have had to run to a budget. Everything Max needed was at his disposal.

He had detectives posing as electricians at Harrington High School and he had DS Bradley and DS Forrest taking turns to 'babysit' at his house. Harry and Ben had been within sight of damn good coppers all day.

He'd had to tell Harry what was happening and, typically, Harry saw it as an adventure. He wasn't in the least worried. Why should he be? Like all fourteen-year-olds, he considered himself immortal. Besides, his dad was the ace detective, wasn't he?

While Max had been chasing round all day, Jill had been at the nick going over every piece of information they'd gathered on this case – and there was plenty. She was still there now.

Max had been talking to Philip McKay, the headmaster, about security for his boys this morning and, when he'd left him, he'd seen Donna Lord.

She'd been a bit cool, probably because he'd turned her

down, but he'd thought Jill's idea had merit. She was right; Donna was on the same wavelength as the pupils.

'I need to talk to you,' he'd told her, 'and I'd far rather do it over a drink. Can I tempt you?'

'Am I getting preferential treatment, detective?'

'You are. If you want it, that is.'

She gave him that coy smile of hers. 'Why?'

'Have you looked in a mirror recently?'

She smiled at that. Flattery went down well with her. 'OK,' she said.

'The Chameleon?' he suggested. 'Seven o'clock?'

'OK.' She tapped her fingers against his tie. 'See you at seven, detective.'

It was seven fifteen and there was no sign of her. He'd give her until seven thirty then take it he'd been stood up. It was a long shot anyway. As ever, he was clutching at straws.

He was emptying his glass when the doors swung open and she rushed inside. It was seven twenty-nine.

'Max, I'm so sorry.' Her hand rested on his arm as she spoke. 'I forgot all about our date. I thought you would have given up on me.'

'Almost,' he said. 'I thought you'd found something better to do.' He nodded at the bar. 'What can I get you?'

'White wine, medium, please. I'll grab us a table.'

As he waited to be served, Max was pleased to see her sit at a table on the far edge of the room. He glanced up at the ceiling; they should be far enough away from the speakers to make conversation relatively easy.

She looked stunning, he couldn't help noticing. The dress she wore was pale grey wool and it clung to her figure like skin. Her curves were in all the right places and her legs seemed to go on forever. In a word, she was gorgeous.

'Here's a coincidence,' she said when he joined her, 'my hairdresser is Sarah Hayden. Martin's sister. I only found out today. I turned up for my appointment, asked where Sarah was and had the shock of my life when they told me. She looks nothing like her brother.'

'No.' He wouldn't tell her they had different fathers. That was the Haydens' business.

'What a small world.' She took a sip of her wine. 'Ooh, delicious. Thank you, Max. Now, what do you want to talk to me about?'

Once again, he flattered her, this time by telling her how he realized she was her pupils' best friend.

'They'd talk to you about things,' he explained, 'whereas they'd be wary of the other teachers. Have any of the kids mentioned anything unusual? Has anyone unusual been seen hanging around the school? Anyone behaving oddly? Have any strangers approached them?'

'I've thought and thought,' she told him, 'but nothing springs to mind. The boys are full of bravado, but they're scared. They're on their guard.'

'That's good.'

'Yes.' She was about to speak, but changed her mind.

'What is it?' Max pressed.

'I'm sure it's nothing,' she said, 'but the other day, I noticed a bloke hanging around at the school gates. Whether he was suspicious or whether we're so anxious that now *everyone* seems suspicious, I don't know.' She gave a self-conscious shrug. 'Probably the latter.'

And probably not.

'What was he like?'

'A good-looking man, as far as you could tell. He was sitting in his car. Mid-forties, perhaps. Fair hair.' She ran a finger round the rim of her glass. 'The thing is – God, this sounds crazy. When I saw him, I had the idea that I'd seen him there before. This is probably the sign of an over-active imagination, but I think he's been there several times – just watching from his car.'

Max was intrigued. 'What sort of car is it?'

'A big, flash silver thing. A BMW, a Mercedes or something like that.'

That description would fit Brian Taylor. Did he go along to see his son, Martin, or did he watch the other kids, too?

'You said you saw him the other day,' Max reminded her. 'Can you be more specific?'

'Yes, it was on Tuesday. I know that because I left early, at the same time as the pupils, and he was parked right in front of the gates, blocking my view as I tried to pull out.'

'I don't suppose . . .' No, of course she hadn't.

'What?'

'I was wondering if you noticed the number plate, but you wouldn't, would you?'

'Sorry.' She grinned at him. 'Hopeless, aren't I?'

'Not at all.' She'd been more helpful than she'd know. What in hell's name was Brian Taylor doing outside the school gates on Tuesday?

Had Taylor tried to get to his son and ended up killing him, losing him forever? Then, blaming Josie for the fact that he'd never known that son, had he killed her in the most brutal way possible? Perhaps he'd then acquired the taste for murder and gone after James Murphy and Jason Keane.

At best, that theory was weak.

'Anything else?' he asked. 'Has anyone said anything?'

'Not to me.'

The music was getting louder and the place was getting hotter.

'What about Martin Hayden, James Murphy and Jason Keane?' he asked. 'Sorry, I know you've been asked about them before but –'

'I have. Countless times.' She took a sip of her wine. 'They were just normal kids. James, I know, is having battles with his parents. They're suffocating him.' She pulled a face. 'Mr and Mrs Murphy come to every parents' evening, every school play, every school fair, every sports day. Their world revolves around James. And poor James just longs to escape the apron strings.'

'And Martin Hayden?' Max asked. 'Did he long to escape the apron strings?'

'Who knows?' She shrugged. 'I would if I were him. Who'd want to live on a farm in the middle of nowhere?'

Max thought of the dull, dreary place that was Lower Crags Farm. 'Not me,' he admitted, and she smiled.

'Someone was telling me that the police over there outnumber the residents now – and I include the sheep in that.'

She was right. With two members of the family murdered, security was tight out at the farm.

'Who told you that?'

'I can't remember. It was just something someone said in passing. Oh, I know, it was Alan Turner.' At his frown, she added with a grin, 'Geoff Morrison's bit of skirt.'

Why had Morrison's boyfriend been out at the farm?

'So,' she said, teasingly, emptying her glass, 'is that it? As I can't tell you anything useful, I suppose I have to buy my own drink?'

'I'll buy it,' Max said on a laugh. 'It might help you remember something else.'

He fought his way to the bar, and waited to be served. One barmaid was moving at the pace of a comatose slug, and the other was taking a personal call on her mobile.

Eventually, he caught the comatose slug's attention. 'A medium white wine,' he said, 'and a double Scotch, please.'

He should take a cab home and leave his car here, but he needed it for the morning. Sod it, he'd have to be totally irresponsible and drive while over the legal limit. He was safe to drive, he just wouldn't be legal. Yeah, and how many times had he heard Harrington's morons come out with that logic?

He carried their drinks to the table and wished his gaze wasn't constantly drawn to her cleavage.

'Does the name Toby Campbell mean anything to you?' he asked. 'He gives guitar lessons. Has anyone mentioned him to you?'

'No. Sorry, the name means nothing. Oh, wait. He's not the weirdo who played at our school concert, is he? The Christmas one, year before last?'

'I don't know.' But he'd like to. 'Tell me about it.'

'Philip McKay had this great idea of putting on a musical – *Joseph and the Amazing Technicolor Dreamcoat*. The music teacher, John Higgs, said he knew a good guitarist and this weird bloke pitched up.'

Toby Campbell was weird.

'What did he look like?'

'Strange,' she said on a laugh. 'Like Quentin Crisp.'

That *was* Toby Campbell.

'He wore strange clothes,' she went on, 'had long hair, and he was knocking on a bit.'

'Yes, that sounds like Toby Campbell.' There was no doubt about it. 'What about the music teacher, John Higgs? How come I haven't spoken to him?'

'He left.' She laughed again. 'Soon after that disaster of a concert.'

'Where is he now?'

'I've no idea.' She patted his knee, and an involuntary shudder trembled through his body. Donna Lord was too attractive for her own good. She was certainly too attractive for Max's. 'I'm not much help, am I?'

'You've given me a couple of ideas,' he assured her.

'I have?' Like a child, she was absurdly pleased.

'You have. Thanks.'

'You're welcome, detective.'

She put her elbows on the table and rested her chin on her hands, pouting slightly as she gazed at him.

'So who are you going home to tonight?' she asked him.

'The same as ever. Harry, Ben and two dogs.' He feigned regret. 'What about you?'

'An empty flat,' she said with a shrug, 'and an enormous bed.'

Silk sheets, he'd bet. Lots of pillows. She'd send a man blind . . .

'Sadly, it really is time I was going. Can I give you a lift or call you a taxi?'

She looked around the room.

'No, thanks. If you're deserting me, I'll have to see if I can find someone else to keep me company.'

She'd have no problems there. Max would bet his life that there wasn't a man in the room who hadn't noticed her. Noticed her and wanted her.

'You're sure?'

'I'm sure.' Her face brightened suddenly. 'Next time, though, I won't let you go so easily.'

He smiled. 'I'll keep you to that.'

She reached up, kissed him on the cheek, then walked over to the bar. Max watched her climb on to a stool next to a guy in his early thirties. Lucky devil.

Max stepped out into the fresh air and walked round to the car park.

Why had Brian Taylor been hanging around the school? How many times had Toby Campbell been to the school? And why hadn't he mentioned it? Because you didn't have the sense to ask him, a small voice mocked. What about John Higgs? Was he connected to this?

Chapter Thirty-Four

It had been a long, anxious day and Jill was shattered. She wanted to get to her cottage, order a takeaway, put her feet up with the *Racing Post* and relax. Last night, she'd only dozed for a couple of hours on Max's sofa.

She was driving through Harrington when she saw the sign for the Blue Lodge Care Home. She drove past it, then stopped the car. Maybe it was worth having another chat with Rose Dee. The place depressed her, and she really did want to get home, but half an hour there wouldn't hurt.

She turned the car around, doubled back on herself, drove along the driveway and parked as near to the front door as she could get. Deciding she wouldn't be sorry if she couldn't see Rose, she got out of the car and walked up the front steps and into reception.

Julie was sitting at the main desk, tapping away at a computer keyboard. A smile of recognition crossed her face.

'Hello, there, it's . . .'

'Jill. Jill Kennedy.'

'Of course it is. And you've come to see Rose? Aw, that's nice. She does like visitors. She's in the conservatory where you saw her last time. Would you . . .' She looked undecided for a moment. 'I'd better come along with you,' she said at last.

They walked along to the conservatory.

'She's had a very good day today,' Julie told her. 'She's been quite lucid at times.'

'That's good then.'

The conservatory was cold again, but that wasn't responsible for stopping Jill in her tracks. It was the sight of
Rose. She looked like a jewellery stall.

'She insisted on wearing her bits and bobs today,' Julie
told her in an over-bright voice. 'It's good to see them take
care in their appearance, isn't it?'

'Er, yes,' Jill agreed.

Julie reminded Rose who her visitor was, not that it
meant anything to Rose, and left them alone to 'have a
nice chat'.

'You're looking very pretty today, Rose,' Jill began. 'Have
you had visitors?'

'I've got to go to work in a minute,' she said, looking
agitated.

Jill's spirits sank. If this was lucid . . .

'Where's that? Where do you work, Rose? At
Rockafella's?'

Rose gazed at a gleaming rubber plant, her expression
blank.

'Did you like working at Rockafella's?' Jill asked her.

'Had to leave,' Rose said, her bottom lip quivering.

'Yes, you had to leave, didn't you? Why was that, Rose?'

'Lies,' she whispered. 'It was lies.' She began pulling at
the string of beads around her neck. 'She told lies!'

'Who did, Rose?'

'It was lies!' The string snapped and plastic beads flew
across the linoleum floor.

'Oh, dear. Here, let me pick them up for you.'

While Jill went on her hands and knees, scrabbling
under tables and chairs in an effort to gather up the beads,
Rose rocked back and forth in her chair, tugging on another
set of beads around her neck.

Jill wished she'd gone straight home . . .

'Here we are,' she said, putting the beads in a dish – ash-
tray? – on the table. 'I'm sure Julie will be able to get them
fixed for you.'

'Lies,' Rose whispered, still rocking back and forth.

Jill might as well not be there.

210

'Who told lies about you, Rose?' she asked softly.

'She sent him away.'

They'd had this exact conversation before. Jill didn't think it was due entirely to Alzheimer's; this was something deeper, possibly brought on by Josie's murder.

'Who sent him away, Rose?' There was no answer. 'Was it Josie? Did Josie send him away?'

Rose started humming to herself, refusing to listen in a way that a temperamental child might.

'Who did she send away, Rose? Was it Terry?'

Rose's agonized scream rattled the conservatory's glass. Her eyes were wide and blazing with passion.

'Terry!' she cried, and she burst into noisy, hysterical tears.

'Now, now, there's nothing to get upset about,' Jill soothed her, putting an arm around those thin shoulders. 'It's all right now, Rose. There's nothing wrong.'

After five minutes or so, with Jill expecting Julie to appear at any moment to evict her, Rose calmed down.

'Brenda told me about Terry,' Jill ventured, breath suspended. 'She said you liked him a lot. He didn't mind that you had a daughter, did he?'

'Terry never touched her. Never.' Each word was delivered with the force of a bullet. 'She told lies about him. She made up filthy stories about him. He didn't harm her. He wouldn't, would he? She was only a baby. Only a baby.'

Rose began to howl again and, this time, the noise did bring Julie.

'Have you upset her?' she demanded, scowling at Jill.

'Not knowingly,' Jill said, 'but perhaps I'd better go. She seems a little distraught.'

'I think you had,' Julie said, clicking her teeth. 'Fancy upsetting her. And what happened to your beads, Rose? I've told you before about that. The last time this happened, you clogged up the Hoover. We can't have that happening again, can we?'

Jill rose to her feet before she was blamed for making Rose break her beads and clog up the vacuum cleaner.

211

'Perhaps I'll call again one day,' she ventured.

No one answered. Rose was still sobbing and Julie was still tutting over the pile of beads, so Jill crept out of the conservatory and left the building.

It was a relief to sit in her car, start the engine and drive away.

Her mind was full of what Rose had said. Max thought Rose was simply gaga, as he put it. Jill believed there was something much deeper. The more she thought about it, the more she thought that Terry had left Rose because Josie had accused him of – what? Sexual abuse? Rape?

Terry? Terry who?

If Terry still had such an effect on Rose, they needed to find out who he was. And fast.

Chapter Thirty-Five

The following afternoon, Jill was chatting to Max in his office and about to head for home, when Grace sought them out.

'I've found your Terry!' she announced triumphantly.

Jill's heart skipped a beat. 'Really? Brilliant! Where is he?'

'Currently pushing up daisies in Blackpool,' Grace said with a grin.

'Oh, for –' Jill had pinned every hope on the mysterious Terry, and now he was dead.

'His name was Terry Potter, and he died four years ago,' Grace went on, 'but he has a sister. She's alive and well and, as far as we know, fully compos mentis and living in Blackpool. Here's her address.'

'Thanks.' Jill looked at the slip of paper. 'How did you find them?'

'I spoke to the old manager of Reno's,' she said, 'and, about fifty phone calls later, I came across a woman who remembered him. She'd been going out with him, apparently, before Rose came along and whisked him away from her.'

Jill looked at Max.

'I think it's a load of crap,' he said, not for the first time, 'but as I have sod all else to go on, we may as well pay her a visit.' He looked at his watch. 'I need to collect the boys from school now, but . . .' He looked at Jill, his expression coaxing. 'How do you fancy a trip to Blackpool this evening? I'll buy you a stick of rock.'

'You're on.'

'OK, I'll pick you up from your place if you like. Thanks, Grace. Good work,' he added.

'You're welcome, guv!' Grace left the office even more pleased with his praise than she was with herself, if that were possible.

Jill drove home, fed her cats, tidied her cottage, sighed at the pile of work on her desk that she couldn't find time for, and went to run a bath.

She got in and lay back in the hot water, determined to relax. She couldn't, though. Her mind was like a tumble dryer filled with a million pieces of paper on which was written an abstract thought. Round and round, over and over, it went.

Terry Potter could tell them nothing. He was dead.

And why, having killed Josie and Martin Hayden, had the killer turned to James Murphy and Jason Keane? Why had Harry been threatened?

While they were chasing dead ends in Blackpool, anything could happen.

She shivered, despite the hot water.

'It's just as well we can see her tonight,' Max said, as he eased the car into the line of fast-moving traffic on the motorway, 'because she's going on holiday in the morning.'

'What did she sound like?'

'Bitter.'

'Oh?'

'Yeah. She said she wondered when us lot – coppers, I assume – would start sniffing round.'

'So she connected Josie Hayden with her brother?'

'Must have.'

'That's interesting.'

'Hmm. Anyway, she's more than willing to talk to us.'

'That makes a refreshing change,' Jill said with a wry smile.

When Max stopped the car outside Alice Potter's home, Jill was amazed by the size of the place. Every other house in the street was a bed and breakfast business, but this was a private residence. Tall, thick hedges shielded the house from the street.

They got out of the car, and walked up three stone steps to the front door. Max rang the bell and it was answered immediately, as if she'd been standing on the other side of it, waiting for them.

'You'll be the police?'

She was a large woman whose face was dominated by thick spectacles. Her hair was black with an inch of grey roots showing. She was wearing a pale green dress with a floral pattern on it.

'Yes,' Max replied, showing his ID.

She inspected it closely, and nodded her approval. 'Come in, then.' She showed them along a wide hallway and into a sitting room. Like Josie Hayden's home, this too was cluttered with a lifetime's collection of bric-a-brac. Two shelves were crammed with Blackpool souvenirs.

'Thank you for agreeing to see us,' Max said, taking the armchair she offered.

Jill was offered another armchair opposite him.

'I gather you were expecting us to call,' Jill began, as Alice Potter sat on the sofa where she could best see both of them. 'How did you connect Josie Hayden with your brother?'

'I didn't, not at first,' she explained. 'It was a friend who put me on to it. When I knew her – or when Terry knew her – she was Josie Dee. Terry was as good as gold to her.'

'Was he seeing her mother?' Jill asked curiously.

'Yes. Rose Dee was working at some nightclub or other,' Alice Potter said, 'and Terry met her there. He was besotted with her. Nothing I said would make him see that she was trouble.'

'Was she trouble?' Max asked.

'Trouble? Ha! Men can be such fools, can't they?'

'They can,' Jill murmured, lips twitching.

'That was my Terry. A fool when it came to her. No

215

matter what I said to him, he wouldn't believe she was using him. She had a string of other blokes in tow.'

'Really?' Jill said.

'Yes, I know her sort. But my Terry was blind when it came to her. Her daughter – that'll be Josie – was around eleven or twelve and, to help her out, he used to sit with the kid until Rose got back from the club. Terry and me were brought up proper, you know, and he didn't like to think of the girl being in that house on her own. Ha! He soon found out the error of his ways.'

'What happened?' Jill asked.

'The daughter, like I said, was only a young kid, but she must have been as wicked as her mother. She got herself pregnant. Or claimed she was pregnant. Rose Dee was a drama queen and her daughter was the same. So Josie, the crafty little cow – pardon my French, but, well – she only went and blamed it on my Terry. She said he forced her to have sex with him.'

Alice Potter gathered her ample bosom.

'Even now, all these years later, it makes my blood boil to think about it. My Terry's only fault was that he was daft. At least, he was daft when it came to women, and he was downright simple when it came to Rose Dee. How that Josie could accuse him of that, I can't imagine.'

'What happened?' Jill asked.

'Well, Rose, to give her her due, didn't believe the girl any more than we did,' she explained, 'but she sent Terry away. Then she went off for a few months – vanished completely. My Terry didn't have anything to do with her again. Rose kept herself pretty much to herself after that, so I heard. Went a bit queer in the head if you ask me.'

'What about Terry?' Max asked. 'What did he do after that?'

'He kept himself pretty much to himself too,' Alice told them. 'In the end, we moved here, right away from Rose Dee and her lying, conniving daughter. Terry kept away from women after that. I told him, you don't know what sort of trouble they'll get you into.'

216

'He never married?' Jill said.

'No. He had me,' Alice said with satisfaction. 'I was better to him than any wife would have been.'

She brushed an imaginary speck of dust from the arm of the sofa.

'If you ask me,' she went on in a confidential tone, 'that Josie Dee – Josie Hayden – was asking for trouble all her life. She made up those dreadful tales about my Terry and got away with it. I bet you any money she tried on the same thing with someone else. It stands to reason in my mind. She deserved all she got.' She paused. 'Not that I like to speak ill of the dead,' she added as an afterthought. 'Our old dad always used to say, if you can't find something good to say about someone, you should keep quiet. And normally I would have. But you did ask.'

'We did,' Max said, and Jill spotted the amusement in his eyes. 'Well, thank you. You've been most helpful.'

He looked questioningly at Jill, but she had nothing further to ask. Like him, she stood up. She'd be glad to get out of this cramped, dark room.

'That place gave me the creeps,' Max said as they walked back to his car. 'Fancy a coffee?'

'Yeah. And fish and chips. On the sea front.'

'At this time of night?'

'Yep.'

She loved the seaside. Even Blackpool. Everyone said it was tacky, and it was, but she still loved to be beside the sea. It had to stem from holidays in Rhyl she'd had as a child. Her sister, Prue, would want to spend her time swimming whereas Jill had always headed for the beach and the donkey rides. She associated the seaside with fun – with donkey rides, toffee apples, candy floss, boat trips, amusement arcades and all the rest of it. Tacky or not, she loved it.

Blackpool was deserted on this chilly December evening, and Max parked on the sea front. They were soon sitting on the wall, huddled in their coats, with a tray of fish and chips each and polystyrene cups filled with hot coffee.

'What did you think of Alice then?' Max asked, throwing a chip to a seagull.

'I thought she was a vindictive old bitch who liked to keep her brother in tow.'

'Hey, don't sit on the fence. Say what you really mean.'

'I doubt she has a good word to say about anyone,' Jill muttered.

'A waste of time?' he asked.

'No. Not a waste of time,' Jill answered thoughtfully.

'If you think about Josie Hayden,' Max said, and they were surrounded by squawking seagulls now, 'she said that Terry had made her pregnant, then she fell pregnant by George and got him to marry her, then she told Brian Taylor that he's about to become a father . . .'

'And your point is?'

'George, as we know, felt conned into marriage, Brian Taylor thought she was trying to con him into marriage . . .' He shrugged. 'She had a pretty impressive track record, our Josie.'

'Or a very unlucky life,' Jill argued.

'Maybe.' Max threw his last few chips to the seagulls and then started on his coffee.

He had a point, Jill supposed. Three men had cause to dislike Josie . . .

Chapter Thirty-Six

Alice Potter hadn't been able to settle since that detective and his sidekick had left. She had guessed they would come sniffing around sooner or later and she'd been ready for them.

They should be grateful she'd spoken to them at all. She could easily have denied all knowledge of Rose Dee and her deceitful cow of a daughter. Thinking about it, perhaps she should have done just that. At the time, though, she'd felt better for being able to give vent to her feelings.

What did it matter, anyway? They couldn't prove anything. Not now. Terry was dead, as was that lying bitch Josie Dee. She'd got what was coming to her all right.

It was thanks to her and her lies that Alice and Terry had been forced to leave Harrington. They'd been happy there, but Alice had known they needed to get away. She certainly hadn't wanted her Terry hanging around there as the target for more lies.

So they'd upped sticks. They moved to Manchester, right away from Harrington. Terry got a job at the factory, and Alice managed to clean a couple of days a week. They'd soon settled down, and Alice had thought they could be happy there.

Two years later though, it all started again.

This time, it was an eleven-year-old, Heather Irvine, who caused trouble. Little bitch she was. Alice blamed the schools for filling their heads with such filth. At the same age, Alice had known nothing about sex. She knew little more now.

Heather Irvine had run to her dad with her disgusting lies. The little madam had said that Terry had taken her into the bushes and meddled with her. She'd said all the kids knew he used to hang around the playing field. That was a downright lie. If the weather was good, he used to eat his sandwiches there at lunchtime. There was no crime in that.

The Irvine girl claimed he used to take sweets for the girls. Perhaps he did. That was Terry all over. He was too soft for his own good.

Not content with taking sweets off him, the lying little bitch had said he took her into the bushes and – touched her.

It was all lies. The little madam should have had her mouth washed out with soap and water. Instead, she'd run to her dad with her lies and he, a big thug of a bloke who spoke with his fists, had knocked Terry about.

Poor Terry had crawled home with his nose and jaw broken and a couple of cracked ribs. It had been left to Alice to clean him up.

Word got out and the next thing, people were spraying filthy obscenities on the outside of their house.

In the end, they'd been forced to move on again.

Alice had decided it was time to make a complete change so they'd headed for the seaside. Blackpool had suited them from the start.

Terry was a fool, though. He didn't learn. One summer's day, Alice saw him talking to a young girl and she watched, horrified, as he handed over a packet of sweets.

It was the last straw.

Oh, Alice knew it was only kindness. She also knew that others wouldn't see it that way. They would soon start spewing out their malicious filth.

'You're to stay indoors,' she'd instructed Terry firmly. 'We'll go out together. I'm not having people telling lies about you again. I won't stand for it . . .'

That's how they'd been forced to live, like prisoners in their own home. All because young girls had their heads filled with disgusting nonsense. It *was* nonsense. Of course it was.

Terry had no children of his own so it was only natural he should take an interest in other people's. That wasn't a crime, was it?

He'd been a good man - soft, gentle, kind and generous. He wouldn't have done anything bad because he knew it would have hurt his sister. Alice had always watched out for him, right from the moment he was born, and he wouldn't have done anything to hurt her. He wouldn't!

She wished she'd never heard of Rose Dee and her cheating daughter, just as she wished she'd never heard of Heather Irvine.

She'd had Terry, and he'd been enough for her so that she'd never wanted a husband or children. If that's how the little devils behaved, she was glad about that.

That policeman and the woman had unsettled her, though. Why did they have to rake it all over? It was all lies. Filthy, unfounded lies.

Alice refused to spare it another thought.

Chapter Thirty-Seven

The following morning, Jill and Max stood in Phil's office. It wasn't a pretty sight. Phil was in a foul mood and he was less than happy about their trip to Blackpool.

'I suppose you took in the sodding illuminations!' he snapped.

They ignored that.

'What I'd like to do –' Jill began.

'And what I'd like,' Phil cut her off, 'is a profile. Is that too much to ask? Even a vague bloody profile. Just who in hell's name are we looking for, Jill?'

'I don't know.' How could she know? 'We have two murders, both members of the Hayden family,' she reminded him, 'and two missing schoolboys. For the moment, I have to concentrate on the murders. I have nothing else to go on. So I'd like to check out places offering terminations in the area around the time Josie Hayden was fourteen. The more I think about this, the more convinced I am that Terry Potter did get her pregnant.'

'Oh, for –'

'Listen, Phil. Josie didn't wrongly accuse George of getting her pregnant. We know that because Andy is the image of his dad. It's the same with Brian Taylor. Martin was a ringer for him.'

'So what if Potter did get her pregnant?' Phil cried, exasperated. 'The bloke's dead. And what the hell does it have to do with James Murphy or Jason Keane?'

'Possibly nothing,' she admitted.

'Jill, we have two boys missing and the parents are in a right bloody state as you can imagine.'

He was wrong. Jill couldn't even begin to imagine the state they were in. Nor could she imagine how Max was feeling right now.

'I'd still like to get the local clinics checked out. It'll be time-consuming, I know, but it might be worth it.'

'You liked Josie Hayden from the start.' He spoke in an accusing way.

'I did, yes, but that has nothing to do with anything.'

Phil grunted, which possibly translated as 'Fine, use all the staff and resources you need.' She doubted it.

'You'll need to give a bloody convincing statement to the media, Max,' Phil said, turning his attention in Max's direction. 'Don't give them the impression that we don't have a clue what we're doing!'

'Right,' Max said.

'Even if it is bloody true,' Phil said, determined to have the last word. 'We've got every available officer on this case,' he reminded them both. 'Every resource available is in place. What more do you need, for Christ's sake?'

'I'm sure it's only a matter of time before we get a decent lead,' Max said.

Jill was surprised he was sounding so calm. She was a wreck.

'Why James Murphy? Why Jason Keane? Hmm?' Phil wanted to know.

'Your guess is as good as mine.'

'Guess? Christ, you're not even bloody guessing, Max.'

'Right, well, we can't waste time,' Max murmured, taking a step towards the door.

'Indeed,' Jill said, taking a step in the same direction. 'I'll make a start on the local clinics.'

'Keep me informed,' Phil snapped. 'I'll catch up with you later, Jill, and I'll expect progress.'

'Right,' she said, and she was out of the door before he thought of something else.

'That was useful,' Max said on a sigh once they were out of earshot.

'Quite.'

'I'm out of here,' he added.

He looked and sounded calm, but Jill knew he wasn't. How could he be when his own son had been threatened with the same fate as Martin Hayden?

'Are you all right?' she asked quietly.

'I'm fine.' He touched her chin in the lightest of gestures. 'Don't worry, Harry's safe. Don't even think otherwise.'

She nodded.

'I'll issue a statement to the press,' he went on, 'and then I'll be at the school. Get the new girl – what's her name?'

'Lucy?' She named the girl who'd joined the force last week.

'Yes. Get her to give you a hand with the phone calls. Although I have to say –'

'You think it's a waste of time,' she finished for him. 'I know. I've got damn all else to do, though.'

'OK, I'll see you later.'

Jill watched him stride along the corridor, car keys jangling from his fingers. She liked a man who was calm in a crisis but she couldn't help thinking he was too calm.

Forgetting Max for the moment, she went in search of Lucy.

Lucy didn't ask questions, thank goodness. She was soon on the phone, pen in hand. Jill started on her own list. How was it possible to have so many maternity clinics in the area? There were hundreds.

By lunchtime, they'd drawn a blank. That was either because they were only halfway through their lists or because hospital records were so sketchy. Or, she thought grimly, because she was on totally the wrong track. Perhaps Alice Potter was right and Josie had made up a pack of lies about a pregnancy.

The more she thought about it, though, the more she believed Josie had been raped as a child. It explained a lot, like the fact that she'd been naive and not keen on sex, like the fact that she hadn't been a virgin when George met her . . .

Lucy brought them a coffee and a sandwich for lunch and they ate it at their desks. It promised to be a long, fruitless afternoon.

'I'm going to drive out to the farm,' Jill announced. 'Will you carry on here, Lucy?'

'Of course.' Lucy, new to the force, seemed to be enjoying herself.

Jill hated Lower Crags Farm. As she drove down the rutted track to the farmhouse, her spirits sank. Although she loved the surrounding countryside, she hated this particular spot. But that was due more to circumstances than anything else. With a welcoming house, cats basking in the sunshine and children playing outside, it could be beautiful.

She pulled up next to a police car and was about to head for the house when she spotted Sarah walking in her direction from the field.

Jill waited for her.

Poor Sarah looked lost. She was a sad thing, and Jill's heart went out to her. Life had never been much fun on the farm, she suspected, but now it was downright unbearable.

'Hello, Sarah,' she said. 'How are you doing?'

'Oh, OK, I suppose,' she said. 'There's a policeman here.' She nodded at the car. 'Dad doesn't want a fuss made, he never does, but it's good of the police to bother. But there, I suppose with Mum and Martin gone, they think one of us might be next.'

She spoke in a flat tone as if she didn't much care what happened to any of them. Who could blame her?

'I'm sure you're safe,' Jill said, not sure of any such thing. Who knew where this maniac would strike next?

'Sarah, can you remember your mum mentioning going away anywhere as a child? When she was, say, fourteen?'

Sarah thought for a moment, but shook her head. 'It's funny, but Mum never spoke much about her childhood. If I ever asked her about it, she'd change the subject. Now she's gone, there's loads of things I'd have liked to ask her. It's too late now.'

Much too late.

'Do you think she had a happy childhood?' Jill asked.

Sarah looked as if she had never even considered the question before. 'I don't know, but no, probably not. Dad might know if she went away as a child,' she added. 'He's indoors.' She began walking to the house, then turned to Jill. 'Why do you want to know?'

'I'm not sure,' Jill said carefully. 'We're looking into your mum's past, to see if we can find anyone who might have done this to her and Martin, but there's nothing local.'

Sarah led the way into the kitchen. George Hayden was standing by the window, a huge mug of tea in his hands.

'Miss Kennedy,' he greeted her.

He still looked lost and totally bewildered. Jill suspected he was filled with regrets, too. Josie hadn't had a fun-filled life with him, and he knew it.

'Hello, Mr Hayden,' she said. 'How are you coping?'

'We're coping,' he replied automatically. 'What can we do for you?'

He was still bluff, but there was a softness to the edges now.

'We're looking into your wife's past, Mr Hayden,' she began, not wanting to give too much away, 'and we're wondering if she mentioned going away anywhere as a child. A holiday, an unexpected trip – something like that.'

'Not that I know of. She never spoke much about life before she met me. She worked in a solicitor's office, and she spoke of that sometimes, but nothing else. She rarely mentioned her mother at all. They didn't keep in touch.'

It had been a long shot, Jill knew that. They were busy checking the local clinics, but Josie could have been booked into a private clinic anywhere in the country. She and her mother might have caught the train to London and been

226

back in forty-eight hours. Yet Alice Potter claimed that Rose had gone away for a few months.

'Religious differences,' George said suddenly.

'Sorry?'

'I think that's why they didn't get along,' George explained. 'Her mother were Roman Catholic and Josie would have nothing to do with the Church.'

'Catholic?' Jill had no idea. She was convinced she'd read C of E on the paperwork.

If Josie had been brought up as a Catholic, there definitely wouldn't have been a termination. If Josie *had* been pregnant, there would be a child somewhere.

'Why was that?' Jill asked curiously. 'Why was Josie against the Church?'

'Who knows?' he replied. 'Apart from calling them a load of hypocrites once, she never talked about it.'

There had been scant conversation in their marriage.

'Will you have a cup of tea?' he asked.

Jill was completely taken aback. Of all the people to offer refreshment, George Hayden would have been last on her list. 'Thank you. That would be very welcome.'

'Sarah, love,' he said, nodding at the kettle.

While Sarah made the tea, automatically handing another huge mug to her father, they chatted about Josie. It saddened Jill to think they had no real happy memories of her. Josie's life had been a drudge. There were no laughing anecdotes.

'Hey,' Sarah said suddenly, 'she did go to Ireland once.'

'Ireland?' George repeated, frowning. 'I never heard of that.'

'Yes,' Sarah said, sifting through her memories. 'One day, me and Mum were sorting out rubbish to take to a charity shop. Mum were a hoarder and she wanted the spare bedroom emptied. In the midst of a load of old junk – plates, china animals, and stuff I'd never seen before – I found a dish. It were an ugly thing – a souvenir from Dublin. When I laughed and asked her where she'd got it from, she said, "Dublin. Where do you think?" She were quite snappy with me. I asked if we were going to throw it out and she said no. Later that day, and she'd been strange and snappy all day, she went and threw it in the dustbin.'

Dublin? Was it just possible that Rose had taken Josie to Dublin to have her baby?

'When did she go, Sarah? Do you know?'

Sarah shook her head. 'I asked her about it, but all she said was that she'd been there years ago and could hardly remember the place.'

'Did she have family in Dublin?' Jill asked George.

'Not that I know of,' he said. 'Like I said, she never talked about her family. She didn't say much at all about her life before she came here.'

'It were a horrid dish,' Sarah said. 'It were white with a green shamrock on it, and it said Good Luck at the top and Dublin at the bottom. Real ugly it were.'

The sort of thing a child might like to remind them of a place, Jill thought. Having said that, the entire farmhouse was filled with ugly china dogs and chipped china birds.

She tried to jog their memories, to see if they could recall Josie mentioning any other towns, but they could think of nothing. Jill knew more about her milkman than they knew about the woman they'd lived with for so many years. It was a sad thought.

Chapter Thirty-Eight

Max was beginning to believe he'd end his days in this interview room. This afternoon it was stuffy and airless, and Grace, questioning Alan Turner with him, had a stinking cold. Even when she wasn't coughing and sneezing, it was almost impossible to catch what she was saying. Max would bet his life he'd catch her confounded germs.

Alan Turner was a cool, arrogant individual. What would he make of Donna Lord's description? Geoff Morrison's bit of skirt, she'd called him. He was medium height, and had dark hair that was messed up. Max suspected it cost a fortune and took time to keep it looking that untidy. He had very full lips, and was inclined to pout.

'How do you earn your living, Mr Turner?' Max asked curiously. 'I know you're in a band, but I can't believe that pays the mortgage. Or does Mr Morrison keep you in luxury?'

He smiled at that. 'No, he doesn't. And no, the band doesn't keep me, either. It brings in a bit, though, and I write songs which some big bands have recorded. Added to that, I produce records.'

'I see. So what is the average day like for you?'

'Well, I'm usually up around six thirty.'

'Why so early?'

Turner sneered at that. 'It's the best part of the day. I usually prepare breakfast for us both, and then Geoff goes for a run. If our newspaper's been delivered by then, I sit and read that with a couple of cups of coffee. I need my coffee in the morning.'

'And Geoff – Mr Morrison – goes straight to the school after his run?'

'Usually, yes.'

'Then what?'

'Then, if I'm not in the recording studio, I play my guitar for a couple of hours before starting work on the song I'm currently writing. I stop for lunch, and usually do the crossword, and then work until Geoff gets home at around five thirty.'

'You're in the house alone a lot then,' Grace said, snuffling.

'Not really. I'm often in the recording studio and I'm out in the evenings.'

'How do you feel about Mr Morrison's job?' Max asked him. 'Don't you mind him being around young boys – good-looking young boys?'

'Why should I?'

Max tried to remember what Jill had said. She'd thought Turner might be jealous, but he couldn't recall her theory.

'No reason, I suppose,' Max said. 'When you and he were out together, did you ever see any of his pupils?'

'Sometimes. Harrington's not that big a town.'

'True.'

Max had had enough. He needed coffee, and he needed air that Grace hadn't coughed and sneezed into. In any case, it would do Turner good to sit and worry for a while.

If Max could drag Jill away from her phone calls to every Tom, Dick and Harry in Dublin, he'd like her to talk to Turner.

He got himself a coffee and set off to find her.

As he walked along the corridor, he wondered what it must be like to have a normal job, in a normal office, where everyone watched the clock and chatted amiably as they waited for five o'clock to arrive. Here, it was frantic. Phones didn't stop ringing, people didn't stop shouting to each other because it was the only way to make yourself heard, people dashed in and rushed out again –

230

He heard Phil Meredith talking to some unfortunate just ahead of him and quickly doubled back. He could do without updating him on the lack of progress. He could also do without another bollocking regarding his lack of delegation skills.

He was almost back at the interview room when he found Jill. She'd also got a coffee in her hands.

'How's it going?' he asked.

'Nothing so far, but I've left a message for a friend of mine. Babs and I were at uni together –' She broke off suddenly. 'You met her.'

Babs? The name meant – 'Oh, yes. Big woman? Can talk for England?'

A smile lit her eyes briefly. 'That's her.'

When he and Jill had lived together, Babs had stayed with them one weekend. She was almost as wide as she was tall and hadn't given two hoots about that.

'A nice woman,' he added. 'She enjoyed my spaghetti bolognese, I seem to recall.'

'She did,' Jill agreed, her eyes on the carpet. 'Anyway, she works in Dublin now. She might be able to help.'

Max thought it doubtful, but he didn't say so.

'Will you come and talk to Alan Turner?' he asked. 'He's an arrogant so-and-so, and I think he's hiding something.'

'Like what?'

'I still think he's lying about being with Geoff Morrison the day Martin Hayden vanished. It's too convenient.'

'OK. I could do with a change of scenery, and a rest from the phone would be good.'

She was about to set off.

'Have your coffee first,' he said. 'It'll do him good to stew for a while.'

'Is he stewing?'

'Most people do when they're in that interview room.'

'True.' She met his gaze. 'You look shattered, Max.'

He felt shattered.

'Being dead on your feet won't keep Harry any safer,' she pointed out.

'You don't look so great yourself. Have you slept?'

She shrugged, and he knew she hadn't.

'Jill, when this is over –'

'But it's not, Max,' she cut him off. 'Come on, let's go and see Turner.'

She refused to discuss a future. All Max had been going to suggest was – well, he didn't really know what he'd been going to suggest. They belonged together though, and he wished she would give them a chance.

He caught her arm to halt her flight. 'You will see us – see the boys at Christmas, won't you?'

'Of course,' she said softly.

'Christmas Day?' At her hesitation, he said, 'Don't tell me you could survive Christmas with your parents. Or with your sister and her brood.'

'Probably not,' she agreed, smiling.

'Good. So I'll tell the boys you'll spend the day with us? Kate's already planning the menu so no worries there. Although what there is to plan, I have no idea. Call me a bluff old cynic, but I bet it'll be turkey and –'

He broke off as he spotted the shimmer of moisture in her eyes. What caused that? Memories of Christmas spent together? Fears for Harry?

'Harry's safe, love,' he promised her.

'I know.' She drew a deep breath. 'Come on. Let's go and talk to Turner.'

They walked to the interview room, which was just as stuffy as when Max had left it. Alan Turner looked as calm as he had when Max had left, too.

Max switched on the tapes and named those present.

'Why have you brought a shrink along?' Turner sneered.

'I'm a forensic psychologist,' Jill corrected him, bristling as she did every time someone called her a shrink. 'Have you ever seen a shrink, as you call them?' she asked.

'No. Why should I?'

'Why not? Plenty of people do.'

'Not me.'

'How about your boyfriend?' she asked. 'Has he seen one?'

'Of course not.'

'Oh, I just wondered. He's had trouble in the past, hasn't he? A few – what shall we say? – misunderstandings? Young boys thinking along sexual assault lines.'

'For God's sake,' he muttered. 'One boy thought he was masturbating in the park. He was having a slash, that's all.'

'So he told you,' she said pleasantly. 'You're his boyfriend. He's hardly likely to tell you he had the hots for one of his pupils, is he? Why should he? People have affairs every day. They don't tell their partners about them, do they?'

Why did Max always cringe when she got on to the subject of affairs? And why did she always get on to the blasted subject?

'Of course they don't,' she pressed on. 'They lie, they pretend, they buy gifts – and they carry on having affairs. They don't confess to them until it's all over.'

Max cleared his throat, and she swung her face in his direction.

'Are you all right, DCI Trentham?'

'Fine.'

She returned her attention to Turner. 'What about you?' she asked him. 'Do you have affairs?'

'No.'

'Really?'

'Really.'

'He watches the boys in the swimming pool, you know,' Jill went on affably. 'One boy said he always made sure he had an erection when he went swimming just to get your boyfriend going. He called him a pervert.'

'Look –' Turner lashed out with his fist so viciously that, for an awful second, Max thought he was going to land one on Jill. Instead, he hit the table.

'You were about to say?' Jill prompted, as he clamped his jaw shut, biting back on the abuse he'd been about to give her.

233

'Forget it,' he snapped. 'You shrinks are all the same. It all comes down to sex, doesn't it? Why's that? Don't you get enough? You wanna take a look in the mirror, sweetheart, and ask yourself why.'

Turner was losing his cool. He didn't like to think of Geoff Morrison looking at anyone else. Max had to agree with him, though; psychiatrists and psychologists always brought everything round to sex.

'I get plenty, thanks,' Jill replied pleasantly. 'More than you, I expect. Your boyfriend's too busy out running, too busy keeping fit, and too busy watching boys swimming with erections or racing around a football field. He's busy with the football team after school and at weekends. Why's that, do you think? Because he enjoys football, or because he'd rather be surrounded by young boys than spend his time with you?'

'Crap!'

'Is it?' She shrugged. 'You never saw Martin Hayden, did you? Well, let me tell you, he was a good-looking boy. The photos in the paper and on TV didn't do him justice. You had to see him in the flesh.'

'I saw him in the flesh!' He realized what he'd said, and a tide of red colour flooded his face.

'Where?' Max demanded.

'In Benedict's,' he said quietly. 'Only once. And yeah,' he said, talking to Jill, 'he had the hots for Geoff. I could see that. But Geoff wasn't interested.'

Martin Hayden in a gay club? Never. Surely not. What in hell's name would he be doing there?

'Nice-looking boy, wasn't he?' Jill said. 'And you're telling me Geoff wasn't interested? Ha! I don't believe that. According to Martin, your boyfriend was all over him.'

'You're lying.'

'Nope. He told his sister all about it. Said he was a perv.' She smiled. 'So what was he doing at Benedict's? How many gays did he know – apart from Geoff Morrison?'

'Why should I know what he was doing there?'

'Then I'll tell you. He was after your boyfriend.'

'No!'

'Yes.' She sat back in her chair, looking relaxed. 'That's rich, isn't it? You give him an alibi – say he was with you the morning Martin Hayden disappeared – and all the while, he was probably with the boy anyway.'

His head flew up at that. 'No!'

'I imagine so,' Jill said. 'When did you see Martin Hayden in Benedict's? I bet it wasn't long before he vanished, was it?'

'It was the night before,' Turner admitted.

'Thought so,' Jill murmured. 'So your boyfriend would have arranged to see Martin on Wednesday at school. I bet he left early that morning, didn't he? Sure to have done. He'll have wanted to be at the school waiting for Martin. He wasn't with you that morning. You lied. He told you to lie, didn't he? He told you to say you were with him but really, he was with Martin Hayden.'

'No!'

'Yes. Oh, I doubt they did much at the school. A kiss maybe, a bit of a fumble –'

'OK, OK,' he cried. 'I lied. Geoff wasn't with me that morning. He did leave early, but he didn't see the boy.'

'You don't know that,' Jill scoffed.

'Yes, I fucking do. Bitch!'

Finally, Turner looked as if he wanted to run and hide.

'You followed him, didn't you?' Jill said suddenly. 'You know he didn't see Martin Hayden because you followed him. He left early, and you were suspicious, weren't you?'

Turner nodded, and he looked close to tears.

'He said he was going jogging,' he admitted, all bluster gone, 'and I didn't believe him. So yeah, I followed him. He drove out towards the park – he often runs there – but then I lost him. I got stuck at traffic lights because the idiot in front of me – well, that doesn't matter. I lost him. But he was heading out towards Burnley. He couldn't have been going to see the boy because he was driving in the wrong direction. He couldn't have.'

235

'What do you know about Lower Crags Farm?' Max asked.

'What? The farm where the boy came from? Well, nothing. I've never seen the place.'

'Liar,' Max scoffed.

'On my life, I have never seen it. I know roughly where it is, but I've never been along that road. I've had no cause to. There's nothing there.'

'So you've never driven past?'

'No.'

'Not even out of curiosity?' Jill said scornfully.

'Never.'

'So if you've never been past the place,' Max said, 'how would you know there are more police than residents there?'

He looked at Max as if he was speaking in Swahili. 'I wouldn't.'

'Someone told me you'd said exactly that,' Max informed him.

'Well, I didn't. I swear on my life that I never said that. Why would I? I've no idea how many police are there or how many people live there.'

'So you're saying the person who told me is a liar?' Max asked.

'No,' he replied. 'I'm saying they've got it wrong. I never said that. Either they're confusing me with someone else or – hell, I don't know. I didn't say it, haven't thought it, wouldn't say it.'

'And we're supposed to take your word for that?' Jill said, shaking her head. 'Why would we do that? You've lied to us before, why should we believe you now?'

'You can believe what you like,' he retorted, those full lips in pout mode now.

'OK,' Max said. 'You've been most helpful. Thank you.'

'Can I go then?' he asked hopefully.

'Yeah,' Max told him, smiling. 'Soon.'

Max nodded to Jill and they both left the room.

236

'Thanks for that,' Max said. 'Do you believe he's never been past Lower Crags Farm?'

'If it were anyone else, I wouldn't. Most people would have to look. They would see Martin Hayden as competition and go along to see where he lived. But Turner, I'm not so sure about. He was satisfied that Morrison didn't go near Martin Hayden. That may have been enough.'

Max checked his watch. 'I need to collect Harry and Ben from school, so I'll have a chat with our friend Morrison while I'm there.'

'Give the boys a hug from me, Max.'

'I will.'

Chapter Thirty-Nine

'That's a nice sight,' Max called out. Striding along the corridor at Harrington High School was none other than Donna Lord.

She turned round, smiling. 'Well, well, well, if it's not my favourite detective.'

'How many do you know?' he asked when he caught her up.

'Just the one.'

She really was a nice sight. How young boys concentrated on their English studies, Max had no idea. She was wearing a tight black skirt that showed off those amazing legs of hers, and a crisp white blouse that embraced her breasts.

'Where are you heading?' she asked.

'To the gym.'

'Ah, you're still talking to Geoff then. You've got that wrong, detective. He's far too squeamish to make a killer. One of the girls cut her arm yesterday and he fainted.' She laughed. 'There wasn't too much blood, but he had to spend the afternoon lying down.'

Max smiled at the story.

'I owe you a drink,' she reminded him, flashing white teeth from ruby red lips. 'How about tonight?'

If he said no, he'd need his head examining.

'I'd love to, really, but I can't make it.' It was official; he needed his head examining. 'Some other time?'

'Count on it, detective.' She took a door on their left. 'See you later.'

'See you.'

He rid his mind of Ms Lord and carried on to the gym.

As luck would have it, the boys had finished their lesson and were putting the equipment away. Did Geoff Morrison look shifty? Max couldn't decide. He certainly wasn't pleased to see him.

'Could I have another word?' Max asked.

'Do I have a choice?'

'Not really, no.'

'Right, you lot,' he shouted. 'No messing around. I want you changed in record time. And no leaving the changing rooms until I get there.'

Muttering, grumbling or giggling, the kids left through an adjoining door.

'So what is it now?' Morrison asked, resigned.

'We've been talking to your boyfriend,' Max explained, 'and he's had a change of mind. He reckons he wasn't with you the morning Martin Hayden vanished. He says you left early to go for a run.'

Morrison's face flushed red. It was difficult to tell if he was embarrassed or furious. A bit of both perhaps.

'OK,' he said at last. 'Yeah, he's right. I left early. I left early that morning because I was sick of him and his jealous, petty tantrums.'

'Oh?' A lovers' tiff. Great.

'Did he tell you we saw Martin Hayden at Benedict's on the Tuesday night?' He sneered. 'Yeah, I bet he did. He reckons Hayden was after me. I mean, for God's sake. He was in a foul mood about it all night. He reckoned I encouraged the boy. Jesus H, I didn't even recognize the kid until we were leaving and then I only said hello. I was too shocked to see him there, of all places, to say anything else. So we had hissy fits all bloody night.'

'I see.' The mind boggled. 'So where did you go on that particular Wednesday morning?'

'I just drove,' he said. 'Anything to get away from him. I ended up driving through Burnley. I stopped on the Burnley to Bacup road. There's a pull-in on the left, as you

239

head to Bacup. It has a nice view – the hills and the wind farm. I sat there, looking at the view, until I headed back and went to the school.'

'Can anyone confirm that?'

'I very much doubt it.'

'That's a shame.'

'It is,' Morrison agreed. 'You can arrest me, I'm past bloody caring, but if you do and the killer strikes again, you're going to look pretty damn silly, aren't you?'

'I can live with that.'

Morrison, deathly pale now, took a quick step back.

'OK, that'll be all,' Max told him. 'You can go.'

'I can?'

'Yes.'

'Gee, thanks.' The bravado was back.

'You're welcome.'

Having driven Harry and Ben home and left them with Kate and DS Forrest, Max was on his way back to the nick when Fletch phoned.

'Brian Taylor's here, Max. Says he wants to make a statement. He'll only talk to you, though.'

'Really? What's that all about?'

'He wouldn't say.'

'OK, Fletch. I'll be there in around fifteen minutes.'

What did Taylor want with him? His alibis really were ironclad. No way could he have killed Martin or Josie Hayden. So what the hell did he have to say?

Max was sitting opposite him less than fifteen minutes later. If Max looked shattered, Brian Taylor looked even worse. He was still chain-smoking, too.

'You want to talk to me?'

Taylor nodded. 'Yes.' He stubbed out a cigarette. 'I wasn't completely honest with you, Chief Inspector.'

You and a few dozen others, Max thought grimly.

'Let's hear it then.'

240

Taylor lit another cigarette. 'Martin – I did meet him. I met him a few times before he was killed.'

Oh, for . . . 'Why the hell didn't you say so before?'

'How would it have looked?' Taylor cried.

'The same as it looks now! Bloody suspicious!' Max tried to calm himself. 'How did you get to meet him?'

'As you know, I occasionally watched him leave the school.' Taylor didn't look at Max as he spoke. Instead, he concentrated on his cigarette. 'One day, I deliberately bumped into him. We struck up a conversation of sorts and I offered him a lift home. When he saw my car, the BMW, he quickly accepted. I saw him a couple of times and . . .' He cleared his throat. 'I bought him his guitar and I used to pay for his lessons. He had no idea who I was though,' he put in quickly. 'He only knew me as Adam. I used my brother's name. Anyway, I'd see him once a week and give him the money for his guitar lessons.'

'He didn't know you?' Max scoffed. 'Come on, he was a bright kid. Who the hell did he think you were? His fairy bloody godmother?'

'He thought . . .' He cleared his throat again. 'He thought I was attracted to him. Sexually. He started taunting me, asking me what I thought his parents would make of it, what I thought the police would think if they knew.'

'He was blackmailing you?'

'Not as such, but I kept giving him money. I didn't know what else to do. I couldn't just not turn up, could I? In the end, I contacted Josie. I thought that, if I could see him, with everything above board, it would be OK.'

'But Josie said no.'

'She wouldn't hear of it. But I didn't kill him. I swear it. You have to believe me.'

Max tapped his fingers on the desk. 'You see your son, he blackmails you and then ends up dead.'

'I know,' he whispered.

'Could he have been blackmailing anyone else?'

'Quite probably,' he answered immediately.

'What makes you say that?'

241

'Look, Chief Inspector, he may have been my son, but he wasn't a good person. He looked out for himself and didn't give a shit about anyone else.'

So everyone said. At least it explained the money Martin Hayden had. It explained damn all else, though. Brian Taylor hadn't killed Martin or Josie, so who the hell had?

'What about cocaine?' Max asked. 'Would you know anything about that?'

Taylor's face glowed scarlet. He opened his mouth to speak, then closed it again.

'I'm conducting a murder inquiry,' Max told him furiously, 'and I want the truth. OK? I don't give a damn about whether or not you snort coke. I want to know if you gave any to Martin Hayden.'

'I did,' Taylor whispered.

'Thank you!'

Max slammed out of the room leaving a sobbing Brian Taylor saying, 'I wish I'd never met him!'

Chapter Forty

Jill was at her cottage, wrapping Christmas presents, when her phone rang. She thought it might be Max again. He'd phoned an hour ago to tell her about Brian Taylor's confession, but he phoned often to reassure her that Harry and Ben were safe. She was grateful for that.

However, it wasn't Max.

'Hello, stranger. I got your message.'

'Babs, hi! Thanks for getting back to me. How are you?'

'Dreading the obligatory Christmas overdraft. You?'

Jill, surrounded by wrapping paper and presents, had to smile. 'About the same. Thanks for the card, by the way. You always send lovely cards.'

'I bought them last January,' Babs told her. 'How's that for efficiency?'

'Sickening. Anyway, it would be no use me doing that. I'd have lost them long before Christmas.'

They spent a few minutes catching up on each other's news. She and Babs had not only studied together at uni, they'd shared a flat. They'd had some wild times.

'So what can I do for you?' Babs asked.

'It's a long story.' Jill filled her in and told her what they knew about Josie Hayden. 'We must have contacted every clinic in England. However, it's just possible that Josie went to Dublin around the right time. I wondered if you could pull a few strings and get old records checked. We think it was 1977. Josie would have been fourteen.'

Babs sucked in her breath at that.

'I know,' Jill murmured.

'I'll see what I can do,' Babs promised.

'Thanks. You're a star!'

They chatted some more, and then Jill returned to her present-wrapping.

Her cottage was well decorated, and Christmas cards sat on every surface, but she couldn't look forward to Christmas. None of them could. The Lord alone knew how the parents of James Murphy and Jason Keane would cope.

If only the boys could be found safe and sound. What a wonderful Christmas present that would be.

She opened a bottle of wine, filled a glass and stretched out on the sofa with it.

Who had they missed?

Every member of the family had been checked out. Everyone associated with Harrington High School had been seen. Toby Campbell, John Higgs, the ex-music teacher – everyone was innocent.

Brian Taylor wasn't their man. In fact, Jill almost felt sorry for him. What must it be like to meet your son and discover that his only interest is in your money?

Her phone rang again and this time it *was* Max.

'Anything new?' she asked, dreading his answer.

'Nothing.'

She breathed a sigh of relief. Every time he rang, her first thought was Harry. Her second thought was that either James Murphy's or Jason Keane's body had been found.

'I've spoken to Babs,' she told him, 'and she's going to see if she can find anything. It's a long shot, I know, but you never know.'

'It is, Jill. If Josie did have a child in Dublin, well, so what?'

'I know.'

Max suddenly laughed at something. 'This dog show on Sunday? It includes Christmas fancy dress, for the dogs that is. Fly is currently modelling his outfit.'

She smiled, wishing she could be with them. 'Tell Ben I'll look forward to seeing it.'

'I will.'

She sighed. 'Who have we missed, Max? We've spoken to the killer, we must have. There's someone we've dismissed, and we've dismissed them because they don't stand out, because they're ordinary.'

'That's what I keep thinking. Martin Hayden was as good as blackmailing Taylor, and Taylor thinks, quite rightly probably, that he could easily have been blackmailing someone else. Martin Hayden thought Taylor was sexually attracted to him so if he thought someone else was –'

'Like Geoff Morrison or Toby Campbell?'

'Yeah, exactly like them.'

'If he was at Benedict's, he could have met someone there. I expect that's why he went. To find someone rich.'

'We've spent hours in that place but we haven't come up with anything. Bruce is there tonight doing his gay boy impression. We talked him out of the gold satin suit, but God knows what they'll make of him.'

She smiled at that.

'What are you doing tomorrow?' he asked suddenly.

'Visiting Mum and Dad, and Prue and Co. Why?'

'Just wondered. Shall we pick you up on Sunday then?'

'Thanks, Max, but there's no need. I'll have to get straight home after the show because I've still got loads of Christmas presents to sort out.' Including Max's. 'Don't worry, I won't miss Ben.'

Chapter Forty-One

The M62 had been stop-start all the way from Liverpool, presumably because people were spending their Saturdays doing Christmas shopping, and Jill was relieved when she joined the M66. Another half-hour and she would be home.

She'd enjoyed her day, though.

The traffic had been light that morning and she had arrived at 27 River View just after ten o'clock.

As ever, pandemonium reigned at her parents' home. Her mother had been busy baking; she was a hopeless cook when it came to meat and veg, but she had endless patience and her cakes had won prizes. This morning, they'd been treated to delicious, light chocolate eclairs. Jill's father had been trying to study form but, in the end, he'd taken himself off to the bookie's for a couple of hours.

'You'd think it was rocket science he was studying,' Jill's mum had scoffed.

The two of them had sat in the kitchen, catching up on news and drinking coffee. It had been good to see her mum looking so fit and well after the operation on her lung.

'Still off the fags, Mum?'

'I am. Mind,' she added, 'I could murder one right now. I don't reckon the time'll ever come when I don't want one.'

'Of course it will.'

'I feel better for it, though.'

She looked better for it, too. Her skin had lost that dull, grey tinge and her cheeks had a healthy rosy glow.

At lunchtime, Jill's sister Prue arrived, complete with husband Steve and children Charlotte, Zoe and Bethany. Prue was putting on weight, Jill noticed, but she looked happier than ever. Her life revolved around Steve and the kids. Unlike Jill, she'd never had any ambitions to leave River View.

Steve, who'd spent too many hours behind the wheel of a lorry lately, looked as if he longed to make the sofa his own and sleep for a few hours. There was no chance of that though with three daughters demanding his attention. For all that, he seemed happy with his lot.

The lifestyle wouldn't suit Jill, but their togetherness touched a chord. Once, she and Max had known the same feeling. They, too, had been a unit.

She'd brushed the thought aside. From the moment she'd been able, Jill had worked to escape River View. While Prue had decided to leave school as early as possible and train as a hairdresser, Jill had spent hours in her bedroom studying. She hadn't studied to end up as a wife and mother; she'd worked to give herself a rewarding, interesting career. A career which she'd put on hold for the time being . . .

After lunch, the women left the men in front of the television and sat in the kitchen with the girls.

'Auntie Jill, why haven't you got a boyfriend?' Zoe wanted to know.

'She has,' Charlotte said before Jill could formulate an answer.

'I have?' Jill asked, amused.

'Yes, but Mum says you're cross with him.'

Jill glared at her sister, who took no notice whatsoever.

'And how is Max?' Prue asked. 'Still working too hard?'

'I imagine so. I neither know nor care.'

'You're full of crap,' her sister scoffed quietly. 'Mum's right, you know. You'll end up a lonely old spinster with only a houseful of cats for company.'

Jill, who'd heard it all before, had to laugh.

'Firstly, I've been married so I can't qualify as a spinster.' OK, so her marriage had been brief and, if Chris hadn't been killed, they would have been divorced long ago, but she couldn't be termed a spinster. 'Secondly, I don't think three cats qualify as a houseful. Anyway,' she added, trying to change the subject, 'I think I'll be down to two cats soon.'

'Is Rabble dying?' Bethany asked with all the casualness of youth.

'She's getting very old and stiff,' Jill told her.

'I expect you'll find another.' Bethany patted her arm sympathetically. 'Jimmy Brown, who I go to school with, has some kittens to get rid of. I can ask him if you like.'

'I've got enough for the moment,' Jill said, chuckling as she hugged her niece . . .

It had been a fun day and Jill vowed to visit more often. Now, however, after a long, boring journey, she wanted to get out of her car. She left the motorway and drove through Waterfoot, Bacup and then into Kelton Bridge. Instead of going straight to her cottage, she turned into The Weaver's Retreat's car park.

Saturday nights were busy at the pub, and this evening it was even more crowded than usual. Jill spoke to half a dozen people as she made her way to the bar.

'Tony Hutchinson was in last night looking for you,' Maureen said when she served her. 'Have you seen him?'

'No.'

'I expect he'll be here in a while.' Maureen handed over her change. 'He said he'd got something for you.'

'Oh? What was that?'

'No idea,' she said as she took another order for drinks.

Jill carried her drink away from the bar and sat to chat with Tom and Julie for a while. A log fire blazed away next to their table, adding to the sense of cheer provided by Christmas decorations that twinkled merrily from every surface.

Despite the number of drinkers, though, the atmosphere was more muted than usual. Kelton Bridge was uneasy.

Two of the village's young boys were missing and villagers took it as a personal affront. People couldn't truly relax until their young were found.

Jill was about to head for home when Tony Hutchinson walked in. She went to join him at the bar as he waited to be served.

'Did you want me, Tony?'

'I did. I've found something . . .' He broke off to ask Maureen for his pint and Jill waited until he had it in his hand.

'I found a photo that might interest you.' Tony put his pint on the nearest table and delved into his inside pocket. 'Here.' He handed her a slightly dog-eared photograph. 'The quality isn't great, but I can get another printed.'

Jill took it from him and found herself looking straight at Martin Hayden, Jason Keane and James Murphy. The three boys were smiling broadly. Martin Hayden was holding a small trophy aloft.

'What's this, Tony?'

No one could remember seeing the boys together and the photo gave Jill an uneasy feeling. Was this the link they were looking for?

'It's probably nothing,' he said, 'but it was what you said about there being no connection between them. I knew I'd seen them together. I've spent hours going through thousands of photos.' He pointed at the trophy in the photo. 'About eighteen months ago, the village set up a quiz league. We were raising funds for new heating at the village hall. The league only lasted about three months, but these three lads formed a team. All bright boys, of course. Anyway, they won. Competition from the adults was stiff, but they beat them.'

It was disconcerting to look at the boys' smiling faces. Martin Hayden looked as posed as ever, but Jason and James seemed genuinely delighted with their victory.

'I knew Jason was very friendly with Martin Hayden, but I didn't think James was particularly pally with either boy.'

'I didn't either,' Tony admitted. 'It's funny, though, seeing them together, isn't it?'

'It is.'

'But I expect it's nothing other than coincidence,' he said. 'Martin and Jason were the best of friends and they would have needed a third for the quiz team. They probably asked James because he's a bright boy. Or perhaps no one else could be bothered.'

He was probably right.

'I expect,' he said, taking a swallow of his beer, 'that if you looked hard enough, you'd find photos of every combination of Kelton Bridge resident.'

'Probably,' she agreed. All the same . . . 'May I take this, Tony?'

'Be my guest. Let me know if you want a better copy and I'll run it through the school's computer.'

'Thanks. Who else was involved in the quiz?'

'Almost everyone. There was a committee – Mary Lee-Smith may have been behind that. She might know more about it.'

'I'll have a word with her.'

Jill put the photo in her bag and then said her goodbyes.

As she drove to Lilac Cottage, she wondered if there *was* any significance to the photo. But like what? A small village quiz league didn't inspire murder. There might be some bad losers in the village but, surely, no one would kill.

All the same, she would ask around and see if any interesting names came to light.

Chapter Forty-Two

It was bitterly cold, far too cold to be hanging around watching a dog show, but at least it was bright and sunny. Jill's garden, along with those mysterious Pennines, had been cloaked in white frost at first light.

She arrived at the leisure centre in time to see Ben walking Fly around the car park. For a second, she thought he was alone, and her heart seemed to stop, but then she spotted Max, Kate and Harry. Max had Holly, the faithful border collie, on a lead. Some distance away, his watchful gaze on them, stood DS Forrest. He was wrapped up against the cold in a blue padded jacket.

Jill spotted Ben walking towards her and went to meet him.

'Hello, sweetheart.' She gave his shoulder a squeeze. 'Fly's looking very smart.'

'Yeah.' He stroked the dog's ears.

'Nervous?' she asked him.

'A bit.'

She wondered if he had admitted as much to Max.

'You'll be fine,' she said, giving his shoulder another squeeze.

Max, Harry and Kate joined them. Max was alert, that all-seeing gaze of his missing nothing. Kate was tense from smiling and pretending she wasn't frightened to death about her grandsons' safety. Harry looked mutinous.

'What's the matter with you, Harry?' she asked.

'I'm fed up. I can't even go for a hot dog without Dad tagging along.'

'That's not the end of the world, is it? I expect you need him to pay for it anyway.' She ruffled his hair. 'Cheer up. It's the last day of school on Wednesday and then it'll be time for Santa to decide if you've been good or bad.'

'Ha, ha!' He groaned, but she saw his smile.

Several vehicles were vying for space so they moved away from the car park and nearer to the hall. The cars' owners were strangers to Jill. She wondered if one of them had killed Martin and Josie Hayden, if they had abducted, and possibly killed, James Murphy and Jason Keane, and if they had threatened Harry.

Seconds later, she saw someone who wasn't a stranger. A young constable who'd joined the force a few weeks ago was climbing out of his car. What was his name? Jeremy or something like that? He was wearing a dark red anorak and his hands were deep inside the pockets. He stood for a moment, his gaze taking in Max, the boys and DS Forrest, and then walked over to the coffee stall.

'Is it business or pleasure for him?' Jill asked Max in a whisper.

'Business.'

She was relieved, although she couldn't help wondering if Max was expecting a move to be made on Harry today. But it made no difference; they had to be vigilant every minute of every day.

Despite watching everyone, Max was managing to look as if everything was under control. She guessed that was for his mother-in-law's benefit as Kate looked awful.

'Here's that photo I told you about,' Jill murmured, taking it from her bag. 'I'm sure it's nothing, but you never know.'

'I'm sure it is, too.' Max held it to the light and inspected it closely. 'Just a coincidence, I imagine.' He gave her a wry smile. 'It's a nice trophy but I don't imagine anyone would kill for it.'

She guessed he was right.

'It's odd, though,' he admitted, 'seeing them together like this.' He put the photo in his pocket. 'We'll look into it. Meanwhile,' he added in an over-bright voice, 'we'd better get this boy a hot dog before he dies of malnutrition.'

They stood eating hot dogs that Jill thought, through no fault of the caterers, tasted like damp cardboard. At least it cheered Harry though, who was soon teasing Ben. Fortunately, Ben was used to it and took no notice whatsoever.

Jill and Kate chatted inanely about the weather and Christmas, Ben tried to keep Fly calm, Harry ate another hot dog, and Max continued to watch everyone.

It seemed an age before, finally, Ben and Fly were called to the show ring.

Kate linked her arm through Jill's. 'If that dog lets him down, he'll end up as cat meat,' she murmured.

Jill, a bundle of nerves for Ben, knew exactly how she felt. 'He won't knowingly let him down,' she murmured. Fly was devoted to Ben. His eyes never left the boy's face.

A huge lump wedged itself in Jill's throat as she watched Ben and Fly walking up and down and across the ring. Fly walked to heel, he sat and waited when told, and he lay down and waited when told. Jill could remember when the rescue dog had burst into their lives. A bundle of nervous energy, he had seemed untrainable to Jill. That a sensitive child like Ben had managed it touched her beyond words.

When they left the ring, Ben grinning from ear to ear as he joined them, Jill's eyes were awash with tears.

Ben accepted their congratulations with typical modesty. 'I need to work on his finishes,' he said, 'but he did well. We'll have to wait and see how the others get on.'

Jill, who had no idea what was wrong with Fly's finishes, hugged Ben close. 'You were wonderful. Both of you. I'm so proud of you!'

A couple of the other contestants provided them with much amusement, especially the dog that escaped the ring, raced off and ended up having a grand time splashing in the river at the back of the field.

The fancy dress parade came next and Fly wore his Santa costume with pride. Ben had to stop him chewing at a poodle's snowman outfit, but it passed without incident and provided them with some much-needed laughter.

Max was sharing a joke with DS Forrest, and the sight relaxed Jill slightly.

Ben and Fly were placed second for their obedience work and, again, Jill had tears in her eyes as she watched Ben proudly accept their rosette and fasten it to Fly's collar.

'If he can do that in the show ring,' Max murmured, 'why does the damned animal behave like a maniac at home?'

Despite the grumble, Jill knew he was bursting with pride. 'He's still a young dog. I expect he needs to let off steam.'

'Mmm. So,' he said, 'are you coming with us for the celebrations? We're stopping for a meal.'

She hesitated. The idea appealed, but she had a lot to do. In any case, she was too edgy to be worthwhile company.

'I'd love to, Max, but I can't. I've far too much to do.'

He sighed. 'Another time then.'

'Yes.' She said her goodbyes, congratulated Ben again, and then drove home.

She loved her cottage, she enjoyed her life in the village, so why did she always feel so lonely when she left Max and the boys? Why did life suddenly seem so pointless?

It was ridiculous to think along those lines so she vowed to keep busy. She tidied up, phoned her parents, and then ran herself a bath.

She was attempting to relax in the hot water when her phone rang.

The machine picked up while she was still wrapping a towel around herself, but she went downstairs to see who had called.

It was Babs, and her message was brief. 'Jill, you'd better give me a call about your Josie Dee.'

As Jill hit the button to return the call, she wondered what Babs could possibly have found out on a Sunday.

'Babs, it's Jill. Have you found something?'

'I certainly have and it's a disturbing story. Right ...' Babs must have written everything down because Jill could hear her turning pages on a notebook. 'Your Josie Dee was brought to Dublin and she had a daughter on the fifteenth of September, 1977.'

'I knew it!'

Josie hadn't lied to anyone. Despite what Alice Potter liked to think, she hadn't lied about Terry Potter. Just as she hadn't lied to George Hayden or Brian Taylor ...

'Josie was fourteen going on fifteen years old when she had the baby,' Babs said sadly. 'Anyway, the child was put up for adoption and this is where it gets –' She broke off. 'I was about to say interesting, but it's more tragic than interesting.'

'Oh?' Jill adjusted her towel, carried the phone to the chair nearest the radiator, and sat down.

'The child was named Hope and was adopted by a David and Heather Perkins,' Babs explained. 'They'd been trying for a child for years and, as you can imagine, they were besotted with her. They lived on the edge of a small village in County Clare. When young Hope was just five years old, there was a car accident. David Perkins was killed instantly, but Heather was alive when the emergency services arrived. It took fire crews several hours to cut Heather and young Hope from the wreckage. Hope was uninjured, but hysterical. Heather, however, died from her injuries the next day.'

Jill's towel was cold and damp, and she was starting to shiver. 'Go on, Babs.'

'Hope was traumatized, but she was eventually fostered by another couple, a Jenny and Peter Ramsland. They'd been fostering children for twenty years, but I gather Hope would have tested anyone to their limits. I managed to speak to Jenny today.'

Jill could tell from Babs' voice that she didn't want to hear what was coming next. 'What did she have to say?'

'When Hope was eight, there was another tragedy in her life. Her best friend, a lad called Denzil, was drowned near their home.'

'Go on.'

'Hope was with him at the time, apparently. When they found her, she was by the edge of the river – laughing hysterically.'

'Laughing?'

'So Jenny said. According to her, Hope had psychiatric treatment for the next five years. In the end, the medical experts said she was fine. Jenny didn't agree; she thought Hope was merely adept at fooling them. Anyway, the family then moved to England.'

'And where's Hope now?'

'Jenny said they'd lost touch with her. She was eighteen when she left home. That's twelve, thirteen years ago.'

'And they have no idea where she is?'

'None whatsoever. She was always a difficult child – terrible mood swings, that sort of thing. Well, Jenny called them *violent* mood swings. But she was very bright. After school, she went to university in Reading. She wanted to be a teacher, I gather.'

A teacher?

'Jenny wrote to her,' Babs went on, 'but Hope never answered and, after a few months, the letters were returned by Royal Mail with gone away scrawled all over them. They think Hope may have changed her name too, but they don't know.'

Jenny and Peter Ramsland might not know, but Jill thought that she might. She was already on her feet, her heart pounding.

'Jenny's emailed me a photo that was taken of Hope when she was seventeen,' Babs explained. 'The quality isn't great, but it might be of interest. I've forwarded it to you.'

With the phone clutched to her ear, Jill went to her computer and switched it on. It took a while for her emails to download.

'I've got it, Babs.'

She clicked on the email but, even before it opened, Jill suspected she knew exactly whose face she would see in the photo.

Chapter Forty-Three

Max was beginning to think they would never get home. After a meal to celebrate Ben and Fly's success, he'd been persuaded to stop at Jane Miller's house so that she could see the rosette. Jane Miller, a friend of Kate's, was a stranger to Max, but she knew all there was to know about him and the boys. As they all sat in her living room, Max could feel life passing him by.

When they finally made their escape from there, Kate wanted to call at Asda.

'Fine,' Max told her, relieved. 'We'll see you back at the house.'

Of course, it hadn't been that simple.

'There are a few things I need,' she'd said, 'but I also thought the boys could treat themselves. What do you say, boys?'

As if she needed to ask!

So they'd bought up half of Asda before, finally, heading for home.

As Max drove, his thoughts were on Martin and Josie Hayden, and on Jason Keane and James Murphy. He remembered what Jill had said. She believed he had spoken to the killer. According to her logic, there was someone they'd dismissed, and they'd dismissed that person because they didn't stand out, because that person was ordinary.

So who the hell had they missed?

Hundreds of people had been questioned in connection

with this. Perhaps by concentrating on his favoured suspects, he *had* missed someone.

Every person on Harrington High School's payroll had
been questioned and checked out. Everyone from the
headmaster, through the teachers to the canteen staff and
cleaners. Everyone who visited the school had been questioned, from the girl who drove the van and delivered the
stationery to the lad who delivered the milk.

In the same way, everyone with a connection to Lower
Crags Farm had been discounted.

His mind drifted back to his chat with Alan Turner. He'd
been adamant that he had never commented on the ratio
of police to residents at Lower Crags Farm. Why? He could
easily have said he'd driven past. That wasn't a crime. The
thing was though that to know how many police officers
were there, one would have to do more than drive past.
The farmhouse wasn't visible from the road.

In the rear-view mirror, he caught a glimpse of Ben
fondling the yellow rosette he'd won. The sight made him
smile. To have such great kids, he had to be one of the
luckiest blokes alive.

If he had Jill, too –

He didn't, not yet, but she was mellowing, he was sure
of it. It was a slow process though. When he'd had his
night of – he couldn't call it passion – in that seedy hotel
room, he'd had no idea that he could hurt Jill as much as
he had. He'd had no idea anyone could be hurt so deeply.

He rounded the corner into their road –

What the fuck –?

The noise was unbelievable. Glass and bricks flew into
the road, and a huge ball of fire engulfed the front wall of
his house.

'Holy shit!' Harry's voice shook.

Max had stopped the car and he swung around in his
seat. 'You OK?'

Harry nodded, a little doubtfully.

Ben looked at his brother, looked at Max, and hugged
Holly and Fly a little tighter.

'Ben?'

Ben, still clinging to the dogs, followed his brother's example and nodded at Max.

'Right. It's OK,' Max told them, 'we're all safe. Now, I want you to stay in the car. Got that? Don't move!'

He jumped out of the car and ran towards his house, but he couldn't get close. He was shaking. Little wonder really. If it hadn't been for the mother-in-law he'd spent the last few hours cursing, they would all have been inside.

He raced back to his car, and while waiting for Kate to catch them up, he phoned the fire brigade. Then he phoned the station.

He was surprised to see his mobile registering seven missed calls. Damn! He'd switched it to Silent when Ben and Fly went into the show ring and forgotten to switch it back to Normal. He didn't have time to see who'd called now. There were far more important things to do and the first job was to get his neighbours out of their houses. If there was another explosion –

Had it really been an explosion? Of course it had. What else could it have been?

Was it a gas fault, or was this the work of the maniac they were after? He had killed twice, at least twice, already. *Tell DCI Trentham that Harry is next.* Had this been intended for Harry? But this wasn't their killer's style –

Max had no idea what the fuck was happening.

While he was getting his elderly neighbour out of her house, he heard the welcome wail of sirens.

Chaos ruled for a good half an hour. At least, it felt like chaos to Max. Fire crews arrived, the road was sealed off, and all houses in the street were evacuated. Everything that needed doing was being done.

Kate was standing some distance away with Harry, Ben and the two dogs. DS Forrest was standing next to them, talking into his radio.

Max was trying to decide what he needed to do next, but he couldn't think straight. Hell, he was struggling to breathe.

Chapter Forty-Four

As soon as she ended the call to Babs, Jill tried Max's mobile. It rang out, but he wasn't answering. She had no idea where they were having that celebratory meal, and she couldn't ring every restaurant in the area.

She carried her phone upstairs and dressed in jeans and a thick sweater. She'd give Max ten more minutes and, if she hadn't managed to reach him, she'd drive over to his house and wait for them to return.

This was frightening her. Where the hell was he? It was unlike him not to answer his phone.

Five minutes later, she locked up her cottage, jumped in her car and headed for his place. On the way, she called his number again, but he still wasn't answering.

What if something had happened to him? A sharp pain, somewhere between her chest and her stomach, told her how she would feel, how she *did* feel about him. She loved him. Always had, she supposed. He'd hurt her, but try as she might, she couldn't master the art of not loving him . . .

Her driving was as erratic as her heartbeat and when she tried to turn the corner into his road, she found it blocked by fire crews and police cars. What the –?

She jumped out of her car and managed to catch snippets from the crowd gathered at the corner. The whole road had been evacuated. Someone even mentioned a bomb.

As Jill ran towards the crowd, she saw that the cloud of smoke was billowing out of Max's house.

She soon had Ben in her arms and Harry standing close. Kate looked on the point of collapse.

'Just as we turned the corner,' Harry was telling Jill breathlessly, 'there was a huge bang. It was like a bomb going off.'

'It must have been a gas leak,' Kate said, her voice all highs and lows.

'Sure to have been,' Jill said, but she was sure of no such thing. 'Thank God you were all out!'

'What will happen?' Ben whispered, one hand tight on Fly's lead and the other just as tight on Jill's arm.

'You'll have to stay with me tonight,' she told him. 'You might end up sleeping on the floor, but there's plenty of room. It'll be fun!'

She saw Max talking to a group. From the way he was waving his arms around, he looked to be issuing orders.

'I need to see your dad,' she told the boys. She patted Kate's arm. 'You all right, Kate?'

'Fine,' Kate replied, but it was obvious that she was far from all right.

'Here.' Jill handed DS Forrest a bunch of keys. 'Drive them all back to my place. Kate can take my car if necessary.' She nodded up the road. 'It's parked back at the corner. And don't, whatever you do, let them out of your sight.'

'Oh, I won't do that,' he promised her.

Kate seemed glad to be told what to do and she was soon giving instructions to the boys. Jill watched as DS Forrest, alert as ever as he spoke into his radio, led them away.

Then she pushed her way through the crowd of police and firemen to get to Max.

He broke away when he saw and walked over to her.

'What in hell's name happened, Max?'

'It might have been a gas leak,' he said, and despite the calm, measured tone, she knew he was taut with rage. He was a master at keeping his emotions tightly in check, but, right now, he looked as if he was a breath away from committing murder.

'It wasn't a gas leak, was it?' Her teeth were chattering as she tried to get the words out. 'I've sent Kate and the boys back to my place. DS Forrest is with them. But we need to find Donna Lord, Max.'

'What?'

'It's a long story, but I think – no, I'm *sure* she's our killer. She's Josie Hayden's daughter!'

For a moment, he was completely still. Apart from the fury blazing in his eyes, nothing registered in his expression. Nothing.

Then, he swung into action. He went to speak to a couple of officers and, as he came back to join Jill, she heard him say, '. . . and organize some fucking back-up!'

He grabbed Jill's arm. 'We'll drive out to her place and, on the way, you can tell me what you've found out.'

As they strode up the road to Max's car, his hand was still biting into her arm. When they were inside, he fired the engine, slammed the car into gear and, with difficulty, manoeuvred around the police cars.

'Right,' he said when they were finally out on the main road. 'Tell all.'

Jill told him of her conversation with Babs, and of the photo she'd been sent.

'There's no doubt that Donna Lord – or Hope – is Josie's daughter,' she told him, concentrating on stopping her teeth from chattering. 'As to whether she's our killer – well, there's no doubt in my mind, but we don't have any proof.'

'We'll get proof,' he said grimly.

'We need to handle her with care,' Jill pointed out. 'She's sick, Max. She needs help. And our first priority has to be finding Jason Keane and James Murphy.'

'I know that.' He gave her a brief sideways look as they sped along Harrington's main street. 'What do you suggest?'

'I'm not sure,' she answered, 'but I do know that we need to tread very carefully indeed.'

Chapter Forty-Five

All Max wanted was Jill and his kids next to him. They were all safe, and he kept reminding himself of that, but it had been a close call. If it hadn't been for Kate's insistence on seeing her friend and then stopping to shop, they would have been in the house. They would most likely have been dead.

Max thanked whatever guardian angel had looked out for them today.

Donna Lord's car was parked outside her house and he slowed to a stop behind it.

'Let's see what she has to say for herself,' he said, striving for calm.

Her house was a traditional terraced building with nothing to set it apart from the others in the street. The door was painted a deep blue and Max rang the bell. Just as he was about to ring it again, the door opened and there she was.

'Well, well, well, if it isn't my favourite detective.'

Surprise had registered in those attractive eyes of hers. Why? Because he was alive?

'And the psychologist,' she added. 'I am honoured.'

'Can we come inside?' Max asked. 'We'd like a word.'

She hesitated briefly and Max noticed that her eyes were dangerously bright.

'Of course,' she said.

They were shown into a large sitting room and offered seats. They both remained standing.

'To what do I owe this – pleasure?' Donna asked lightly.

'We need your help,' Jill told her, and Max suspected he was the only one to hear the catch in her voice. 'We need to find Jason and James and we think you can help us.'

Donna Lord shook her head. 'I wish I could but . . .' She shrugged. 'I've told you all I know. And I can only spare you a minute or so because I'm on my way out.'

'Donna, listen,' Jill said gently. 'We've been talking to your parents – your foster parents.' She paused, letting her comments sink in. 'We know about the car accident, Donna. Or should I call you Hope?'

'What?' She looked to Max, eyes glittering more brightly than ever. 'What's she talking about?'

'I'm talking about the car crash, Hope,' Jill said, her voice soft and almost hypnotic.

Max wanted to grab Donna Lord by the throat and drag answers from her by force but, for now, he was prepared to go along with Jill.

'The car crash that killed your adoptive parents,' Jill went on, 'was truly awful, wasn't it? You were only five years old and you had to watch your mother die. You were trapped in your seat, crying for your mother, watching her die.'

'I don't know what you're talking about!' Donna Lord cried. 'It's all nonsense – I don't understand.'

'Your friend drowned too, didn't he? His name was Denzil. You must have missed –'

With lightning speed, Donna lunged forward. She'd pulled a knife from the back pocket of her jeans and it was heading straight for Jill's throat.

Thankfully, Max was quicker and managed to knock her to the ground.

'While you were grieving for him,' Jill continued as if nothing had happened, 'you discovered that your mother – your real mother – had given you up for adoption, didn't you? How did you feel, Hope? Abandoned? But Josie didn't abandon you willingly. She loved you.'

As Max was calling for back-up, Donna swung her head round and spat in his face.

'Now that's no way to treat your favourite detective,' he ground out, tempted to punch that lovely face of hers.

Four officers burst through the door.

'Get her cuffed,' he shouted at them, 'and then I want this place ripped apart.'

'Tell us, Hope,' Jill said, bending to speak to her as two officers managed to put handcuffs on her. 'Tell us what you've done with Jason and James.'

'They need to learn,' Donna said, twisting and kicking as an officer lifted her to her feet. 'They have to learn that Mummy doesn't come. I had to learn. They have to. They can cry all they like but Mummy won't come. She never will.'

'We'll make sure you get the help you need,' Jill persisted. 'Just tell us where the boys are. Please!'

'Go to hell!'

'Why did you kill Josie? Why couldn't you –'

'She left her own child. She abandoned me. Not the others, oh no. She didn't leave that little shit Martin Hayden. He was golden bollocks. Not that bitch, Sarah Hayden, either. No. I was the one she abandoned. Me!'

'She was fourteen,' Jill said. 'She had no choice. She didn't give you up willingly. She was raped. Her life was just as terrible as yours.'

Donna Lord was kicking at an officer, spitting out obscenities with every breath, and insisting that boys had to learn. She'd had to learn, Martin Hayden had had to learn and now James Murphy and Jason Keane had to learn.

Then she was suddenly still.

'Where's Harry Trentham?' she demanded.

Max was in the process of smashing a door, one that he suspected led to a cellar, but he stopped and turned round.

'At home, I imagine,' he told her.

Two officers smashed the door for him and, sure enough, there were steps down to a cellar.

'That's where I left him,' he continued, walking towards her. 'Why? What's the sudden interest in Harry?'

She burst into hysterical, manic laughter and, just as Max was about to hit her with all the force he could muster, an officer called out, 'We need an ambulance down here!'

Chapter Forty-Six

Amazed that she had overslept, Jill leapt out of bed, pulled back her curtains and almost clapped her hands in child-like delight as the snow-covered landscape was revealed.

If only this had arrived yesterday, she would have relieved the bookie of a couple of hundred quid. She'd checked at midnight, but there hadn't been so much as a hint of a flake. Now, they had a good couple of inches. Sadly, snow on Boxing Day didn't qualify as a white Christmas.

It was an amazing sight nevertheless. The hills were majestic in their regal white mantle. In her garden, a robin was hopping from shrub to shrub, his red breast the only splash of colour against snow that was unspoilt except for one neat, straight line of cat's paw prints.

There wasn't a sound; the world was muffled by its snowy blanket.

'Oh, my –' Jill chuckled. So much for her beautiful, unspoilt snow.

Someone had let out the dogs. Holly ambled through it as if it were an everyday occurrence. Fly, however, was racing around at breakneck pace and trying to shovel it up with his nose.

Harry and Ben followed and Jill watched as they began to build a snowman.

It had been a joy to have the boys at the cottage. The invitation had been made on an impulse, to get them away from their burning home and to reassure Ben that all would be well, but Jill had assumed it would only be for one night. She'd thought Max would argue that her cottage was far too small for so many humans plus assorted pets. He hadn't. Quite the reverse in fact. He'd seized on her invitation.

It had been fine, though. She'd found it strange, to say the least, having Max in her cottage, but he'd left for his office early each morning and hadn't returned until late. Jill hadn't seen much of him.

She'd enjoyed having time with the boys, though.

Her back door banged shut again and then Max was in the garden. Jill inched back from the window to watch him.

He was making snowballs and throwing them for Fly. The dog leapt into the air to catch them, and then, as they disintegrated around him, raced around the garden hunting for them.

Max looked more relaxed today. She knew it would be a long time before he stopped thinking about what could have been, but he was finally beginning to relax.

Christmas Day had been OK. It had passed in a hectic blur of present opening, cooking, eating and drinking. Kate, who was staying with friends for the time being, had spent most of the day with them and Jill had been on the phone to her parents a lot. She'd been tempted to allay their worries about her spending Christmas alone by telling them that Max and the boys were with her but, thankfully, she'd resisted. She would never hear the last of it!

So yesterday had been fine and, this morning, they were all going to Gerald and Emma Murphy's house for drinks.

James and Jason had been found unconscious and severely dehydrated in Donna Lord's cellar. Both boys had several fractures, but James had been allowed out of hospital on Christmas Eve and Jason, also destined to make a full recovery, was expected home at the beginning of next week.

Christmas could have been a very different affair for Kelton Bridge but, as it was, the village was quietly giving thanks. It had seemed to Jill that every single resident had turned up at the church for the Christmas Eve service. Even Sarah Hayden had been there.

'After Christmas,' she'd told Jill, 'I'm moving to Burnley. With Martin and Mum gone, there's no point me staying at the farm. I'm going to share a flat with a friend.'

Jill had wished her well. Christmas at Lower Crags Farm would be a sad, painful affair, but she hoped the new year would bring brighter futures for them all.

Jill dragged her attention away from the garden and began hunting through her wardrobe for something suitable to wear.

An hour later, the four of them set off for the Murphys' house. Jill guessed that the crisp snow would soon turn to grey slush but now it crunched satisfactorily underfoot. The boys went on ahead, their heads bent as they discussed whatever it is brothers discuss.

'You OK, Max?'

He looked at her and smiled. 'Yes, I'm OK. You?'

'I'm good,' she told him.

They'd had an enjoyable Christmas together and, when life settled down again, perhaps – well, who knew what the future would bring?

'I hope Donna Lord gets the treatment she needs,' she murmured.

'What she needs is banging up for the rest of her days,' Max retorted. 'What she'll get is the best set of shrinks the taxpayer can afford.'

Max had little sympathy for her plight. Correction. He had no sympathy whatsoever. Jill supposed that as his son's life had been threatened, his house deemed uninhabitable for the moment and his life and that of his family almost wiped out, he had good reason.

'She was five years old, Max.'

'But people get over things. They have to.'

'Usually they do, yes. But no five-year-old spends hours trapped in her car seat watching her mother die and then gets over it without one hell of a lot of love and care.'

'Christ, Jill, if everyone who'd suffered some sort of tragedy went on a killing spree, we'd be knee-deep in corpses!' He sighed. 'The five-year-old died in that car accident. As for the thirty-year-old, I only hope to God I never have to lay eyes on her again!'

'It's over,' Jill said quietly. 'Let's just enjoy the day and be grateful that we can.'

She sensed some of the tension leave him.

'Oh, I almost forgot,' he said suddenly. 'Your dad called earlier with a dead cert for you. It was –'

'Whoa! Hang on a minute.' She stopped so abruptly that she almost slipped on the snow. 'What do you mean, my dad called? You answered my phone?'

He'd put out a hand to steady her. 'I could hardly ignore it, could I?'

'Why the hell not?' she demanded, shaking herself free. 'Oh, for God's sake!'

'Your mum sounds well, doesn't she?'

Jill walked on. 'This is your idea of a joke, isn't it? You're just winding me up. You didn't speak to my mother at all.'

Max shrugged in his helpless little boy way, and she knew damn well he had.

'So how,' she demanded through gritted teeth, 'did you explain the reason for them hearing your dulcet tones?'

'I explained about my place having an argument with a bomb, said you must have forgotten to tell them we were staying –'

'You know damn well I hadn't forgotten!'

'And then said that I'd left you in bed to have a lie-in while –'

'What?'

'You're screeching, Jill.'

'Bloody hell, Max!'

'I couldn't lie, could I? Not to your parents of all people.'

'Max.' Jill took a deep breath and silently counted to ten. 'You didn't have to lie. You didn't have to answer the damn phone in the first place but, having done that, you certainly didn't have to say that you'd left me having a lie-in. What sort of crap's that? For Christ's sake, they'll assume . . .'

'What?' His expression was pure innocence. 'You reckon they'll think we're sleeping together? Well, I shouldn't worry about that. They've always struck me as broadminded individuals. They see it all on River View.'

Jill was speechless.

'I said you'd call them later,' he went on. 'Your dad planned to stay at home to watch the racing this afternoon but your mum was off to the sales.'

'To buy what?' Jill demanded on a near-hysterical laugh. 'A new hat? A box of confetti? Wedding invitations? Bloody hell!'

They were at the entrance to the Murphys' drive.

'I can't believe you spoke to them. I can't believe you could let them think that we were . . . that I was . . .' They were walking up the drive to the Murphys' house. 'The sooner the work on your house is finished, the better I'll like it,' she finished.

'Ah. Did I tell you there was going to be a bit of a delay with that?'

'What?'

'You're screeching again, Jill!'

The Murphys' front door swung open. From inside came a babble of voices interrupted by the popping of a champagne cork and a burst of laughter.

'Harry, Ben!' Emma greeted them. 'Run inside and find James. Jill, Max, lovely to see you both. Thank you so much for coming!'

'Thank you for inviting us,' Jill responded, giving Emma a hug.

As they crossed the threshold, Jill managed to keep her warm smile in place while muttering to Max, 'I'll deal with you later.'

'Promises, promises . . .'